ONE WAY OUT

www.penguin.co.uk

ONE WAY OUT

A. A. Dhand

BANTAM PRESS

TRANSWORLD PUBLISHERS
61–63 Uxbridge Road, London W5 5SA
www.penguin.co.uk

Transworld is part of the Penguin Random House group of companies
whose addresses can be found at global.penguinrandomhouse.com

Penguin
Random House
UK

First published in Great Britain in 2019 by Bantam Press
an imprint of Transworld Publishers

A CIP catalogue record for this book
is available from the British Library.

ISBN 9781787631755

Typeset in 11.5/15 pt Aldus by Jouve (UK), Milton Keynes
Printed and bound in Great Britain by Clays Ltd, Elcograf S.p.A.

Penguin Random House is committed to a sustainable
future for our business, our readers and our planet. This book
is made from Forest Stewardship Council® certified paper.

MIX
Paper from
responsible sources
FSC® C018179

1 3 5 7 9 10 8 6 4 2

For my boys, the true
Dark Knights of my world.

PROLOGUE

THE OUTDOOR CINEMA SCREEN in City Park cut out. The children's movie went black. Most of the thousand-strong crowd didn't notice, too busy playing in the fountains, a welcome respite from the sun's inhospitable rays.

Then a message started to flash on the screen, bold and threatening:

IMMINENT SECURITY THREAT. LEAVE CITY PARK IMMEDIATELY.

No 'please'.

No hint that this was optional.

Confusion rippled through the park. People stared at one another, wondering if this was some sort of joke. The screeching of car tyres and the overhead roar from two helicopters answered their doubts.

Police officers jumped from their cars with megaphones, screaming for the crowd to disperse. They did not enter the park but kept to the perimeter.

At first, the shift was slow but the domino effect didn't take long to come into play and the few became the many. Bodies jumped from the pool and ran, some barefoot, others holding their shoes. Parents grabbed their children as the stampede began. Bradford was under siege.

ONE

Ten minutes earlier.

CITY PARK HAD NEVER been so full, the people of Bradford making the most of the July heatwave. Midday was approaching as the mercury soared past thirty, heading towards a forecasted record-high of thirty-four. At its centre, the park's powerful fountains had created a magnificent pool of water, where adults relaxed at the edges and children waded in for water fights. Around the perimeter the restaurants were heaving. The Wetherspoon's pub had a queue two dozen deep.

Detective Chief Inspector Harry Virdee sat beside his mother, Joyti, and rested two cups of tea on the shallow wall surrounding the fountains. No matter the heat, it was always 'tea' with her.

'How much were they?' she asked, watching her four-year-old grandson, Aaron, splashing in the fountains.

'Does it matter?' replied Harry, shaking his head.

He watched his mother prise the lid from the container and frown at the colour. 'I knew it would be like this.'

'It's how people like it, Mum.'

'If I had a stall here and made my Indian tea, these English people would never drink this filth.'

'I'm English. I drink it.'

Harry's mother frowned. 'Your blood is Indian, your brain English.'

'I'm more English than you think. I stand in queues, prefer sandwiches to samosas and, most importantly, when you hit seventy, I'll be tempted to put you in an old people's home.'

His mother shook her head disapprovingly and sipped the tea, wincing at its taste. Harry slipped his arm around her and gave her a squeeze. God, he had missed this. With his brother, Ronnie, in India with his family, Harry was looking forward to a bit more time with his mother. He was determined today not to think of his father. Not if he could help it.

Harry's phone rang, interrupting his heat-hazed peace. He saw it was work and ignored it. These moments with his mother were precious; five years apart had been five years too many. Today was the first day of a fortnight's annual leave, and he would be creating memories he could call upon during those frequent nights when his job dragged him to the city's darkest corners.

He kept his arm around his mother as she rested her head on his shoulder, both of them watching Aaron innocently splashing in the water.

Today, even more than usual, City Park was a vibrant display of Bradford's citizens. Women in burkas played with their children while beside them girls in Western swimwear were sunbathing. Boys, both Asian and white, had stripped off their tops and were flexing their muscles. Everyone was laughing and enjoying the weather.

'Do you like the watch?' his mother asked him.

Harry sighed, glancing at the Rolex on his wrist. 'It's a bit extravagant, Mum. You didn't need to.'

'Rubbish. You never had a proper wedding, so I never gave you a gift.'

Usually the watch stayed inside its box but when he met his mother he made a point of wearing it so she could see that he appreciated the extravagance. He'd looked up the value on the internet.

Five grand.

Harry wasn't a flash bastard and, while he did have a thing for watches, he'd never indulged it. A detective's salary didn't stretch that far.

Harry slipped off the wall and stepped into the water, soothing his sunburnt bare feet. He lifted Aaron and pointed towards the ice cream van.

'You want one?'

Aaron nodded.

'I think we'd better get dry first.'

'We come back here after, Daddy?'

'Maybe.'

Aaron kissed Harry's cheek. 'I love you, Daddy.'

Harry smiled and started towards his mother, who was ready with a towel. 'Love and affection when you want something, just like your mother.'

Harry's phone rang again.

Work.

Again, he dismissed it and flipped the phone to silent.

'Don't take the piss, I'm off,' he muttered to himself, annoyed.

As Harry's mother towelled Aaron, she took every opportunity to steal a kiss from him. Harry closed his eyes, taking a mental photograph. He hoped Saima would get here before his mother had to go.

She was due to meet Harry after Friday prayers.

Distracted from his son by an unfamiliar noise, Harry looked up to see a distant swirling of helicopter blades. More than one. As he saw them, the enormous cinema screen at the far end of City Park went black, before displaying a flashing red message, timed perfectly with the deafening roar of what appeared to be two military helicopters now almost directly overhead.

IMMINENT SECURITY THREAT. LEAVE CITY PARK IMME-DIATELY.

Only moments later, the same message boomed from the speakers.

Time froze in City Park. Everyone stared at the screen.

Nobody moved.

The message sounded again.

Harry watched as, in agonizing slow-motion, the panic started.

'Shit,' he said, feeling his phone vibrating in his pocket again. He pulled it out and put it to his ear, taking Aaron from Joyti and moving her out of the main flow of people as City Park started to fracture.

'What's happening?' said Harry. On the borders of City Park officers exited two armed-response vehicles, weapons raised, but came no further. More police vehicles were arriving every second and in the distance Harry could see uniformed officers pulling bright yellow tape taut to establish a cordon around the site.

The cinema screen now displayed another message, this one far more sinister: a skull and crossbones, a timer below them, counting down from twenty minutes. An obvious hack – there was no way that was protocol.

Harry listened to his boss, jaw tense, his eyes drifting down to his watch.

13.10.

Twenty minutes.

Before the call hit thirty seconds, he disconnected it, turned to his mother, tightened his grip around Aaron and said, 'Run.'

TWO

Pandemonium.

HARRY HAD NEVER WITNESSED anything like it.

People running in all directions. Screaming, shouting, adrenaline tangible in the hot, thick air.

Two helicopters continued to hover in the sky, not directly overhead, a little distance away. Harry knew there was only one reason for that – City Park was a blast zone. Police were ushering the public out of the area, loudspeakers bellowing for everyone to evacuate.

Terrorism.

Had to be.

Even Harry wasn't immune to the panic.

They'd only moved a short distance, people pushing past them, when his mother stopped, her face crippled in pain. Aaron started to cry in confusion.

'It's OK, little man, just a game we're playing,' he said.

'You go, Hardeep, get my boy to safety. I'm too slow,' Harry's mother said, panting, her hand gripping his.

'The hell with that,' replied Harry, lifting her arm and putting it around his shoulder. He threaded his hand round his mother's waist and tried to support her. It was her bad hip.

'Come on, Mum, I've got you.'

They moved slowly, too damn slowly.

Bodies glanced off Harry as people rushed forward and he saw several fall to the ground, skin grazing on concrete. Above them the sun continued its assault. Around them a mess of car horns, packed buses trying to move through stationary traffic. Everywhere was chaos.

Harry was struggling. Aaron grew heavier with each step, his mother pulling down his right arm. He felt as though he were back playing rugby, the second-row forward trying to support a collapsing scrum. He did what he did then, commanding her forward, pushing her with his arm.

They crossed the road, hit Hustlergate. She wouldn't last much longer – no chance she'd make it to the car.

In his peripheral vision, Harry saw people with mobile phones in their hands, social media no doubt awash with rumours. He could only imagine the speculation. His thoughts went to Saima but his hands were full and he had no chance to call her.

His mother finally stopped outside Waterstones, the old wool exchange building, sweat pouring down her face, breathless.

She tried to push him away. 'You go, take my boy and leave!'

Aaron cried louder, his face red and not just from the heat.

Harry couldn't leave Joyti. He glanced for somewhere to hide.

From what? A bomb? A terrorist attack?

Joyti pushed him again. 'I said go!'

Harry looked around, utterly lost. He would not leave her. As he stared down the street opposite, Piece Hall Yard, a British flag caught his eye.

The Bradford Club.

He waited for a frightened crowd to tear past him, then made his move. His mother didn't resist.

They slowed as they turned off the main street, Harry afraid the cobbled path might hinder her further. The eerily abandoned street was a welcome interlude from the chaos behind. The chatter and pounding of footsteps on concrete faded. In the quiet, Aaron's cries reduced to a whimper.

'Hardeep, what is happening?' asked Joyti, panting.

'I don't know, Mum,' he replied, kissing Aaron and trying to soothe his little boy.

They reached the door of the Bradford Club and Harry tried to open it.

Locked.

He rang the bell and hammered on the door. His mum leaned against the wall, getting her breath.

Harry used the internet on his phone to find the club's telephone number and hit the Call button, praying reception in the area wasn't compromised. The phone started to ring. Harry kept pounding on the door.

'Hello?' said a frightened voice on the other end of the phone.

'This is Detective Chief Inspector Harry Virdee. I'm outside the club and I need you to open up. Now.'

'Why? What is happening out there?'

'Open the door or I'll be forced to arrest you for hindering an investigation.' It was a bluff but Harry didn't care at this point. He just needed to get inside. An old Victorian building like this must have had an old cellar, even an old air-raid shelter.

'I'm coming,' said the voice and hung up.

Harry immediately tried to call Saima but she didn't answer. He sent a frantic text, *Call me ASAP*, then glanced back to where they came from. He could see a chaotic stream of terrified people running away from City Park. As some fell, others jumped over them to escape.

Harry squeezed Aaron a little tighter, trying both to comfort his son and to keep the feeling in his left arm.

13.21.

Nine minutes until the countdown finished.

What was going to happen then?

The sound of robust Victorian locks being opened jarred his thoughts, then the grand wooden doors parted.

Harry grabbed his mother and pushed her inside, past a grey-haired man. Harry quickly established he was Philip Jones, the fifty-three-year-old manager.

'Close the doors, Philip. Seal them,' said Harry. He let go of his mother, who almost fell into a nearby leather chair.

Harry switched Aaron to his right-hand side and shook out his left arm.

'Alone, Philip?' said Harry, hearing the locks being secured.

'Yeah. No one wants to be in here in the dark with the sun out like that.'

Harry placed Aaron into his mother's lap and turned to face Philip, now shaking both his arms to encourage blood flow. He looked around at the building, a spiralling staircase revealing three magnificent floors, 200-year-old architecture steeped in wealth and history.

'Is there a cellar here?'

'What the hell is happening?' said Philip.

'Do you have a cellar, Philip?' His tone was clipped as he massaged his shoulder, trying to recharge his muscles.

'Yes. Although, well, I haven't opened it in years.'

'Old air-raid shelter, right?' asked Harry, more in hope than knowledge. This place had survived two world wars and been a meeting point for wealthy wool merchants. Surely they would have had a shelter in it.

'I'm not sure,' said Philip.

'Where is it?'

'Down here,' said Philip, moving past Harry towards a shadowy oak-panelled corridor.

Harry picked Aaron up and helped his mother to her feet.

They entered a grand drawing room where Philip stopped in

front of a massive wooden door. He struggled with four rusted bolts, pulling them free before opening the ancient door, grunting at the effort it took.

Darkness.

'Lights?' said Harry.

'Be surprised if they still work,' said Philip. He slid his hand along the left-hand side of the stone wall and flicked a switch.

A slight delay, then light breathed life into the void.

Harry pushed his mother inside but she hesitated. Harry checked his watch: 13.27. Three more minutes.

'You just leave me here, take Aaron with you,' she replied, clearly afraid.

'Not happening, Mum.'

Harry handed her Aaron, his face blotchy and streaked with tears. Harry stepped through the doorway on to a staircase that circled down into the cellar. It was easily wide enough for two people side by side.

Those Victorians knew how to design emergency cellars.

Harry flew down the steps, naked bulbs over his head illuminating the route. Satisfied they would be as safe as possible this close to the blast zone, he charged back up the staircase to his mother and told her to hold Aaron tightly. Harry then picked her up, telling Philip to follow them and close the door.

The silence was disconcerting after the madness of City Park. They sat on the cold stone floor, their breaths forming a white mist in the icy cellar.

'What now?' said Philip.

Harry put his arms around Aaron, checked the time and said, 'We wait.'

13.29.

One minute to go.

Harry hugged his family a little tighter, thinking of Saima. She wasn't far away, at the mosque observing Friday prayers, about a quarter-mile from City Park.

He watched the tiny hand on his Rolex ticking down the seconds until the time hit 13.30.

Harry felt the tremors first, then a deafening explosion that shook the ground. The light bulbs surged then popped simultaneously.

Joyti screamed.

THREE

SAIMA VIRDEE WAS ALMOST at the end of her Friday prayers, engaged in the final act of turning her head on to her right shoulder, back to the centre and then on to her left. Her eyes were drawn by the wide windows of the new Mehraj mosque, built on the site of an old wool mill that had been abandoned for decades. She could see much of the city from its elevated position.

More than just a place of worship, the enormous mosque had become a community hub. It had four levels. The basement, technically not part of the actual mosque, was an organized 6,000-square-metre space accommodating aid purchased from worshippers' charitable donations, which could be transported around the globe to areas often destroyed by war. On the ground floor was the grand hall, suitable for weddings and other religious gatherings. The first floor was for prayers, with separate male and female areas, and the top floor housed an impressive white dome, modelled on the Taj Mahal.

Local and national press had described it as the most striking piece of religious architecture in the north, using marble from India, stone from Saudi Arabia and calligraphy artwork from Pakistan. Saima had fallen in love with the place.

She was whispering 'Assalamu alaykum wa rahma tullaah' when something happened. It felt like the foundations of the mosque shook and she heard the windows vibrate.

Saima hesitated, her head momentarily pausing and her eyes darting back towards the windows. Ahead the elderly lady leading Friday prayers also hesitated. Only a fraction of a pause.

'Assalamu alaykum wa rahma tullaah.'

The collective voice of the female worshippers had changed – a subtle change but Saima clearly heard it.

Fear.

What on earth *was* that?

Prayers completed, Saima left her mat on the floor and hurried out towards the doors, other women falling in behind.

They exited the hall into a wide, marble foyer to find the men already there.

The air filled with nervous chatter and loud cries for God to help them all as people started to turn away from the windows, rushing downstairs.

Saima was horrified to see an immense plume of black smoke rising high above City Park, where a fire of herculean proportions was raging. A cloud of ash was beginning to block out the light. She chewed her lip, afraid, thinking of Harry and Aaron, her hand shaking, clawing at her pocket for her phone. For a few seconds, in her mind, the clamour around her faded to silence.

The ash cloud hit the mosque and everything went dark.

Screams came from the foyer. Shouts to close any open windows. People were running down the stairs. A fall, a scream, cries for help – other calls for calm.

Saima retreated into the prayer room.

Hellfire. It was a common enough word in Saima's childhood home and one her mother had used to frighten Saima into obeying God.

She tried to call Harry. No reception.

Her hands scrabbled to send a text.

Message failed.

She rushed to the rack where her shoes were and hurriedly put them on before charging back into the hallway. Saima pushed through the crowd, thinking only one thing.

Aaron.

She desperately needed to connect to Harry, her finger continually hitting Redial.

Just as she reached the ground floor the imam's voice came over the internal speakers.

'Please everyone return to the grand hall. You must not leave the mosque, it is not safe. The doors are locked. Please make your way to the grand hall immediately.'

He repeated his request in Urdu. While some followed the order, others, including Saima, headed for the front door. She was dismayed to see people turning away from it, finding it locked.

With little option but to follow, Saima entered the grand hall but stayed at the back. When the time came to leave, she would be first out.

She never stopped hitting Redial, praying for mobile reception to return.

It took an age for everyone to convene inside the hall. Saima thought she heard men grappling with each other outside, several others appealing for calm.

Saima glanced out of the windows. The smoke was starting to lift. She couldn't prevent visions of the end of times flitting across her mind.

Imam Hashim, dressed in his usual Islamic robes, appeared on the raised stage at the front of the hall and the thousand-strong congregation fell quiet. A dozen or so men surrounded the doorway.

Saima heard her mother's voice again. *Hellfire.*

Imam Hashim stared into the crowd, face serious, arms resting by his side. 'We have been informed by the police that we cannot leave. The doors, my friends, are locked.'

FOUR

HARRY PLACED HIS SON in Joyti's arms. Aaron tried to resist, afraid, and Harry kissed his forehead. They were OK, but was Saima?

'I'll swap you a child for your phone, Mum,' Harry said into the darkness. He checked Philip was OK, relieved to hear he was. The force of the blast could have given the man a heart attack.

They had all survived. That was something.

What exactly had happened?

Harry unlocked Joyti's phone, his date-of-birth the PIN, and turned on the torch, breathing life into the gloomy cellar. He glanced at Aaron, wounded by the sight of his little boy's terrified face, tears streaming down his cheeks. He tried to call Saima.

No reception.

She was fine. Secure inside the mosque. He had to believe that.

Harry handed Joyti her phone and made to leave. 'Wait here for me to come back,' he said, reaching down to reassure Aaron once more. 'Don't worry, little one. I'll be back very soon.' Aaron cried harder, alarmed Harry was leaving, but he had no choice.

Almost ten minutes after the explosion, he stepped outside the

Bradford Club. He'd been expecting the July heat to hit him as he left but, even so, the force took him by surprise. The thick smoke made it worse.

Terrorism.

The smell made him recoil. Dust and ash coated his clothes immediately. Those famous images of 9/11 flooded his mind.

What had been hit to produce an ash cloud like this?

Harry dealt with fear every day but this was unfamiliar territory. A bomb. Had to be.

Harry hurried down Piece Hall Yard, checking his surroundings constantly for threat. He felt vulnerable and didn't like it, particularly not with Aaron and Joyti so close by. He needed to get them to safety but he couldn't do that until he knew what he was up against.

Harry turned right on to Hustlergate and stopped dead in the street.

The clear blue skies were no more. An enormous mushroom cloud of black smoke had bloomed over City Park.

Visibility was poor. He could feel the heat from an angry fire but he couldn't see it.

Harry heard sirens in the distance, the sound of helicopter blades too.

He struggled with who to call first. His instinct was for Saima, not his colleagues at Trafalgar House, but it didn't matter.

No reception.

Harry imagined the cell masts were overloaded, the whole of Bradford calling their loved ones. Surely Saima would have been safe inside the mosque – it was far enough away.

Dismayed, he put the phone away and hurried into the smoke – towards the heat of a fire.

'Christ,' he whispered and inhaled a mouthful of smog that made him cough until he retched.

City Hall was on fire and the clock tower, which had survived the second world war, had been destroyed.

City Park was no longer there. The fountains were no more. The entire landscape had sunk several feet below ground level. All the shops around the perimeter had been obliterated.

The park was a hole in the ground.

Locals had referred to the centre of town as a hole in the ground for more than a decade while they awaited an expensive regeneration project that had never materialized. Now the phrase took on new meaning.

He hoped everyone had got out.

Dust, smoke and heat stung Harry's eyes and he raised his hands to shield them from an approaching gust of heavy air. The sound of sirens was growing ever louder. He doubled over and coughed a lungful of soot out of his system.

Forced to retreat, he saw people in doorways venturing to have a look, their faces filled with perplexed disbelief.

Harry was thinking so many things:

Was Saima OK?

How could he get his mother and Aaron to safety?

Was another blast coming? Again his thoughts went to images of the 9/11 disaster. Nobody had envisaged a second plane until it hit.

He turned back into Piece Hall Yard, now staggering from the cumulative hurt only smoke could inflict.

He couldn't bring Aaron out here yet.

In the club he locked the doors behind him and turned to see Philip standing unsure in the hallway.

'Detective? What's happened?'

Around an angry coughing fit, Harry told him what he had seen, then made for the cellar.

'Hardeep?' his mother said, voice sharp with concern before he reached the staircase.

'I told you to stay put.' He tried for stern but the sight of her face softened him. 'I'm OK, Mum.'

She threw her arms around him. Harry knew that embrace, a mother's desperation to keep him safe. It hadn't diminished with age.

'Seriously, Mum, I'm OK.'

'Daddy, I don't like it here,' piped up Aaron with his usual matter-of-fact delivery.

Harry stepped away from his mother and scooped Aaron into his arms, embracing him tightly.

Aaron recoiled a little. 'You smell funny, Daddy.'

'We're going to leave soon, baby. OK?'

'I want to go now,' said Aaron, burying his face into Harry's neck.

Harry turned to his mother and informed her in Punjabi, a language Aaron didn't understand, what he had seen. Philip looked confused and Harry simply nodded towards the front door, encouraging him to take a look.

Joyti's face mirrored the ones Harry had seen outside.

'I know,' said Harry.

'What . . . what are we going to do?' said Joyti, looking worriedly at Aaron.

'I don't know but I need to let Saima know we're OK. She'll be worried.'

He checked his phone.

Still no reception.

Harry was thinking of his next move. He lived a mile from here but needed to get Aaron further away than that. His mother lived in Thornton, a leafy suburb far enough for Harry to feel they would be safe.

He could hear Saima's voice inside his head.

Get our boy to safety.

Harry kept tight hold of Aaron. Philip hadn't ventured outside, looking afraid and unsure of himself. Harry told him of his fears about a secondary device and that he needed to make his own decision on whether to stay. To his mother he said, 'Come on, Mum, we're leaving.'

She stopped him as if reading his mind and said, 'Saima?'

Harry rubbed Aaron's back.

'She'll be safe at the mosque. Right now, I need to get Aaron and you to safety.'

FIVE

SAIMA STOOD AT THE back of the room, watching carefully.

Imam Hashim, at age forty one of the youngest imams in the city, stood centre stage in the grand hall of the mosque. Behind him was a large screen where a video clip had started to play – a clip also released on social media and, unknown to the worshippers, currently trending on Twitter.

It showed a dozen men, nothing more than silhouettes, sitting silently while a voiceover relayed their message.

Today we, the Patriots, unleashed the largest bomb to have been detonated on UK soil since the second world war. We have planted a similar bomb inside one of the hundred and five mosques in Bradford. This bomb will be detonated should any worshippers in any of these mosques attempt to leave.

A wave of nervous whispers rippled through the crowd. Saima felt her heart racing, her mind a mess with worry for Harry and Aaron.

Our demands are simple. Bradford is home to a group who call themselves Almukhtaroon – the chosen ones. Their slogan is 'Death to the West' and they seek to impose their ways on the UK and its citizens. This group, led by a man called Abu-Nazir, incite religious hatred but they have so far managed to stay on the right side of the law. The UK government has tried and failed to secure prison sentences for leaders of the so-called Almukhtaroon, making a mockery of our justice system.

Saima knew all about Abu-Nazir. He was a white convert to Islam, born and raised in Newcastle, before moving to London where something had caused him to veer towards extremist ideology. He was considered a disgrace to the Islamic community. She watched the video, her mood souring.

No more. Today we issue this demand, that the leaders of Almukhtaroon are to be taken into custody and brought to us at the mosque where we have hidden the bomb.

Once the bomb has been located, if the security services attempt to storm the mosque, we will detonate.

If worshippers attempt to leave any mosque before we say so, we will detonate.

If any of our demands are not met, we will detonate.

The other hundred and four mosques in Bradford will be allowed to evacuate once the bomb's location has been verified by the police.

We are testing the Islamic community. Will they come together to ensure the safety of their worshippers? One hundred and five mosques will need to demonstrate that when a threat is brought to their doorstep, their resolve to protect one another is robust.

The wider community need to ask themselves a vital question: are the lives of four toxic individuals who seek to bring harm and division to the British way of life of equal value to the many lives of innocent Muslim worshippers?

Sacrifices must be made. Difficult decisions undertaken.

Our capabilities must not be underestimated.

This morning we provided a twenty-minute warning to evacuate City Park. We will not do so again.

We require the leaders of Almukhtaroon by 06.00 tomorrow.

Non-compliance will result in significant loss of life.

The transmission ended.

A stunned silence filled the room.

In spite of their predicament, Saima seized on the positive news that City Park had been given a twenty-minute warning. Harry would have escaped with Aaron in that time, wouldn't he?

She had to believe it.

Saima had already lost most of her family by marrying Harry. She had a sister, Nadia, with whom she had become reconciled the year before, but they were not close. Truthfully, all she had was Harry and Aaron.

Saima saw life and death on a daily basis in the A&E department where she worked. She was able to keep her head in difficult situations, but this was on another level.

She was still clutching her mobile phone to her ear but the networks remained down. In the far window she saw smoke continuing to rise from City Park. Such appalling devastation.

Who could survive that?

The dread was twisting her insides, making it hard to breathe.

Nervous chatter was sweeping the room. A man at the front stood up and shouted, 'Why should we stay here like caged animals?' Others joined him.

Imam Hashim raised his hands and asked for calm. He was starting to lose the hall.

Saima didn't know what to think. There was simply no way they could keep thousands of people inside a hundred and five mosques. How on earth would the terrorists know if people left? The improbability of the Patriots keeping watch on all the mosques seemed clear to Saima.

Why couldn't the imam see that?

His voice boomed from the speakers, the microphone crackling. He ordered everyone to stay where they were and be calm. Saima had never heard him speak with such force. She didn't think anyone had.

The crowd fell into stunned silence.

'Let me speak. Listen to me. Then we can discuss our options,' he said.

He raised his hands for the dozen or so men who had stood up to sit back down. Hashim told the hall that the Patriots had given the security services advance warning of what was happening in Bradford before their broadcast had gone live on the internet – only a short window. The information had been cascaded to the mosques and an urgent decision taken to seal their doors. Nobody had known exactly what was going to happen and the consensus had been that the worshippers would be safest inside. Hashim was clear about what needed to be done now.

'We speak about solidarity. We hold charitable events for Palestine, Syria, Iraq, and our Rohingya Muslim brothers and sisters. The persecution of our people is everywhere – a continual test. The intelligence is apparently extremely credible that one of our mosques contains an explosive device. Our responsibility is as a collective. If we walk out of our doors and somewhere in Bradford that bomb is detonated – because of *our* fear and *our* need to save *our* own lives – then we, as a community, will have failed. We have limited information on other potential threats. For now, we are safest in our places of worship. The hour is dark, but if we panic it will become darker still. On our own doorstep, will we not save the lives of our neighbours?'

Hashim moved his head right to left, surveying the crowd, who had become subdued.

'I ask for your restraint. I ask you to trust this great city to defuse this unprecedented situation. Failure today will condemn us – across the world and inside our own minds. We must not act with haste.'

He paused. The room remained painfully silent, the atmosphere heavy.

'The doors have been sealed. You are not prisoners here. This mosque can never be viewed in such a way.' He pointed towards the window where ash from the blast was still clearly visible. 'Think about what might happen now. People may start hunting the leaders of the so-called Almukhtaroon. They may see every Muslim as a target. The Far Right may mobilize. These are uncertain times. Division is here, it has been building. Are we any safer out there than we are in here?'

He smiled, a warm, comfortable sight.

'You are thinking, what if this bomb is inside *this* mosque? I can see it in your faces. We will coordinate a thorough search, just like every other mosque is doing. What I ask from you is to remember that the other hundred and four mosques are with us. Now I ask those of you who insist you still want to leave and put at risk thousands of lives, to raise your hand.'

He looked carefully into the crowd.

Hashim repeated the message in Urdu.

Nobody raised their hand.

'Thank you,' he said. 'Our time to show we can endure has arrived.'

He bowed his head and began whispering a prayer. In spite of her insides feeling like they were on fire, Saima focused on the prayer: the only thing she had now.

SIX

HARRY'S DECISION TO LEAVE the Bradford Club wasn't lightly taken. Again, his thoughts went to 9/11 and the second plane. If a secondary device detonated here, gas-main ruptures could lead to raging fires. Staying put and waiting to see what happened just didn't seem right.

The streets of Bradford felt alien to Harry as he hurried away from Piece Hall Yard, holding Aaron and supporting his mother. Philip had decided to stay put. Harry kept Aaron's face pressed into his body so he wouldn't inhale the thick, black dust swirling around them. His mother was struggling with her hip but forced herself on.

The smog enveloped them in a choke-hold. Aaron was starting to freak out, sensing all was not right.

And all the while, Harry knew he needed to get to Saima. She was at the mosque and would be safe. He couldn't though rest until she was with him.

Harry's car was at the Midland Hotel carpark. His mind was filled with questions about potential next targets. He couldn't see any danger here. It would be the shopping centre next, and they'd left that behind.

People's faces held disbelieving stares. Buttons on mobile phones were being pressed. Harry saw dismay that networks were still down.

He secured his family in the car then started it, maxing out the air-conditioning and ignoring Aaron's pleas for him to lower the windows. As they pulled out on to the road, the car still thick with summer heat in spite of the air-con, he saw an armed police car tear past, lights flashing, siren screaming.

Harry headed towards Upper Piccadilly, away from the city centre, reaching to turn the radio off. He needed a clear head.

More police cars tore past.

Above he could hear helicopter blades getting closer.

The roads were quiet, shock and fear keeping people away.

Harry ignored the traffic lights and the speed limits, cutting through the side streets, heading towards Thornton Road. He used one hand to unlock his mobile phone, scrolled to the Favourites and hit the top entry before handing it to his mother, the car veering as he did so.

'Keep trying Saima,' he said, ignoring another red light.

'It says Unavailable,' said Joyti.

From behind, Aaron started to whine about wanting his mum. Harry glanced at the clock: 14.05.

'Keep trying, Mum,' he said.

'Still nothing,' said Joyti, staring at the iPhone.

'Just keep pressing Redial,' said Harry, glancing at her to make sure she was doing it right. 'Anything?'

'No,' replied Joyti.

A speed camera flashed at Harry as the speedometer of his BMW tore past sixty on the forty-mile-an-hour road.

The flash made Harry wince.

Whoever had detonated that bomb was no ordinary terrorist.

Surely there was more to come.

SEVEN

THIS IS BCB RADIO'S Grace Chia reporting live from Bradford city centre, where a devastating explosion has reduced City Park from the well-loved mirror pool to nothing more than rubble and smoke. The heat of the fires raging through City Hall and the clock tower can be felt even from a good fifty or so metres away. Sources have told me that at around 13.10, a frantic twenty-minute warning was given to those in City Park, some two thousand people, to immediately evacuate. The cinema screen allegedly stopped playing a children's movie, instead flashing an urgent message for everyone to leave. Sources have confirmed that soon after, a further message featuring a skull and crossbones cast an entirely different light on this evacuation order. A video circulating on social media by a group calling themselves the Patriots, a seemingly new nationalistic group, has claimed there is a bomb inside one of the hundred and five mosques within the city. This claim is as yet unsubstantiated and I understand this group is unknown to security services. They are demanding the arrest of the leaders of the well-known radical group Almukhtaroon, who were due to give a speech in Bradford tonight, but what is to happen after that is unclear. Almukhta-roon, of course, have long been a contentious topic, especially for the current Home Secretary, Tariq Islam, who failed to get their organization banned last year. Islam himself is in Bradford and, according to sources, was evacuated from Bradford City Football Club, where he was opening a new Asian football academy. At exactly 13.30, the bomb detonated. We do not yet know the extent of the damage caused. The emergency services are expecting a number of casualties, and we understand the Prime Minister has convened a COBRA meeting. As I stand here, smoke continues to bellow into the skies, and you can probably hear – raising her voice over the sudden noise *– dozens of sirens behind me, police cars, ambulances and fire engines all desperate to save the lives of anyone trapped in the area.*

Grace moved the microphone towards the centre of City Park. *I don't know if you can hear that –* almost shouting now *– but there seem to be further explosions around the City Park area. The emergency services are ushering me away. I'm hearing something about a gas pipe.*

EIGHT

HARRY PASSED THROUGH THE black iron gates of his brother Ronnie's grand Victorian house in Thornton. His brother was the model son, buying a big house and moving his elderly parents in with his own family. He'd even gone along with Asian hierarchy – this was his house, but while his parents lived there, they had the authority. It was not a house Harry was welcome in. His father had disowned Harry for marrying a Muslim and the rest of the family had been forced to follow. Harry had only recently been reconciled with his mother, but his father was a different animal entirely.

He hated being here. It was a place laden with the terrible memory of the night his job had brought him to this house to tell his brother and wife that their eldest daughter, Tara, had been murdered.

Harry did not want to leave Aaron here. He didn't trust his father not to react badly but he had no choice.

He turned to his mother and was about to speak when she raised her hand.

'He's my grandson,' she said fiercely in Punjabi, 'and, Hardeep, I love him more than I love you. He is *my* baby today and nothing your father says or does will change that. Put it out of your mind and go and get my daughter-in-law. Make sure your family is safe and I will do the same.'

Harry smiled. He needed to hear it. But he couldn't help glancing up at the house once more. He had been inside only once, when he had delivered the heart-breaking news about Tara. His father flashed before his eyes, his words from that night coming back to haunt Harry,

'This morning when I woke up, it was a good day. If I had known I would have to suffer seeing your face, in this house, on this day, I would have wished my own death.'

Harry grimaced. Punjabi could be such a coarse tongue, insults delivered with a force the English language could never muster.

Joyti put her hand on Harry's chin, forcing him to look at her. Harry realized she had seen the pain in his face.

'Today is not the day to think of the past,' she said firmly. 'Go and get Saima.'

He got out of the car, the humidity immediately sucking at his energy levels, and lifted Aaron from his car seat in the back.

'Listen, I'm going to leave you here with Grandma,' said Harry.

Aaron looked startled. 'No, Daddy, you stay here too.'

'I'll come back later with Mummy.'

'No, Daddy, I come with you.'

His pleading got to Harry, who felt a lump in his throat. He'd never left Aaron here before. The fact his father was inside and likely to treat Aaron with contempt troubled him deeply. At least they were surely safer here in Thornton than anywhere close to City Park.

Joyti arrived by his side and tried to take Aaron, who shied away from her, putting his arms tightly around Harry's neck.

'Daddy stay too!' he cried.

Joyti went to take him forcefully, which made it worse.

'Mum, leave it a minute,' said Harry, spotting a bright red, ride-on mower parked on the grass. 'Aaron, look at that,' said Harry. Aaron did, and stopped crying immediately.

'Mum, I'm going to take Aaron with me so he can't play with the tractor,' said Harry solemnly, looking at Joyti.

She nodded, understanding the game. 'Yes, I put it here so Aaron could play with it, but if he is going with you, I'll have to lock it away.'

Harry saw the change in Aaron's face, eyes widening with excitement.

'Come on then,' said Harry, turning away from the tractor.

'No, Daddy,' said Aaron, struggling to get free.

Harry put him down.

Aaron looked at him matter-of-factly. 'I stay here . . . I play with tractor with Grandma and you get Mummy and come back?'

Harry shook his head. 'I don't know. You said you wanted to come with me?'

'No, Daddy, I sit on the tractor.' He paused, thought about it some more and added, 'I good boy.'

Harry crouched and ruffled Aaron's hair. 'OK. Because you're a good boy, I'll leave you here with Grandma.' He kissed him twice and stood up to leave, giving his mother one final look.

'Sunscreen's in his bag and make sure you give him lots of water.' Harry stared up at the house. 'And, Mum, make sure he's –' Harry struggled for this next word, an image of his angry father flashing across his mind – 'safe,' he said.

Joyti came across and took Harry's face in her hands, kissing him. 'Go and get Saima.' She let go of him, picked Aaron up and held him tightly. 'My life flows through his veins. Nothing and nobody is hurting this boy while I'm here.'

NINE

WEST YORKSHIRE ASSISTANT CHIEF Constable Steven Frost was no stranger to fast-moving operations in Bradford, but the sight he was looking at on his TV screen was unprecedented. The whole of City Park was no more. He had quickly established a Gold Command centre at the Dudley Hill police station to handle the emergency unfolding in his hometown. They'd evacuated Police HQ at Trafalgar House, less than a half-mile from City Park. Their switchboard had been forced to section off work to other centres around the country. It seemed like the whole of Bradford had hit 999 within the last hour.

They knew relatively little about what was happening but one thing was certain. Once this was all over, whatever *this* was, every decision he made would be scrutinized. This afternoon could come to define Frost's career, for good or for bad.

No pressure.

The regional counter-terrorism centre was located in Leeds and the assistant chief constable for that department, Peter Weetwood, was on his way.

Frost's current priority was avoiding any loss of life. All his officers who didn't need to be present at Gold Command were making their way to City Park. They would establish a hot zone where secondary terrorist activity might be imminent, a warm zone where casualties could be treated, and a cold, safe zone where operational teams could base themselves.

Frost also needed to try to prevent the media from getting ahead of him, no easy task in an age where social media could quickly manipulate the news. That meant making sure his officers weren't about to leak information to the press. It could jeopardize the whole operation.

The West Yorkshire Police had seen the video the Patriots put out on Twitter. They had also received a further video which had not been shared publicly. This second one showed a detailed, step-by-step demonstration of the make-up of a bomb, the bomb that was currently inside one of the hundred and five mosques of Bradford. A CTU bomb-disposal expert had briefed Frost on the video, giving an initial assessment that it looked credible. The assembly was flawless and clearly organized by someone proficient in bomb-making. Most importantly, the level of explosives it contained was enough to kill thousands.

'I've got no way of knowing if this is the bomb inside the mosque, sir,' he'd been told. 'I can tell you that if these are the Patriots on this video, then they know what they're doing. They're very much capable of carrying out their threats. Perhaps, even, of more.'

Frost picked up his phone, dialled the main switchboard and said, 'Get me the Prime Minister's office.'

TEN

THE MEHRAJ MOSQUE WAS opposite Forster Square retail park and the only way Harry could get to it was by driving past the blast site. Saima was the only thing on his mind as he stopped his car half a mile from City Park, where a yellow police cordon and two patrol cars were blocking the route. He showed his identification to uniformed officers and waited as they made a gap for him to pass.

Harry managed another quarter-mile before he was forced to stop. The roads surrounding the immediate perimeter of the park were blocked off by more police cars, these ones unmanned.

He started to jog towards City Park. He reached the site of the old Odeon cinema and immediately felt the heat, the air thick with smoke. The only way to reach the Mehraj mosque from here was on foot. Not far, if he cut through the side streets.

His phone rang.

Saima.

'Hey, I'm fine and Aaron is fine,' he said quickly, afraid reception would cut out.

'Oh, thank God!' She burst into tears.

Harry retreated into a dark side street, abandoned mills to both sides, afraid the sound of deafening sirens would alarm her.

'Saima, calm down, we might not have much time before reception cuts. Are you OK? Where are you now?'

She sobbed again and asked how Aaron was.

'He'll be playing with Ronnie's lawnmower for a good while this afternoon. Not a scratch on him.'

'Have you seen social media?'

'No. I've had no signal. What's going on?'

'You need to see the video on Twitter, Harry. I . . . I . . . can't explain.'

'I'm coming to get you first. Twitter can wait.'

'No, Harry. I can't leave the mosque.'

'What?'

'The terrorists have said nobody can leave any of the mosques or they will blow one up.'

Harry kept her on the line as he opened Twitter on his phone. He held his breath while it loaded, painfully slowly.

'Stay there, Saima, I can't afford to cut the connection with you. We might not get it back.'

It was the first thing in his newsfeed. He must have gone silent.

'Harry?'

He swallowed a lump in his throat, energy sapped from his body, and put the phone back to his ear.

'Yeah,' he said, completely flat.

'I don't know what to do.'

Neither did he.

'People are sweeping the mosque now to see if they can find anything.'

Harry put his head in his hands, closed his eyes.

'Harry? Are you there?'

'I'm here, Saima.'

'I can hear lots of sirens. Are you sure you're OK?'

'It's a mess down here. I was on my way to see you. Still am.'

Harry didn't know what else to do. He just wanted to be close to her.

'No,' she said firmly, almost angrily.

He knew what was coming.

'Aaron needs you. *That* is your priority. Not me. You cannot change what is happening or going to happen but you damn well can and bloody well will look after that boy of mine.'

'That boy of ours,' he said quietly. He'd seen the blast site, he'd been there for the warnings and now, with the Patriots' video, he knew there was nothing he could do to stop this.

'Promise me you will go back and look after Aaron.'

'Aaron's safe, I—'

'Harry Virdee, you swear to me now.'

He blew his cheeks out and stared up at the sky, angry smoke blocking out an even angrier sun. He couldn't find the words.

Saima's tone changed.

'You've always looked after me, Harry, but today it's about Aaron, not me.'

Harry said nothing.

Terrorism was not his expertise. As far as Bradford went, for now, he felt like a civilian, powerless.

'I'll look after Aaron,' he said.

'Promise me you will stay away from here. From every mosque in the city.'

'There's a mosque everywhere, Saima. What do you want me to do? Leave Bradford?'

'That's exactly what I want you to do. Take Aaron with you.'

She meant well but it irritated Harry.

'This isn't the time for your macho shit, Harry. You haven't promised me yet—'

'—and I'm not going to.'

'Harry—'

'—Saima, I don't want to fight with you. Not today.' His tone silenced her pleas. 'All I need to hear are three little words.'

'I trust you,' she said.

'Not those, you muppet.' He smiled.

'I love you.'

'I love you, too. Now hang up, conserve your battery and text rather than call – this is going to be a long day.'

'OK, OK,' Saima said, calmer than before. 'And for God's sake, stay safe. You know I can't raise our boy on my own.'

Harry sank to the ground, placing his phone on the warm concrete pavement. His phone beeped, notification of several voicemails. Harry saw they were all from his boss. He listened to the first one. A desperate plea for all hands on deck. Harry ignored it, unable to shake the fact that Saima was inside one of the mosques.

A Gold Command would be set up somewhere, probably Dudley Hill.

The Counter-Terrorism Unit would take control. Assistant Chief Constable Frost was no doubt shitting himself that this had landed on his watch, in his city.

Christ almighty – why Bradford?

He thought back to the Patriots' video.

One hundred and five mosques, one bomb.

Only Greater London and perhaps Birmingham had a higher number.

Harry picked up his phone to watch the video again when it started to ring.

Unknown number.

He answered, surprised to hear the Home Secretary, Tariq Islam, on the line.

'Harry, are you OK?' said Tariq, voice quiet, tone serious.

'Bloody wonderful. Was in City Park when the evacuation order came in and Saima is inside one of the mosques. So, yeah, I'm pretty fucking terrific. You?'

Tariq paused and when he spoke his voice was uncertain.

'I need you to come and meet me, Harry.'

He knew better than to ask for details on the phone. 'Where?' asked Harry, getting to his feet.

Islam told him.

He couldn't have heard it right.

'Your silence says everything, Harry, but you heard me just fine. Meet me there as soon as you can. We need to get a handle on this. I'll be waiting.'

The line went dead.

It hardly seemed possible, but Harry's day had just got worse.

ELEVEN

STANDING OUTSIDE HER HOME, Joyti had felt a deep unease as she watched Harry's car disappear out of the driveway.

Her husband would not be convinced to change his mind about Harry. To Ranjit, Harry was a disgrace. He would not forgive his Sikh son for marrying a Muslim woman.

Joyti understood her husband's position. Her acceptance of Saima had not been without its own challenges. The stereotypical depiction of Muslim women and their culture was not confined to white society.

Joyti held Aaron's hand a little tighter.

He was innocent, a beautiful product of Harry and Saima's relationship. And for her, all the more beautiful for looking just like her son. Being with Aaron brought back wonderful memories of Harry as a child.

Joyti started to cry and wiped her face immediately, not wanting Aaron to see.

Standing outside her home, she felt more afraid than ever.

'Grandma, you live here?' said Aaron, letting go of her hand, once again focusing on the tractor he was sitting on.

'Yes,' she said, and lifted the bag Harry had left her, unzipping it to find a bottle of children's sunscreen inside. She was grateful they were far enough away from City Park that the ash cloud from the blast was absent from the sky. She squirted some cream on to her hand and rubbed it into Aaron's face, then his arms. He didn't struggle but did close his eyes.

She stared at him, blinking hard, trying to regain her composure.

Ranjit could not hate Aaron, could he?

What kind of a man would that make him?

In truth, she was afraid of the answer to that question.

'Grandma, this your tractor?' asked Aaron, grabbing the steering wheel and making driving sounds.

Just like Harry, she thought. As a child, he would sit in Ranjit's car doing the same thing.

She nodded and stroked his sweaty head, the heat unforgiving. She needed to get Aaron inside. Sitting out here in thirty-plus temperatures wouldn't do.

'My daddy coming back? He going to drive it?' said Aaron.

Another nod of her head. Another stroke of his clammy hair.

Joyti gritted her teeth, the contempt she felt for her husband's stubborn position suddenly cold and venomous.

Aaron was *his* grandchild also. Surely he could not vent his rage on a child? If he did, Joyti would not tolerate it.

She looked up at her home.

Four walls and a roof.

Not a home.

Joyti hadn't felt like anywhere had been a true home since they had sold their corner shop and the flat they had lived in above it. They'd moved in here with Ronnie not long after. This place, whilst luxurious, felt cold without any memories of Harry.

A mother was incomplete without her children, that was how she felt. No matter what he had done. She was proud of him, always had been.

In some respects, even when Harry had chosen Saima over his family, deep down a spark of warmth had comforted her. He had chosen love over hatred. What mother could not be proud of a son making such a difficult choice? To simply judge a person on who they were.

Joyti looked at Aaron.

She leaned down and kissed him dozens of times until he recoiled, then picked him up, ignoring his cries to be left on the tractor.

'Ice cream inside,' she said, knowing exactly which buttons to push.

'Magnum?' he said, eyes wide, smile broad.

She nodded.

'I don't like white one.'

'I have chocolate,' she said, carrying him towards the front door.

'I have two, Grandma?'

'No.'

'At home, Mummy gives me two.'

'No she doesn't,' she said, squeezing his chubby cheeks.

Inside, Joyti took Aaron into the kitchen, sat him down and got a Magnum ice cream.

'No, I open it!'

She nodded and handed it over, unopened, sitting beside him.

Footsteps coming down the hallway startled her. Ranjit's shoes clicked on granite tiles. Joyti's heart began hammering, sweat prickled her temple. Her chest felt tight and a momentary lightheadedness afflicted her mind.

She watched as Aaron bit into his ice cream, the sound of smooth chocolate breaking as Ranjit strode commandingly into the kitchen, chest stuck out, long hair loose down his back. He had learned of the blast and made his own assumptions, laying the blame firmly where it felt comfortable for him.

'Joyti! Have you been watching the news? Have you seen what these bastard Muslims have done now?'

TWELVE

QUEENSBURY TUNNEL.

This was Ronnie's domain. How in hell did the Home Secretary know about the place where Harry's brother buried the bodies?

Ronnie controlled the supply and distribution of heroin in a city only second to Greater London for its drug problem. Ronnie insisted he supplied only a clean product and claimed to be helping rid the city of dealers who cut the heroin with any old crap in the interests of making more money. Clean heroin, he said, was no more toxic than alcohol.

Harry hadn't given up the fight to bring his brother over to the right side of the law, but it was a long struggle.

He parked near the tunnel, BBC Five Live reporting from the 'Bradford terrorist attack' on the radio. He heard that Bradford City Football Club had been evacuated where Tariq had been, opening the new academy that encouraged young players from ethnic minorities to enter the game. The news report said the Home Secretary was currently en route back to Whitehall.

No he bloody wasn't.

Harry's brain couldn't handle any more stress right now.

How did Tariq know about this place?

Was he working with Ronnie, too? Harry pushed the thought from his mind. Tariq was the Home Secretary, of course he wasn't working with Ronnie. He was not though just a cabinet minister. Before entering politics, Tariq had been in the army, in an elite special forces group, no less. There were rumours that he had also been part of a covert group whose very existence was nothing more than speculation.

Eyes closed, hands gripping the steering wheel, he wondered if Tariq and his associates had ventured into the tunnel and found the bodies of the past.

The weapons hidden deep inside.

The secrets which could ruin them both.

Harry didn't like helping Ronnie out from time to time but blood ran thicker than water.

Harry exited his car, hurried to the boot and took off his expensive Rolex, shoving it in his laptop bag; the tunnel was no place for it.

As he looked down towards the entrance, it hit him. There was only one way Tariq Islam could know about this place. He'd been wary of Harry and his methods since a high-profile case threw them together. Tariq must have had him watched.

Queensbury Tunnel was once a busy thoroughfare for passenger trains between the city and Halifax. The Highways Agency had been planning to fill it with concrete and consign it to the history books until a private investor had purchased it for a bargain price. Ronnie.

He used it to remind those bastards who dared cross him just what the entrance to hell felt like.

Dark.

Infested.

Forgotten.

Harry hurried down the steep, parched embankment, barren shrubs scratching at his naked arms. The city needed rainfall, especially today, he thought, remembering the fires raging in City Park. He jumped into the canyon, grateful for the shade.

Pulling a rusted, creaking doorway aside, Harry saw Tariq Islam with a torch on the ground pointing towards the concrete ceiling.

No suit and tie today. Still smart, though: white shirt, dark jeans. That shirt was too clean for this tunnel. Harry suspected Tariq never got his hands dirty. Not any more.

Harry left the door ajar, stepped inside and took up his place opposite Tariq, hands in pockets, waiting.

'Lots of questions, no doubt,' said Tariq.

He didn't reply. He didn't trust his voice not to betray how uneasy he felt.

'What needs to happen now, Harry, are a series of fast, extremely pressurized decisions which might shape the future of this city as well as the next decade's foreign policy and civil liberty programme.'

Harry raised his hand to silence Tariq. Then he pointed deep inside the tunnel where there was nothing but darkness.

'You know this isn't the place for politics. When you walk through that door' – Harry nodded towards the entrance – 'everything is off the record.'

Tariq nodded, arms folded across his chest now. 'You want to know how I came to find out about this place?'

Harry shook his head. 'It's obvious. You had me followed.'

Tariq raised an eyebrow.

'I helped you last year. I did you a massive fucking personal favour. Oh and of course, while I was at it, I got you a career-high poll rating.'

Tariq chewed his lips, listening intently.

'We had an agreement' – Harry pointed to Tariq, his voice gaining an edge now – 'but you couldn't let it lie, could you? Put one of your team on me and realized one day this place existed. Have a snoop inside, did you? Find anything interesting?'

Harry's words were bitter, mostly because he didn't have a hand to play. Tariq knew everything about him.

'Some brother you have there,' said Tariq.

'In another life, you two would get along.'

Tariq nodded. 'Maybe. Something you said to me before really stuck out. Know what it was?'

Harry shook his head, waited.

'You said, Bradford isn't like anywhere else. You've got to stay in the shadows, become the city. Understand its energy, the good and the bad . . .'

Harry remained motionless, recalling those exact words.

Tariq continued, quoting him, '. . . and there are some dark times to come, maybe darker than we've ever known.' He paused. 'Remember that, Harry?'

'I do.'

'Almost like you were predicting the future.'

'This is Bradford. Its future is not without challenges. You know I had nothing to do with this. I was there with my little boy.'

Tariq unfolded his arms and stepped a little closer to Harry, blocking some of the light from the torch, silhouetting half his face. 'Dark times,' he repeated.

Harry stared at the one eye he could see, a sense of dread growing. 'Who the fuck am I speaking to here? The Home Secretary? The ex-special forces commander? Or someone else entirely?'

This time, when Islam spoke, it sounded altogether like military talk, pure facts, no padding – about as far removed from political speak as it got. 'One hundred and five mosques, one bomb. Worshippers are afraid now but in a few hours they'll want to leave, some of them – maybe all. *Impossible* to contain so many people. The guy with a pregnant wife at home, the daughter with chronically ill parents, they're going to want to get back to their loved ones. We've got, I reckon, three hours before the Muslim community starts to crack. With the best intentions in the world, the imams, the police, the politicians, we can urge for calm but ten thousand people spread across a hundred and five sites? We can't control that.'

'Why am I here, Tariq?'

'We also have a blast site to contain,' Tariq continued, as if Harry hadn't spoken. 'A city to sweep for secondary devices and, amidst all that, four dickheads who refer to themselves as the chosen ones to locate and set up in a safe house, while troublemakers in Bradford, maybe even vigilante groups, try to compete with security services to track them down.' He paused, then said, 'Four dead or a thousand? That's what this might come down to if we cannot find that bomb and disarm it without the Patriots knowing.'

Another pause.

Harry had no idea where this might be going.

'We've got a deadline of six a.m. Sunrise.' Islam checked his watch. 'About fifteen hours from now. These . . . Patriots haven't destroyed this city and pulled off this plot without planning it for months. This might come down to choices we simply cannot make.'

'We?' said Harry, feeling the chill of the tunnel on his skin.

'Security services.' Tariq waved his phone at Harry. 'Twitter,' he said, shaking his head ruefully. 'Let me read you some tweets that sum this up.'

Tariq's finger scrolled through his feed.

'*Let the bomb inside the mosque blow! New national holiday #takebackourcountry.*'

It shouldn't have bothered Harry. Twitter heroes were cowardly people.

It did.

Tariq read another. '*Find the leaders of Almukhtaroon and make them Saints! #anothermuslimterroristattack.*' He scrolled for more.

'I get it,' said Harry.

'One more,' replied Tariq. '*Far Right brothers and sisters! Our day has arrived. #whiteandproud.*'

Harry put his hand out and lowered the phone in Tariq's hand.

Islam backed off, holding Harry's gaze. 'What happens if the security services find these four leaders of Almukhtaroon? They have no cards to play. The government does not negotiate with terrorists and that policy will not change simply because thousands of lives are at risk. There are always lives at risk. Either we will get them into safe custody and then pray we're able to disarm the bomb, or we somehow negotiate a truce with the Patriots. If the bomb blows, we will have the start of a new crisis in this country. It could be a generation of nutters born from those who lost loved ones in this siege or a massive surge in popularity for the Far Right who will play on these fears. Either way, we lose.'

Harry knew Tariq was right.

Lose–lose.

With sudden clarity, Harry knew what was coming.

'There is one more option,' said Tariq.

Harry stepped back, leaning against the cold wall of the tunnel, a welcome distraction from the fear burning in his mind.

'If it does come down to the choice between four lives and thousands of lives, I want to be able to make that call, off the record. I need Almukhtaroon in my custody. To do that, I need someone to find them for me.'

THIRTEEN

SAIMA WAS STANDING BY the window in the foyer of the Mehraj mosque. From here she could see the ash as it continued to bloom into the sky from City Park, emergency services all around as fires burned in the distance. It looked like a war zone.

Saima continued to tap at her mobile. Joyti wasn't answering. Why not?

Had something happened? She tried to phone Harry but his phone went straight to voicemail. Outraged, she kicked her foot against the base of the window.

Saima had managed to speak to her sister, who thankfully was not inside a mosque. They had shared an awkward conversation about whether Nadia should inform Saima's parents about her predicament. Their parents had moved to Pakistan soon after Saima had married Harry. That had always been their plan but had been expedited by Saima's decision. The cultural shame, the damnation from the community. Saima had ordered Nadia not to inform their parents. She didn't need the added drama today of all days.

She'd left the grand hall, preferring to watch what was

happening outside. Inside, a search was under way, the men taking control because *clearly* women couldn't find a bomb.

Almost as worrying, dissent was rising. They all wanted to get out of this alive and unharmed. Yet all hundred and five mosques across Bradford would not stand together as one for long. In here, divisions were already forming. Saima heard people whispering about making a break for it.

Out the window she could see the one thing that might stop them. Dozens of officers creating a cordon around the mosque.

Somehow, amid all this chaos, she felt totally alone in the world.

She turned away from the window and glanced at the battery life on her phone: 33 per cent. She couldn't keep trying to call her mother-in-law. She couldn't just stand here, either.

Screw it, she was just as good as anybody else at searching.

Those men would accept her help whether they liked it or not.

FOURTEEN

HARRY HAD SPENT TOO many sombre nights in Queensbury Tunnel.

Usually as the voice of reason.

Now and again as something darker.

What Tariq was asking was impossible.

'Even if I wanted to, I couldn't. Almukhtaroon will be sought by every security service in the country. If they're smart, they'll already be in hiding.'

Harry pointed at Tariq's phone, still in his hands.

'Bet Twitter trolls are putting Almukhtaroon at the top of their most-wanted list. I might know this city better than anyone else but I also know when I'm out of my depth.'

Tariq turned his phone off, the screen fading to darkness, his face no longer illuminated by it.

'Out of your depth?' he said.

'Yes. The whole world is looking for four ghosts who could be anywhere in Bradford right now. How do we even know they are here?'

'They had an organized talk scheduled for this evening. It's on their Twitter page. They're around, all right.'

Harry glanced down the tunnel. 'Maybe so, but I'm beaten here.'

Tariq stayed silent.

'Anyway, murder's not my thing.'

'So, what then?'

Harry shook his head. 'Nothing.'

'I should be talking to your brother?'

'No. I mean, if I had these guys, I'd leave it to Bradford to choose their fate.'

'What do you think Bradford would decide?'

Harry thought about the city's intolerance for anyone who tried to bring it to its knees. If the four leaders of Almukhtaroon were left on the streets, they'd simply become part of its history.

'I think I'd be having dinner with my wife before the sun sets this evening.'

'Mob mentality?'

Harry started to reply, reconsidered and said, 'Street justice.'

'What if you had a head start?'

'I don't.'

'What if—'

Harry suddenly stepped towards Tariq. In the darkness, he would have expected a lesser man to flinch. Tariq didn't move.

'My wife is in one of those mosques, my kid and my mother nearly got caught up in the blast, so, Tariq, why don't you just cut to the chase? What have you got on them?'

Islam looked at his watch.

Harry held his ground.

'I need to be briefed on the COBRA meeting within the hour,' said Tariq.

'Yet you'd rather be here, with me.'

'I'd rather not be at either. They'll assume I've been waylaid by the fallout up here. And all we need to stop Bradford from falling is four fuckers I can't do anything about because they're British citizens.'

He was starting to lose it and Harry didn't like it one bit.

'Abu-Nazir was born here, everyone knows that. The white Geordie ginger lad who moved to London, converted to Islam, went to Syria and returned with an English girl, Amelia Rose, also a Muslim convert. They set up Almukhtaroon.'

Harry knew the cases. They had caused a media sensation when the current Far Right leader, Tyler Sudworth, had a public altercation with Abu-Nazir, calling him by his English name, Kade Turner. Sudworth had handed out a beating to Nazir and all hell had broken loose as Almukhtaroon supporters and Far Right extremists had locked horns. Arrests in their dozens had been made and Sudworth, the self-appointed 'saviour' of white people, had been jailed for six months, gaining an even larger following inside prison.

'Like we said, the security services lose either way on this one – with Almukhtaroon in safe custody or not,' said Tariq.

Harry felt his phone vibrate. A text from Saima.

You OK, and Aaron? What's happening out there? Everyone in here scared. So am I. Miss you. XXX

'I agree you can't win,' said Harry.

'But you can.'

Harry replied to Saima.

I'm fine. Aaron perfect. We'll get through this. We always do. XXX

He put his phone away and focused on Tariq. 'I don't follow.'

'Group-13.'

That got Harry's attention.

The covert para-military organization who officially didn't exist except in internet chat rooms, where arguments raged about who were deadlier, them or the USA's Navy Seal teams. He inched closer to Tariq, recalling speculation that the Home Secretary had once been a member of Group-13.

The men stared at each other.

In a tunnel rich with secrets, the silence they shared for those few seconds told Harry everything he needed to know.

He inched closer still.

'Call them in,' whispered Harry.

'It is being considered. Most cannot be pulled from ongoing missions.'

Tariq stared past him into the darkness of the tunnel.

Harry felt the hairs on the back of his neck stand on end. 'What are you not telling me?' he said.

'It is more complicated. Group-13 don't engage with matters like this,' replied Tariq.

'Then what do they do?'

Tariq didn't answer that. 'If they get caught or pictured here – even a sniff of their existence – it opens up a box of explosives far more dangerous than what is currently ongoing in Bradford. I cannot say any more than that.'

Harry didn't understand. He turned around, looked into the darkness. Tariq arrived at his shoulder, both men now side by side.

'What's down there?' asked Harry.

'Nobody from Group-13,' said Tariq.

'So, who then?'

'Decision time, Harry. If you walk down there and find out then you're involved until this siege ends, no matter the outcome. No going back.'

Aaron. Saima. He couldn't risk them.

'Why do I want any part of this?' asked Harry, focusing on the darkness.

'Because I think you want to be in control of what happens in Bradford today. To the city, to Saima, to your son.'

Tariq was right, of course he was.

Harry didn't want to leave this to chance. He held Tariq's stare for a moment, then stepped into the darkness.

FIFTEEN

THE LIVING ROOM OF the Virdee household was panelled with dark oak and had an ornate fireplace with brown Chesterfield couches either side. Joyti was standing by the living-room window, watching Aaron. He'd eaten his ice cream and was back on the tractor, pretending to drive. Ranjit was sitting behind her, the atmosphere strained, the silence deafening. Joyti had become accustomed to this over the years, always finding solace in standing by the window, watching the world go by. Joyti often used to find Harry standing as she was today, arms folded, deep in thought. Her boy.

She didn't know what to say to her husband. Ranjit had found her with Aaron and stormed out of the kitchen, muttering words and curses that made her relieved her grandson couldn't speak Punjabi.

For so long, her life had been about subservience, always deferring to Ranjit. Even when it lost her a son. However, she had come to see that his was not the only way.

She couldn't – she *wouldn't* – allow Ranjit to take this from her. Her newly formed relationship with Aaron was more important than Ranjit's hatred of what Harry had done.

The stillness felt like a noose around her neck.

How to break it?

'Did you think when we first came to this country that we would ever live in a house with a little tractor to cut our grass?' she said, speaking in Punjabi.

Ranjit said nothing.

'You had two pounds in your pocket. We couldn't speak English. Do you remember how cold it was? How we yearned to go back to India?'

Still nothing.

Joyti smiled, focusing on Aaron, lost in his own little world. 'Do you think, in our fight to succeed, to make a life for ourselves and for our sons, we lost sight of the simple things that make life beautiful?'

She allowed the silence that followed to settle, wondering what was going through Ranjit's mind. He had only glanced at Aaron. Yet in that moment she was certain he had seen what had once taken her breath away – a carbon-copy of their little boy. She might have been wrong, but she thought she saw in Ranjit a flicker of something that wasn't hate.

'He cannot stay here,' said Ranjit finally.

Joyti did not detect the usual force behind his words.

'There is nowhere else,' she replied, keeping her back towards Ranjit. If she saw contempt in his face, she didn't trust herself not to react.

'These people have very large families. There is always some-body there.'

'These people,' said Joyti, shaking her head.

'Muslims.'

'He is my grandchild – our grandchild. *We* are the family to look after him.'

'That man is not my son. Therefore, it is impossible for that boy to be my grandchild.'

'Well, a grandchild of mine must surely be one of yours also,' said Joyti, unable to keep a spiteful edge from her voice.

'You see what happened in Bradford two hours ago? Shall I put on the news for you, woman?'

She turned around to face him, irate. 'Did I see? *Did I see?* Take one look at me, Ranjit. I am covered in ash. We were there, in City Park, only moments before the bomb went off. Do you even care?'

'You see? They nearly take you from me! Nearly bring *more* suffering to our family, and still you entertain these people!'

Joyti steadied her voice. 'My son, his wife and my grandson are not simply "people". Harry saved my life this morning. You would have been proud.'

Ranjit swallowed hard, his eyes alight with rage. 'How many dead this morning? Do you know?'

'That has nothing to do with this.'

'They live in his house. Those who did this.'

Joyti was used to the tired, clichéd arguments. 'If you are referring to Saima—'

'Do not say her name in my house!'

'My house also,' she replied, turning back to face the window. It dawned on her that the bomb blast she had witnessed a couple of hours ago wasn't the most harrowing thing she would experience today.

Joyti could not have the same argument with Ranjit again. She had tired of trying to convince him Saima was not a terrorist simply because she was a Muslim. She focused on Aaron, who was now jumping up and down on the seat of the tractor. She envied him; such innocence, oblivious to the hate that existed in the world, in this room. She would do anything to keep it that way.

'He cannot stay here,' said Ranjit. 'If he does, I will leave and never return.'

She knew he meant it. His anger knew no compromise.

'My house is pure. We left Hardeep and his *filth* behind.'

The words sounded harsher in Punjabi. Again, she managed to remain calm. She paused a moment, thinking of her next move.

'OK,' she said, focusing on Aaron, feeling guilt at what she was about to do. She paused a beat then moved towards Ranjit, stopping in front of him. 'I will take him from this house but I want you to do something for me.'

'Which is?'

'I want your word – your kasam that you will honour my request.' She knew he would not go back on his kasam, a sacred Asian promise made on penalty of death.

'Not until I hear what it is.'

Joyti mocked him, shaking her head. 'A man like you should be willing to do *anything* to protect his home.'

Ranjit got to his feet and nodded solemnly. 'You have my kasam.'

Joyti glanced back towards the window; another glimpse of Aaron, another pang of guilt. She had no choice but to try this.

'I will leave this house with Aaron, but before that, you must look that little angel in the face and tell him yourself that he is not welcome here.'

SIXTEEN

A FEW PACES INTO the tunnel, where the air grew colder still, Harry found an Asian boy, blindfolded and unconscious. He bent to check he was still alive, felt a strong pulse and backed away.

It wasn't the first time he'd seen someone like this in here. But he usually had Ronnie to thank for that.

He glanced at Tariq. 'Am I supposed to know who that is?'

Tariq set the torch on the ground. Water dripped from the roof of the tunnel, thudding to the ground by his feet. The air was chilly, enough to make Harry wish he had another layer on.

'No,' said Tariq, stuffing his hands in his pockets and staring down at the kid.

Harry waited for an explanation.

'One thing you learn in the army, especially special ops, is that in a crisis, fast decisions save lives. You ponder, assess, hesitate too much and, more often than not, it's the difference between life and death. Sometimes it takes just a heartbeat.'

Harry crouched near the kid to get a better look.

Thin, almost painfully so. Long, delicate fingers wrapped around his knees. He looked bound, although it was difficult to see in the light of the tunnel. Patchy stubble.

Harry was certain he'd never seen him before.

'Who is it?' asked Harry.

'Your first impression of him?'

'Scared kid. Not much more to say.' Harry stood up. He wished Ronnie were here. Christ, he needed his counsel today. Ronnie might be the vicious one but he was also the smart one. IQ off the charts. When they were kids, he'd been headed for Oxbridge, until he'd gone to prison in place of Harry, protecting him from a murder charge – albeit one that had saved their mother's life after a bungled armed robbery at their corner shop.

Harry had never forgiven himself.

And now here they were, one brother upholding the law, the other breaking it. Complicated wasn't the word.

'Who's the kid?' asked Harry, pulling himself back to the present.

'It's Isaac Wolfe.' Tariq smiled, almost rueful, as if he'd hoped the name would trigger a response. When it didn't he unlocked his phone, accessed a video file and handed it to Harry, who only needed to watch the first few seconds before he hit Pause.

'What the fuck,' he whispered, looking from Tariq to the kid in disbelief.

The video was a typically vile broadcast by the leaders of Almukhtaroon.

Standing beside Abu-Nazir was Amelia Rose, the black widow mooted as his long-term partner and widely speculated to have been responsible for the recruitment of many vulnerable young Muslims to travel to Syria and join the 'resistance'. Then there was Fahad-Bin-Azeez, the muscle behind the pair's organization, and finally a young, naive-looking kid.

The same kid who was unconscious on the floor of the tunnel.

Tariq's voice was cold, his gaze steady, as he explained. While officials took advice on the legitimacy of the threat and pored over the Patriots' videos – both the one released on social media and the one sent directly to the police – Tariq had put his trust in a member of his close-protection team.

'How did he know where to look?' asked Harry.

'Intel on the police database.'

'How did he get access?'

'Trusted sources.'

'Auditable ones?'

'The security services got the video from the Patriots fifteen minutes before it was released to social media. The bastards gave us that window to get the message through to the imams in the mosques to seal their doors. I used it to consider what would happen after the bomb exploded. Like I said, it's the decisions you make in the seconds after learning intel that can define what comes to pass. The police database showed Isaac had a record for assault and that he'd been in a youth detention centre until a year ago. His last known address was listed and we took a punt. Bingo.'

Harry rubbed a sweaty palm across his stubble.

This wasn't happening.

Tariq continued, calm, measured. 'I can't be anywhere near this for obvious reasons. Realistically, neither can Group-13. Manhunts are not what they do. Time is our main enemy here, Harry.'

Harry felt his blood boil. This was a major threat. He did not like Tariq's dismissive tone. He turned to voice his displeasure to find Tariq had his hand raised in anticipation.

'There are many things you don't know. Group-13 do not officially exist and even if I could speak to . . . certain people, they would arrive here far too late. The world's media is upon us, an entire city is in lockdown, and with every security service we have pulling together, Group-13 could not even be ghosts here.'

'And you think I can?' said Harry, perplexed.

Tariq looked around the tunnel. 'You seem to have a

particular set of skills, which today might just give this city a fighting chance.'

With Ronnie in India, Harry had no leverage and no access to the muscle Ronnie employed. Harry's 'particular set of skills' in this instance would just be his determination to keep his family safe.

'I'm alone here,' said Harry. 'You've got the wrong man.'

Irritation flashed across Tariq's face. 'If we walk away from this . . . mess and it all turns to shit, will you ever look back on this moment and forgive yourself?'

Harry thought of Saima.

Scared, alone.

He rubbed his hand across his face again, head hurting.

For the next fifteen hours, Almukhtaroon would be the most hunted people on the planet. Harry had seen the videos they put out on the internet. Abu-Nazir was a charismatic son-of-a-bitch and now, with everyone looking for him, he'd be rallying those closest to him, those he could convince to bring about carnage on the streets of Bradford.

Go out in a blaze of glory.

Harry folded his arms across his chest, a chill zipping down his spine. He sighed.

'What do I have from you?' he asked Tariq, without looking at him.

A hand on his shoulder, squeezing it firmly.

'Anything and everything I've got.'

Alone now, Harry had allowed Tariq to leave, having formed the loosest of alliances. Tariq had given him a cheap burner phone with his number programmed into the memory. It would be the only way they would communicate. Tariq intended to set himself up at Gold Command. With Bradford on lockdown, he could not get out of the city back to Whitehall. Harry could only imagine what ACC Frost would make of that.

Harry had ventured deep into the belly of the tunnel and unearthed a bag Ronnie kept for times like these.

When someone needed to be broken.

Harry wouldn't do it here. Looking at Isaac and knowing his background, the tunnel might serve to deepen his resolve.

No. For this particular task Harry needed to change the game.

SEVENTEEN

TWO HOURS SINCE THE bomb had gone off and West Yorkshire Assistant Chief Constable Steven Frost had just finished his first full Gold Command meeting. Together he and his opposite number in the Counter-Terrorism Unit, Peter Weetwood, had established five critical areas to focus on.

1. Stabilize City Park and contain any ongoing terrorist activity.
2. Identify the previously unheard-of terrorist group calling themselves the Patriots.
3. Locate the four leaders of so-called Almukhtaroon and get them into safe custody.
4. Maintain police presence at as many of the 105 mosques in the city as was possible.
5. Increase general police presence to ensure Bradford did not fall into civil unrest.

'I don't need to remind you all,' he'd said to the crowded briefing room just before he'd dismissed them, 'this is as serious as it gets.

There is nothing too small to warrant our attention here. Everything is relevant. I want all eyes and ears open. And don't do anything stupid.'

The Prime Minister had offered him whatever resources he needed. Officers and patrols from Newcastle to Humberside were currently en route to Bradford. There'd soon be more police here than Frost knew what to do with.

The wild card was the hostage situation. Frost had thousands of people inside the mosques on lockdown. For now, the worshippers were afraid enough to stay there – uncertain of just what was happening in Bradford. He didn't think it would be long before that dynamic changed. If the mosques started to empty, the pressing question became whether to enforce the confinement, something only achievable once the added manpower from the north arrived.

Frost could not be sure of the risks involved. But he felt certain it wouldn't take much for things to go very wrong. He did not want that happening on his watch. For now, the safest place they could be was inside their mosques. The threat of the supposed second device had not yet been verified.

The blast in the park had been right next to Britannia House, where the city's CCTV surveillance was housed. It was currently offline, meaning most of Bradford was unmonitored. Work was frantically under way to restore the network but that might take hours and, as the Patriots had made clear, the clock was ticking.

Frost knew all about Almukhtaroon. It was hard to forget their leader, the man known formerly as Kade Turner who, on converting to Islam, had taken the name Abu-Nazir. He now enjoyed a cult following – the white jihadi with bright ginger hair and a distinctly blond beard. He certainly made an impression.

The Home Secretary, Tariq Islam, had tried to prosecute both Nazir and his partner – and second-in-command – Amelia Rose eighteen months before, and suffered a humiliating defeat when the European Court of Justice ruled the UK had violated *their* human rights. The result had seen support for the Far Right surge.

The muscle behind the leaders was Fahad-Bin-Azeez, commonly referred to simply as Azeez. He was a former power-lifting champion who'd fled Somalia as a teenager and served time for petty thefts and grievous bodily harm. It was in prison that he had been radicalized by sympathizers of Almukhtaroon. Once released, he had joined the organization, quickly climbing the ranks until he sat alongside Abu-Nazir and Amelia Rose.

The fourth and newest senior member of the organization was just a kid: Isaac Wolfe. His role had seemingly been to attract a younger audience – angry teenagers, easy to manipulate. Isaac had recently been released from a youth detention centre and had spoken on social media about how his generation had been forgotten by British society. He was the only one with a registered address in the city. It looked like it had been his mum's place, but she'd died not long before he'd been convicted. The other leaders of Almukhtaroon were listed as NFA – no fixed abode – which made them harder to track down, requiring intelligence. Officers were on their way to Isaac's home to take him into protective custody. Frost didn't have much hope they would find him there. His name was all over the news. While Frost was setting up the Gold Command room and delegating roles and priorities, Isaac Wolfe would have had time to escape.

For all Frost knew about Almukhtaroon, he knew next to nothing about the Patriots or what they were capable of.

Initial reports from City Park suggested no casualties, which Frost didn't believe. The blast site covered 4,000 square metres. City Park was nothing more than ash.

Without the twenty-minute warning to the public, the death toll might have been in the hundreds. Why give the warning? What sort of terrorist wanted to prevent major loss of life?

Frost played the YouTube video again. The national cyber agency hadn't yet sent through their analysis. The Patriots were targeting Almukhtaroon to show the rest of the UK that those with obvious animosity towards the country and its Western values would no longer be tolerated – this was extreme Far Right ideology.

Perhaps it was the inevitable outcome after so many years of terror attacks.

Frost didn't like the look of it. A damn slippery slope to total anarchy.

He saw it clearly. Gold Command had to secure Almukhtaroon before anyone else got to them.

EIGHTEEN

LOOKING OUT FROM THE front door at Aaron still driving the tractor, Ranjit could not quite believe his grandson was half Muslim.

His father would be turning in his grave. The man who had called Muslims a virus, who had declared them toxic, a danger to his family and to the world.

His father, though, had not seen this little boy, this tiny version of Hardeep.

He pushed the uncomfortable thoughts from his mind and focused on Aaron.

This had to be done.

Hardeep had no idea just how difficult he had made life for his father. People in his community had shunned him, even after he had disowned Hardeep. How could a senior member of the Sikh Temple have allowed this to happen? Ranjit had stepped down from the committee. Some said he should have killed Hardeep.

He thought back to the night Hardeep had told him he was going to marry that wretched girl. There had been a moment of anger,

Ranjit had drawn his sword, but Joyti had put herself between father and son.

Would he have done it?

He'd asked himself that question every day since.

And 'Aaron'. Who were they kidding? A white name for an already confused boy. He would grow older and embrace the Muslim faith. And then what? Aaron would go on to marry a Muslim and the Virdee bloodline would forever be ruined.

If the elders in India ever found out . . . it didn't bear thinking about.

He stepped from the house, the sunshine warming his face.

Ranjit approached Aaron, his hand reaching to scratch his forehead, his turban uncomfortable in the heat.

Joyti watched from the window, fists clenched, eyes watery. She was only now aware that she might have placed her boy in danger. Ranjit's demeanour was clear. He had opted to put his turban on, marching out to meet Aaron with his Sikh identity at the forefront.

She wanted to run outside and protect the boy as she watched Ranjit crouch in front of him so they were both almost level with each other. Aaron stuck out his hand, smiling brightly.

He had never looked more like Hardeep.

A tear slid down Joyti's face, the tension unbearable as she watched her husband staring at Aaron, not saying a word.

She thought of Harry's words: *Look after my boy, Mum.*

Joyti felt her feet moving but stopped – she wanted to have faith in this moment, in this man.

She dug her nails into the palms of her hands, breaking the skin.

'Shake his hand, you shake it,' she hissed, trembling in anger, blinking away tears.

He didn't. He got to his feet and walked away, back towards the house, quicker than she had seen him move in a long time.

Joyti moved too, towards the front door.

She marched into the hallway, ready to unleash her anger at her husband, but was stopped dead as Ranjit barged past, their shoulders colliding. He wasn't quick enough that she didn't see his face. Or the tears sliding down it.

NINETEEN

HARRY PULLED UP AT an old farmhouse frequented by Ronnie when he needed a softer location to carry out some of his work. There was nothing for miles around, just field after field.

Perfect.

A quick sweep of the house confirmed it was empty.

Checking that the burner phone Tariq had given him was turned off, he went to get Isaac from the car.

The kid was still unconscious. For how much longer, Harry didn't know. Tariq said they had injected him with a sedative that usually lasted a couple of hours.

Harry carried him into the house and laid him down on an old leather couch in the living room.

He patted the boy down.

No mobile phone.

No wallet.

Nothing hidden under his Islamic robes.

Harry took in more details about the boy. He was extremely fair for an Asian kid, his skin was light and his dark hair had a red tint to it. Harry wondered if one of his parents might have been white.

He checked Isaac's hands, feeling his pulse again. Harry frowned at the thumb on the kid's right hand, markedly thinner than his other. He'd seen this before.

What he really needed was robust intel on the boy and the only place to get that was Isaac's home, an address Tariq had given him.

Police would be there by now, tearing the house to pieces.

Removing his phone, Harry saw several missed calls, all from his boss, Detective Superintendent Clare Conway, but she didn't pick up when he called her back.

16.15.

Waiting around here for Isaac to wake up without a plan was futile.

Harry secured the boy's feet to the base of the couch using handcuffs, ensured his hands were still tightly bound and put a crude gag around his mouth.

The only thing that gave him a fighting chance was information. And the only place he was going to get that was at Isaac's.

TWENTY

PRAYERS FILTERED THROUGH THE Mehraj mosque's PA system as Saima made her way towards the basement. Full of aid boxes and constantly in a state of disorder, it was the obvious place to hide a bomb.

Saima had to take her mind off Aaron, left in the care of grandparents he barely knew.

She whispered for God to give her boy strength.

It wasn't just Aaron she was thinking of. Her mother's voice would not leave her mind.

Hellfire.

Marrying Harry had been bad. But the year before she had done something much worse.

Her life had been on the line.

She knew she'd had no choice. Saima had not forgiven herself for taking a man's life. And Harry . . . Ronnie . . . all the dark things they did, surely . . .

Was this the inevitable damnation for their sins?

She whispered another prayer and forced her mind to focus. She could do nothing with those thoughts now.

For the first time, all the mosques in Bradford were united. Sunni? Shia? Ahmadi? It didn't matter. It was only temporary, Saima knew that.

Once the bomb was located, what then?

Saima had a child who needed her – could she really put the solidarity of her faith before that? She knew she wouldn't be the only one having these thoughts.

The Muslim community spoke proudly of what it saw as its collective responsibility to care for one another. What better way to test that resolve?

She walked down a narrow corridor and checked her phone.

Nothing from Harry.

She wanted to try Joyti again but resisted. Hearing Aaron's voice would send her over the edge.

Saima arrived at a large set of automatic doors. They opened for her and she entered. Seeing the large wooden crates marked *Clothes*, *Dried fruits*, *Water* and *Canned goods* she was reminded of an article in the local *Telegraph & Argus* about how the council was also using some of the space for its own aid programme, lauded as a cross-working collaboration between the Muslim community and the wider population of Bradford.

Hearing voices, she stopped. Men were checking the boxes one by one. Many crates had been opened, with two teams of men taking responsibility for specific areas.

From the shadows, she watched as another was opened. A man was using a tool to remove what she assumed were metal clips, judging by the noise they made. It took a few minutes before several men carefully pulled the wooden cover free.

It was bottled water. They spent a few minutes inspecting it thoroughly, then moved on to the next.

Saima wanted to help but she knew these men would not take kindly to a woman interrupting their work. She was looking for something she could do when she heard a change in the other team's voices. She heard gasps and one of the men cursed.

Inside a mosque?

Their voices turned to whispers, then prayers.

She stepped out from the shadows, the men unaware she was there, creeping up behind them, peering into the container.

For a moment, she didn't know what had caused the commotion.

Wires.

Dozens of cylindrical structures.

Then it hit her.

'God help us,' she whispered.

TWENTY-ONE

HARRY ARRIVED OUTSIDE ISAAC Wolfe's home, a small terraced house on a side street not far from a large amusement park in Thornbury, and found it sealed off by a yellow police cordon, with two armed officers at the front door and uniformed constables on the street. He had taken his work laptop from the boot and checked to see if there was any pertinent information detailed for Isaac.

Harry imagined the CTU detectives inside. They wouldn't be searching the place thoroughly, more of a once-over. Technically, this was a 'locate and protect' exercise. Isaac hadn't broken any laws.

Unless, that is, CTU thought Almukhtaroon were complicit in an ongoing terrorist plot. It wasn't impossible. At any given moment, the Counter-Terrorism Unit was dealing with thousands of operations.

Harry called his boss. DS Clare Conway answered. Judging from the noise in the background, she was at Gold Command. Phones rang, voices were raised, doors slammed.

'Harry? Where are you? Are you OK?'

He told her about his day, everything but his meeting with Tariq.

'Jesus, Harry, I was hoping to call you in but I can't have you working after that. You're sure you're not in shock?'

Her concern sounded genuine, but he heard the tinge of disappointment that she was a member of her team down.

'I'm outside Isaac Wolfe's house, Clare.'

'What? Harry, I don't expect you to be operational – not after what you've been through this morning. Not with Saima in one of the mosques. You're compromised.'

'Less sympathy, more focus, Clare. I'll let you know if it gets too much,' he replied flatly.

He heard her sigh in relief.

Harry thought she might have asked how he knew of the address – another reason he had used his laptop to log on. But she didn't.

'What has Frost tasked us with?' asked Harry.

'It's fluid, Harry. Right now it's finding the four leaders of Almukhtaroon and seeing if there's anything connecting them to the Patriots.'

Perfect.

'Who's in charge inside the house?' he said, opening the driver's door.

'DS Taylor, CTU.'

'Veronica Taylor?'

'Yes.'

'Got it. We were in the academy together. I'm going to assist, Clare. See if there's anything of interest.'

There were photos everywhere of Isaac and a woman Harry assumed to be his mother.

No sign of a father.

The place should have felt like a home but it was a mess. Dust swirling in the wake of the detectives, clothes and dishes everywhere and, in the kitchen, a bin overflowing with empty McDonald's milkshake cups. The sweet smell lingered.

Harry moved through the house with authority. Unlike the other officers, Harry was looking for something very specific – a weakness.

Upstairs, Isaac's bedroom was a typical teenager's room, full of clutter and disorder that was clearly there even before the detective started rooting through everything. All over the walls were vibrant posters of superheroes – the Hulk, Superman and Judge Dredd.

DS Taylor handed Harry some paperwork. 'Get up to speed,' she said, not unkindly. The state of the house suddenly made sense. The batch of papers Harry was looking at included a death certificate. Isaac's mother had died from breast cancer two years ago.

Harry did the maths. Isaac had been taken into custody and placed in a youth detention centre two months after his mother's passing.

'Christ,' he called out as he leafed through the remaining papers. 'This kid got straight A* at GCSEs. He did four A levels, getting top marks. Puts him what? Highest one per cent of the country?'

DS Taylor grimaced at him.

'The house is clear, Harry. There's nothing here to help us find him. He could have gone anywhere.' She ran her hands through her hair. 'This is a nightmare.'

With resources at breaking point, she discharged the firearms officers, leaving two uniformed constables protecting the cordon.

'SOCOs are on their way from Wakefield but they'll be another hour. All of ours are out in City Park.' DS Taylor looked tired already. Harry could sympathize.

'I'm just going to look around, get a feel for all this. See you back at base.'

She nodded and took two steps towards the door before she turned back to him. 'Everything all right, Harry?'

Harry smiled at her. 'Fine. I was in City Park earlier – taking a while to shake it off.'

'I'm not surprised. Don't do anything stupid,' DS Taylor said as she left the house.

Alone now, inside Isaac's bedroom, Harry set to work, hoping for some information he might use to test Isaac's loyalties. This wasn't some stupid, impressionable kid. Something had gone badly wrong here. He just needed to find out what.

Lifting the mattress, a rage overcame him. Saima was in one of those mosques, her life in danger because of these people. What he wanted to do was tear Isaac limb from limb, put him through the kind of pain guaranteed to get him talking and find out where the other three leaders of Almukhtaroon were.

It could take time. And he only had a little over twelve hours until the Patriots' deadline.

Harry systematically took the bedroom to pieces, starting with the bed and working his way around. He wasn't really sure what he expected to find.

The wardrobe was interesting. Traditional Islamic clothes for the most part, yet in the back, wrapped in protective plastic covers, he found designer clothing. No price tags. These were clothes that had been worn then carefully stored; they were clearly special to Isaac.

The desk was chaotic. Yet piled neatly to one side were several A4 drawing pads featuring incredibly detailed sketches of what appeared to be a comic superhero called Isiah. The character reminded Harry of Popeye, who would eat a can of spinach and transform himself from weed into hero. Isiah was identical, except he was Asian and ate lentils. His nemesis was a character called the Undertaker, a figure cloaked in black whose superpower was to be able to read other people's minds, control them and, if they did not comply, make them kill themselves. The detail was stunning. Harry put the drawing pads aside to take with him.

The bottom drawer had books on mindfulness and spirituality

alongside several blisters of medication. He pulled it out and emptied it on the bed.

The medication was recent, the labels only a week old. Propranolol hydrochloride 10mg and Amitriptyline 10mg tablets. Harry had no clue what they were for. Maybe the kid needed them. Harry wasn't about to be the one to kill him.

He made for the door. He couldn't risk being here when the SOCOs arrived.

He stopped in the doorway and turned around.

Something was missing.

He cast his eyes over the room once more.

Nothing religious.

No textbooks.

No teaching materials.

Absolutely nothing.

He looked at the posters, the all-action heroes. Judge Dredd was apparently the boy's favourite.

Something wasn't right here.

Outside, Harry put two large carrier bags in his boot along with a change of Western clothing for the boy. He wasn't concerned the uniformed officers had seen him; they were too junior to think of it as anything other than a detective doing his job.

Harry Googled what Isaac's medication was for. He relaxed a little. For the first time, he felt like he was in the game.

Harry started his car and pulled away from the house.

He knew exactly how he was going to break the kid.

TWENTY-TWO

THE MEN WHO FOUND the bomb immediately locked the entrance to the basement. They had been shocked to find Saima there and surprised to see her hardly react.

This was Saima's worst nightmare.

Not being locked in a basement with a group of unfamiliar men.

Not being close to a bomb.

No. It was losing control of her destiny. Whether she left this mosque alive or not was in someone else's hands. Saima hated to feel powerless.

Someone had gone upstairs to discreetly alert the imam. They were awaiting his arrival – his counsel.

'What now?' one of the men said.

Nobody answered.

Saima took out her phone and saw that she had one bar of reception.

'We phone the police,' she said.

They turned to look at her.

Saima saw an opportunity to seize back some of the power the Patriots had taken from her.

'My husband is a police officer. I'll call him. We can't call 999 and report this. We need to know whoever we report it to won't leak it and encourage the other mosques to break out – it's this bomb that goes off if they do. How we control this information is critical.'

There were nods of agreement.

'And we should keep this to ourselves until such time as Imam Hashim is ready to inform the rest of the mosque. There's no knowing how people will react. If we have a stampede because people want to run, we might all die.'

She delivered her words with authority and clarity of mind.

Saima stared hard at the men in the room.

Some looked resilient. Others like they would run at the first chance they got.

It wasn't that Saima was not afraid. She absolutely was. But the fact the bomb was here was something she could not change.

Her heart was aching thinking about Aaron. Yet Saima had to focus on the one positive. Harry was out there. And Harry always came through for her.

Saima scrolled to Harry's number and hit Call. Three rings. Seven.

'Saima?' he said.

It sounded like Harry was driving. She told him to pull over, waiting until he had.

'What is it, Saima? Are you OK?' he said, clear concern in his voice.

She took a breath.

'It's here, Harry. The bomb. I'm looking at it.'

TWENTY-THREE

ACC FROST HAD ENOUGH on his plate without having to babysit the damn Home Secretary. Leeds Bradford airport had closed down as a result of the bombing, as had rail services. With no quick way to return to Whitehall, Islam had posted himself at Gold Command, promising to send COBRA real-time updates.

Frost had heard the exchange between Islam and the Prime Minister. As operational leader of this incident, he wanted to know everything, including what politics were at play. He'd been silently patched on to the call.

The PM did not want Tariq anywhere near this. Politicians needed to shift blame, he had said, especially if things did not go according to plan. This was no place for a Home Secretary, even if he was ultimately responsible for security arrangements within the UK.

Tariq wouldn't hear of it.

'I'm the first Muslim politician to have ever climbed this high. Bradford needs me to be visible, so to hell with the politics.' Frost would not have entertained his subordinate talking to him in this way. 'If I went running back to London, I would forever be remembered as the cowardly Muslim Home Secretary who fled for the sanctuary of Whitehall in one of the country's darkest hours.'

It would ruin him.

Tariq had cut the line before the PM could counter his argument.

Frost had put the phone down, pissed off on the PM's behalf.

Now Tariq was waiting in the conference room for Frost. He could wait a little longer.

Three hours post bombing and Bradford had been secured. Motorways into the city had road blocks. The official line was 'security protocols'. In reality they were doing two things: trying to stop the leaders of Almukhtaroon fleeing, and also stop an influx of potential protesters, Far Right or otherwise. Social media was rife with speculation of a demonstration later that evening.

Frost received updates from his team every fifteen minutes. The latest briefing was coming to an end.

'Nothing at Isaac Wolfe's house, sir,' said DS Taylor.

'Nothing?' he asked, incredulous.

She shook her head. 'The good news is that we've received confirmation that we have five hundred officers from Humberside and the North East en route to Bradford as we speak.'

Frost nodded to dismiss her. He made his way to the conference room, where Tariq Islam was speaking with Peter Weetwood.

'This is really not what we need,' said Frost, closing the door. He could feel eyes on him – the whole floor stealing glances through the glass partition wall. Frost didn't close the blinds. They needed to see who was in charge here and it certainly was not the Home Secretary.

Tariq raised his hands passively and stepped away from Weetwood. 'Before you launch into some prepared speech—'

'Prepared speech?' Frost closed the gap between the two men and pointed angrily. 'We're three hours into this shit-storm. It's moving faster than anything we've dealt with before. The only prepared speech I have is the resignation I've wanted to submit since you fucked up policing in this country.'

Fucking politicians.

'Not the time or the place for politics,' replied Tariq, looking a little flustered.

Weetwood put a hand on Frost's shoulder, his attempt to calm the hostility.

Frost shrugged it away. 'Then why are you here?' he snapped at Tariq.

'If I was playing politics, I'd be on my way back to Whitehall. I'm here to be accountable.'

That stopped Frost. Accountable – he didn't think politicians knew the meaning of the word.

'Whichever mosque the bomb is inside will potentially have hundreds of Muslims inside, right?' said Tariq.

Frost nodded and beckoned for them all to sit down. He remained close to Weetwood, both men firm in their resolve not to fall victim to whatever game Tariq Islam was playing.

'If this goes badly, we need everyone to know that not only did we do everything in our power but that every rung of the ladder played its part. We're at a crossroads where both Far Right and religious extremists are vying for power. We cannot give it to either. The Patriots say that I failed to jail the founders of Almukhtaroon last year – that is my responsibility. Let me speak to them – let them know I am here and willing to negotiate.'

'Negotiate?' Frost and Weetwood spoke at the same time.

'Standard protocols went out the window the moment that bomb went off. I'm not saying I can give them anything but maybe talking about it buys us time.'

'And maybe the Patriots realize you are playing a game and all rules go out the window,' Weetwood said, almost to himself.

Tariq leaned closer, his face turned away from the glass wall of the conference room. He didn't want anyone outside to lip-read what he was about to say.

'Four leaders of Almukhtaroon dead or many, many innocent civilians. What if it comes down to that equation? We all know it might.'

Frost didn't say anything. He glanced at Weetwood, who avoided eye contact.

'How many officers do you have looking for them?' said Tariq.

'Over thirty.'

'How confident are you?'

A pause.

'Gentlemen, we are currently *off* the record.'

Frost shook his head. 'They go underground and it's a lottery. We might get one or two, but all four?'

'Is that our absolute priority at the moment, getting the four leaders of Almukhtaroon into custody?'

'*Safe* custody,' replied Frost.

'Damn it, Steven, we are off the record here.'

'What are you saying, Mr Islam?'

'I am saying that I do not believe that four lives are of more value than hundreds of lives.' Tariq gathered himself up. 'Gentlemen, I'm here to facilitate things which perhaps you can't sanction. All I need is for you both to stand up and walk out of that door if you are content for me to stay and explore every option. If not, remain where you are and we can debate some more.'

Tariq folded his arms across his chest and waited.

The men were interrupted by a harsh knocking on the door and a flustered-looking detective entered without being asked. He told Frost that DCI Harry Virdee was on line two, apparently with crucial information.

Frost nodded and waited for the detective to leave before hurrying to a phone in the corner of the room. He put it on speaker.

'Virdee, sir. Saima found the bomb.'

TWENTY-FOUR

HARRY FELT NUMB. HE let the car idle in the driveway of the Queensbury farmhouse. The Mehraj mosque, Bradford's newest, was the largest in the city. If he were honest with himself, Harry hadn't been all that shocked when Saima had told him she'd found the bomb. There was no higher profile location it could have been.

He had just finished his call to Frost.

'Do you think we can trust Saima to be our eyes inside there, Harry?'

'Absolutely,' Harry said. He wanted Saima distracted so she didn't go crazy worrying about him or Aaron. Frost needed someone with a cool head to relay information about the bomb to CTU and, as far as Harry was concerned, Saima was the perfect candidate. She dealt with pressure every day in her job at A&E.

'And do you think we could task her with taking pictures and some video of the device?' Frost's voice was rich with concern but also sounded desperate.

Harry gave him Saima's number and told him he backed his wife to do it. He hung up, tried to call her and, unable to connect, sent her a text.

Frost is going to call. Head of this investigation. He needs help from inside the mosque and I trust you to do it. Stay in control, Saima. We will get through this. I love you x

Harry knew Saima was more than capable of the job.

How long could Frost contain this information?

Harry's heart was racing.

Inside the mosque, if the imam lost control of his worshippers, this might all unravel quickly. Frost was all over it, he knew. But he had more reason than ever to find the Almukhtaroon himself.

Frost had understood Harry's request, with his wife's life at risk, to stand down from this operation and return to his son. Harry had told him he'd return once he was certain Aaron was OK.

Time was against them. Saima had told him there were a dozen men with her. In Harry's experience, that was too many to contain a secret. Somebody would leak it. Then what?

Harry threw his phone on to the passenger seat, angry, an imaginary clock pounding inside his head. He looked down at the two McDonald's milkshakes in the passenger footwell. He'd bought them for Isaac on his way back, before Saima had called.

Was he putting his neck on the line for nothing?

Was he risking Saima's life by not handing over Isaac to Frost?

No, his boss would do this by the book. And Tariq was right – the book might not serve Harry in this instance.

He had little choice but to at least try, though he didn't like his chances of apprehending the other three leaders of Almukhtaroon before sunrise. Bradford had over three hundred thousand inhabitants; this was a fucking needle in a haystack.

Harry closed his eyes; his head felt like it was about to explode.

Christ, he missed Ronnie. Today of all days his brother's counsel would have been welcome. Last Harry had heard, Ronnie and his family were headed for the remoteness of Shimla – north India, a cooler climate than the rest of the blistering country. It was 11 p.m. in India. He'd tried to call him while waiting for the shakes at McDonald's – no reception.

He didn't like to ask himself what Ronnie would do in this situation. Harry wasn't keen to beat Isaac Wolfe to a pulp, not unless it was strictly necessary. He thought about the kid's stellar school grades, the untimely death of his mother and the stretch inside the youth detention centre. That was the key – who had he mixed with there and what impact had it left on the vulnerable boy? Harry thought of the sketches he had seen. Each one dated, and all of them before his time in the secure unit – that was who Isaac Wolfe really was.

That was who he needed to find.

Harry entered the living room and saw Isaac awake, still secure, still gagged.

The boy glared at him, more in anger than fear.

Not a good sign.

A strong smell of urine hit Harry as he untied Isaac's hands but kept the cuffs around his feet secure.

A pool of piss around Isaac's feet.

Harry removed the gag, expecting rage and got none. Isaac remained silent.

Harry placed the milkshakes on the table.

'Banana or strawberry?' he asked, waving them at Isaac.

No reply.

He looked as though he'd been crying, eyes red raw.

He stuck the strawberry shake in his lap, retreated and sat on a chair opposite.

Isaac bowed his head.

It was the urine. The smell. The evidence of it around his ankles. The embarrassment alone made what Harry hoped to achieve that bit harder.

Harry replaced his shake on the table, took Isaac's from his lap and stooped to free Isaac's feet.

'This is very simple,' said Harry, backing away. 'If you try anything, anything at all, you'll force my hand and I won't be nice.'

Harry paused, then added, 'And trust me, this is me being nice.'
Isaac's head remained bowed.

Harry was struck again at just how immature the kid looked – a twenty-one-year-old who looked no more than sixteen.

'I know what you think this is, what you think is going to happen. If that were true, I wouldn't be telling you to go upstairs, take a shower, then change into some clothes I lifted from your place.'

Isaac met Harry's gaze, anger fractionally diminished.

Harry was impatient. He didn't have time for any of this. He knew though that force would make Isaac more resistant. It would make him shut down, revelling in the knowledge that all the Western hostility shit he had no doubt been brainwashed with was valid.

He forced a smile. 'None of this is going to be like you thought it was, Isaac. As soon as you've had a shower, drunk your milkshake and given me a chance to show you why, you'll see that the only person in control here is you.'

TWENTY-FIVE

ACC STEVEN FROST WAS in a peculiar situation. The fact Harry's wife was inside the Mehraj mosque with the bomb was both of great concern and, at the same time, offered an interesting opportunity.

Two further experts had given their views on the video of the bomb the Patriots had disclosed to them. They needed more information – a closer look, picture and video clips, maybe even a live stream. And for that, they now had a candidate. If Harry thought Saima was capable, Frost was more than happy to go along with that.

Council planning documents listed the new mosque as having a maximum capacity of 1,500 people. That number had made Frost's legs wobble.

It couldn't happen.

While they were waiting for estimates of how many people were inside, Gold Command had spent the past hour discussing their strategy for the other hundred and four mosques, all of which were still under lockdown. According to the Patriots' demands, now they had located the bomb, they needed to let this be known, then they could begin to free those trapped in the other mosques.

Hashim would need to inform his followers and then, ideally, Frost would get high volumes of uniformed officers at each mosque in turn to ensure they evacuated in an orderly fashion and were subject to no hate-related attacks. The command room had now received solid information that the Far Right were making a bee-line for Bradford.

Moving that volume of men around a stalled city would take time. And the longer Frost waited to evacuate the other mosques, the greater the risk they would break out of their own accord, triggering the bomb. He would not have that on his watch.

Frost did the only thing he could. He increased the manpower of the team he had tasked to liaise with the imams of the other mosques, ordering them to organize an orderly evacuation of their sites, but only once Imam Hashim had informed his worshippers the bomb had been located.

Frost may have been the Assistant Chief Constable and 'in charge', but this had all the makings of an impossible situation. He couldn't help but feel out of his depth. They were four hours into this mess and, so far, none of the Almukhtaroon leaders had been found. If they were smart, they'd have gone underground and wouldn't surface until after sunrise tomorrow.

His job was to protect their lives. Social media was already rife with death threats made against them from a whole host of angry groups – Muslims looking to defend their places of worship, Far Right activists jumping on the opportunity to incite hate, and smaller, local groups just wanting to cause bedlam. The four leaders of Almukhtaroon were currently the most hunted in the country. While Frost would have traded the bastards in a heartbeat for the people inside the Mehraj mosque, it was simply wishful thinking on his part. If he got them into protective custody, he wouldn't be able to hand them over to the Patriots. All he could do would be to send the military into the mosque. If he didn't capture them, he would not risk the population inside the Mehraj mosque and would still be sending the military in, before the deadline expired.

Damned if he did and damned if he didn't.

Lost in his thoughts, he didn't notice a junior member of staff knock lightly on his office door until he coughed politely.

'Yes?' he asked abruptly.

'Sir, we've had word from Imam Hashim.' He paused, as though unsure whether he should continue.

Frost waved him on.

'There are one thousand and nine people in the Mehraj mosque.'

Frost felt sick.

Senior military commanders were currently analysing their options with regards to the mosque and he had a conference call with COBRA scheduled in fifteen minutes. He would have to let them know what they were dealing with.

First, though, Frost dialled Saima's number. DS Conway had offered to do it, having met Saima several times, but Frost needed to hear Saima's voice himself – feel her confidence, or lack of it. He hoped she was as resilient as Harry had suggested.

Her number failed to connect the first time. Second time, he heard it ring. In his peripheral vision, Frost could see the military commanders huddled together, working on their strategy – a hostile entry into the mosque. Unless they could disarm the bomb from the inside, it was inevitable. Frost desperately wanted to avoid that, for one main reason.

It was nothing more than a fifty–fifty chance.

His call connected.

'Is that Saima Virdee?' he asked.

'Hi, yes, it is,' she said. Saima's voice crackled noisily, her reception poor.

'This is Assistant Chief Constable Steven Frost. I—'

'I know who you are. Harry told me you would call.'

'I'm pleased. Are you able to speak in private?'

'Yes. I'm at the far end of the basement.'

'Good, because, Saima, we need you to help us.'

TWENTY-SIX

SAIMA WAS BACK INSIDE the grand hall, watching as Imam Hashim took to the stage to tell the rest of the mosque that the bomb had been found in their place of worship. She had many things running through her mind. She needed to send Frost pictures and footage of the bomb. The quicker they got this, the quicker it might all end. First the worshippers needed to know it had been found. A dozen or so already knew. They couldn't wait any longer in case it was leaked. Saima thought this was going to be the most important speech Imam Hashim ever gave. If he didn't secure the trust of his worshippers – if they panicked and went for the exits – this would all fall apart. It was why Saima had told Frost he would have to wait before she attempted what he had asked of her. He sounded dismayed but understood.

Saima noticed the mosque's committee members were by the exits. She had also taken the time to glance out of the foyer windows and seen a considerable increase in police officers a short distance from the mosque.

She was also worried about Aaron. Had he eaten his tea? Was he OK? Saima wanted to call Joyti but this wasn't the time. She could not deal with Aaron sounding upset. The mother inside her felt dirty for thinking it but, for now, her focus was solely on Imam Hashim. Everything depended on how he broke the news.

Two men were standing either side of Hashim, mobile phones raised. He had told the hall what he was about to say would be live-streamed on social media.

Was that wise?

Saima feared the hall would descend into chaos once the news broke.

Hashim raised his voice, commanding everyone to be silent, and waited. He stared at the congregation and smiled. Speaking softly in English, he asked those who could translate into Urdu for non-bilingual worshippers to do so. He waited a few moments, then started.

'Our life is a test. We have read this many times, heard it spoken even more so. Today, our time to be tested has arrived. As Muslims, we speak of a collective responsibility to account for one another. This city works tirelessly to support our brothers and sisters caught up in war zones across the globe. Today a terrorist organization calling themselves the Patriots want to test this resolve. They think our collective responsibility is a show – nothing more. They do not realize that, as Muslims, looking after one another is in the very DNA of our belief system. They mock us and want to show the world that we are nothing but liars!'

His voice changed, not quite combative but certainly more powerful. He paused, stared into the crowd and continued.

'Do you know what I see? A room full of a thousand united Muslims. A benchmark for solidarity and compassion – the very thing that makes us, as a community, unstoppable.'

The passion in his voice was mesmerizing. Saima felt the hairs on the back of her neck stand up. There were nods from around the room and murmurs that he was right.

'Have the other mosques emptied and abandoned our community? No! Have we panicked and turned on one another? No! Will we do so?'

His question was answered with a muted 'No'.

'Is that all you have to offer me?' He smiled and asked the question again, this time getting a more forceful answer.

'No!'

'We have built our lives around not only our faith but one another. So it is not with fear that I tell you all that the threat of a bomb located inside a mosque in Bradford has been verified.'

He quickened his speech, not giving the crowd time to react.

'And I ask you all to look at the life of our beloved Prophet, peace-be-upon-him, and to analyse the many times he was tested. Every time he overcame. Every time he endured and came out stronger. Often it was by his peaceful actions and the wisdom of his words. Now, on perhaps the biggest stage our community might ever be given, we have the chance to show the world how we deal with adversity. How we come together to ensure our faith withstands this test. And withstand it we will.'

His words were working. The energy in the room was palpable. Saima observed hands being held, arms wrapped around one another as if they all knew what was coming.

Hashim continued, his tone softer now.

'Our mosque has been chosen to withstand this test. No greater test are we likely to face in our lifetime than this. It is time to ask ourselves how much we care for the safety of one another. These so-called Patriots want to see if a single person inside this room will put at risk the thousand-strong group that we are. If just one of us tries to leave, the bomb will detonate and the people who doubt the strength of our faith will be proven correct. The wider ramifications for the Islamic world will be crippling. Since we claim to feel the pain of our persecuted brothers and sisters around the world, is it nothing more than a show if we cannot, here and now, endure and stand together? We will be seen as traitors to the very message we work tirelessly to promote – service over self – and I ask you all here and now, are you all traitors?'

The deafening answer echoed through Saima's body.

Hashim asked them all again – this time louder, and the response in the room was equally loud.

The two men standing either side of Hashim turned their phones towards the crowd, getting the images of solidarity before focusing back on him.

'And to the Patriots I say – you have asked your question. And now you have heard our answer.'

He stepped closer to one of the phones, taking the microphone with him.

'A final message for Bradford. There is a resolve among Bradfordians not to allow division, hate and racism to prosper, irrespective of faith. Our time to unite as a city has arrived and, as ever, we will not go down without a fight. Let us show the world, once and for all, that this is truly God's own county.'

The mobile phones either side of him were lowered, the sermon over.

Hashim went back to his stand and stared into the crowd, looking for signs that his speech had pierced the heart of everyone in the grand hall.

Saima could see that it had.

Hashim asked them, with God as his witness, how many of them would go against his request for unity? How many would try to escape, knowing everyone else would almost certainly die?

The answer was unanimous.

Not a single hand was raised.

TWENTY-SEVEN

THE NEWS WAS OUT. Harry's newsfeed was alive with speculation about the bomb inside the Mehraj mosque.

He texted Saima.

How's things in there?

She replied immediately.

Calm for now. I'm in the basement about to send info to Frost. Everyone else upstairs. How's Aaron?

Fine. Call you later. Keep battery conserved. BE CAREFUL. Stop if you feel you cannot do it.

20% left. I got this. Promise me u will chk on Aaron.

Promise. Love you.

Love u 2. XXX

Harry only had 38 per cent of his battery life left, with twelve hours of this siege yet to play out. Not enough.

Isaac was in the shower, door open, window locked. Harry wasn't concerned with the kid trying to do a runner but he sat in the hallway just outside the bathroom to make sure he didn't get any ideas. He had his police laptop open, accessing the Police National Database and seeing what information was listed on the other three leaders of Almukhtaroon. Abu-Nazir had an impressive record, mostly of 'disturbing the peace' by organizing demonstrations around the country. Amelia Rose had a decade-old record for drug use, but the real star of this shit-show was Fahad-Bin-Azeez. He had multiple entries for assault, grievous bodily harm and theft. Exactly the type of character Abu-Nazir targeted. None had listed addresses.

Harry put the laptop aside and examined the drawing pads he had taken from Isaac's house. Each sketch seemed to start with Isiah, a small, weak boy, getting bullied, then a kid from the local town would go missing – kidnapped by his nemesis, the Undertaker – requiring Isiah to eat lentils and explode into a hero to save the day. They were good, really good.

This kid had so much going for him.

What had gone wrong? What had made him join Almukhtaroon?

Pulling a gun he had lifted from Queensbury Tunnel from his pocket, Harry sighed. He thought of Saima inside the mosque, Aaron alone at his mother's house and the shit-storm out in the streets of Bradford. He couldn't afford to get this wrong.

At the kitchen table, Isaac greedily drank his milkshake. Harry hoped the sugar-rush would perk the kid up. Now refreshed and wearing jeans and a T-shirt, Isaac's previous bitterness seemed to have softened.

'I'm not helping you,' said Isaac, slurping the dregs of his shake.

Harry pointed to the drawing pads he had been reading. 'These sketches are good.'

He thought he saw a flash of pride but it disappeared as quickly as it surfaced.

'Reminds me of Popeye. He was one of my favourites as a kid – probably before your time. You know it?'

Isaac nodded.

'An Asian superhero. Don't get many of those. You should have tried to get these published.'

'Nobody wants to read about an Asian superhero. All we're good for is being terrorists.'

Harry shrugged.

'That what you think I am? A terrorist?'

'I've watched Almukhtaroon videos online. Death to the West. A new caliphate.'

Isaac held his gaze.

'Not exactly patriotic, is it?'

'The way the West lives is corrupt,' said Isaac forcefully. His expression didn't match his tone of voice. This was something he had been taught, not something he believed.

Harry's heart quickened. This could work.

'You know what's going on in Bradford right now?'

Isaac nodded. 'A little. Before I was taken from my house – before they injected me with that . . . stuff, they told me some people calling themselves the Patriots were terrorizing everyone. Bomb in a mosque? And they want us in return.'

'That's about right.'

Harry wondered what Isaac knew about the men who had lifted him. 'Any idea who took you from your house?'

'You guys? Police? Least that's what I thought until they hit me with that needle. So what's the deal? Are you here to deliver me to the Patriots?'

'No. I'm here on something different. You and the rest of your crew – Abu-Nazir, Fahad-Bin-Azeez and Amelia Rose – some friends you got there.'

'I'm not sharing anything with you. Torture me all you want.'

'Fine. Let's talk about you, then,' said Harry, flicking through the sketches. 'You believe all that stuff? A new caliphate? Death to the West?'

Isaac nodded weakly.

'Strange, because none of these drawings show that.'

'I believe it.'

'That's what I was hoping for.'

Isaac tensed in his seat. 'Why? So you can do me in?'

'On the contrary,' said Harry, standing up.

He turned his back and closed his eyes, thinking of the earlier bomb blast, the fear on his son's face, the YouTube video of the Patriots' demands, and Saima sitting in the basement of the mosque sending pictures of the bomb to Frost.

He turned towards Isaac again and pulled his revolver from his pocket.

'I knew it,' Isaac spat, slamming his fists on the table, rage flooding his face. 'See a Muslim, take him off the streets and torture him – fucking typical of you pigs!'

This time, Isaac's rage felt real.

'Death to the West,' said Harry quietly, inching closer to Isaac. He stopped a foot short, got on his knees and turned the gun in his hand so he was holding the barrel.

'Thing is, Isaac, I don't think you're an extremist any more than I am.'

One of Isaac's drawing pads lay in his lap. Harry rested the gun on it, watching as Isaac's mouth fell open.

The kid was taking one medication to stop him wetting the bed and another to ease anxiety. The thumb on his right hand was a lot smaller than the one on his left. Harry guessed it was because Isaac still sucked it, just like Aaron did. Harry was betting Isaac wasn't about to blow his brains out.

He didn't have it in him.

'There are one hundred and five mosques under lockdown, and my wife is in one of them.'

Isaac's brow furrowed.

Harry nodded. 'That's right. My wife is Muslim. Saima. I know all about feeling marginalized and persecuted. Do you know what I had to do to marry her? I left my family. I was disowned by my community – the Sikh who married a Paki and it ruined him. You're not the only one in this world on the wrong side of hate. You can choose to leave this place with me and do something good, be a hero. Thousands of innocent Muslims are trapped in those mosques: women, children, the elderly. They are all at risk. You don't need to be in Syria or Palestine to help the Islamic world right now. Today the fight is on your doorstep.'

Harry took Isaac's hand firmly and placed it on the gun, noting the tremble in it.

'You want to bring down the West? Now's the time. The gun is loaded. All you have to do is point and pull the trigger. You'll kill a serving police officer. Got to be worth some brownie points with Abu-Nazir. Or you can look me in the eye, see how much I want to save this city, my wife and all the people inside those mosques. Let's change the narrative and leave this house together. I told you: the only person in control here is you.'

TWENTY-EIGHT

SAIMA WAS STANDING IN front of the large shipping container that contained the bomb. Imam Hashim was by her side, holding a powerful torch, both of them alone in the basement. She needed him to help with this. Sweat was dripping down her forehead into her eyes in spite of it being considerably cooler down here.

Upstairs Hashim had left the worshippers in several large prayer circles and a trusted team keeping watch over them all. It was a smart move, and Saima had wished she could join them. She was silently praying, having doubts about whether she was the right person to do this.

Her phone began to ring, a Facetime request from Frost. She answered, hand shaking. Frost asked her if she was still OK to attempt this and when she confirmed she was, he handed the phone over to a man who identified himself as one of the CTU bomb experts, 'Paul'. He spoke calmly and slowly, asking Saima first to switch off the torch on her phone and rely on the one Imam Hashim was holding.

She put the phone on speaker and listened carefully to instructions, then stepped slowly inside the towering wooden box. Her heart was pounding; it felt louder than Paul's voice coming from her phone.

Mouth parched.

Hands shaking.

She closed her eyes, whispered another prayer, then inched her way in. Hashim's torch was powerful, revealing six towering cylindrical shapes, filled with some kind of white substance. In the centre was a large, square contraption full of wires and lights with a keypad. A timer was counting down to the deadline of 6 a.m. It was that which was most disconcerting.

Saima knew nothing about bombs, yet something told her this was a sophisticated device.

Using her phone, she very slowly mapped out every inch of it, creeping ever closer. Her bladder suddenly felt heavy even though it was empty.

She focused now on the white material inside the glass cylinders.

'What am I looking at?' she asked, trying not to panic.

'Don't you worry about that, Saima,' said Paul. No matter how experienced Paul claimed to be, she heard the change in his voice.

'Paul, this only works if you tell me exactly what is going on.' She didn't really need him to confirm what she was looking at: the cylinder directly in front of her was full of glass and nails. It was nerves that made her ask. Something to fill the silence in the claustrophobic environment of the box.

Paul asked her to focus on the computer-like device, which she did.

Saima angled her phone towards it and confirmed that she could see three red wires, three blue and two yellow. They streamed from the device towards the cylindrical containers.

Saima kept glancing at the one holding the glass and nails.

Designed to injure as many people as possible.

Since there was nobody down here, only she and Hashim would feel that pain.

Her mind was wandering and she asked Paul to repeat what he just said. He did so. Saima crouched by the central device and tried to find a serial number or any markings of note. She found a ten-digit number and said it slowly and clearly, confirming it a second time. Paul asked her to wait. Her eyes once again found the glass and nails, though she tried not to.

What kind of sick bastards did that?

Paul returned and asked her to lift a small metal box next to the wiring and confirm whether she could see a way to take the lid off it. Saima didn't move. She didn't want to touch it.

She closed her eyes and wiped sweat from her brow. The need to urinate was becoming critical.

She could hear Paul's voice but not the words. Head spinning. Vision blurry. She recognized the symptoms of an impending faint. Without realizing it, she had been holding her breath.

Open your mouth.

Breathe.

She wiped a sweaty palm on her clothes, focused solely on the box and tried to lift it.

When she spoke, her voice was shaky. 'The top feels like it might come away. Do you want me to try?'

'Please. Take your time. Softly. If it resists, leave it be, Saima.'

'I need to put my phone down. Use both hands. Can I?'

'Can Hashim hold your phone so we can watch you?'

Saima saw the torchlight flicker as Hashim came carefully towards her. She saw his hand by the side of her face and handed him the phone, waiting until he had positioned it so Paul could see.

Carefully, Saima applied the gentlest of pressure and lifted off the top of the small rectangular box. It came away easily, revealing a maze of messily arranged wires and several lights, blue, red and opaque.

'Excellent,' she heard Paul say.

Feeling like they were making progress, Saima was about to replace the box when it started to beep, lights flickering.

'Shit,' she whispered, unclear what was happening. She nearly dropped the damn thing.

The torch light wavered, Hashim's hand suddenly unsteady.

The noise and urgent flashing of lights from the device continued before stopping abruptly.

Saima heard Paul's voice, firm, alarmed.

'Saima, stand absolutely still and do not move.'

TWENTY-NINE

ABU-NAZIR WATCHED THE NEWS with indifference. The imam's speech inside the Mehraj mosque had caused quite a reaction, *#Hashim* even knocking *#prayforBradford* off the top trending Twitter spot. For the moment, Abu-Nazir was not the most talked about Muslim person in the city. It wouldn't last long. He had just uploaded a video on to YouTube, an old one but one that always got a reaction before being deleted. A video demanding a new caliphate in the West. This time he reckoned it would be viewed millions of times before it got removed.

Timing was everything.

A documentary filmed in 2012, featuring the current leader of the Far Right, Tyler Sudworth, and Abu-Nazir, had been viewed over a million times since the blast in City Park. The two men had come together after a high-profile altercation to try to find common ground. They had found none. Tyler Sudworth had been fierce in his criticism of Abu-Nazir, unable to comprehend why a white British national had crossed over to Islamic extremism. That was, however, Abu-Nazir's USP.

The documentary had been great exposure for Abu-Nazir, a

primetime TV slot. Criticism of it had been widespread but by then the damage had been done.

The news went live to a woman from the BBC, reporting that armed police were now positioned throughout the city, forces from across Yorkshire pooling their resources. Skirmishes had been reported and footage was shown of clashes between Far Right activists and Asian youths.

Abu-Nazir smiled and turned the television off. He moved into the bedroom, checking on Amelia. She was still asleep, snoring lightly. He'd have to wake her soon.

It was over four hours since the bomb had gone off and he'd heard nothing from the boy, Isaac. He'd known where to come in an emergency. They had discussed it many times.

He doubted the boy would make it here now.

Every war involved sacrifice.

Even Isaac Wolfe.

THIRTY

ISAAC WASN'T SITTING ON the chair in front of Harry any more. He was standing over him, gun down by his side.

When he had moved to stand, just for the briefest of moments Harry had thought he might have seriously underestimated the boy.

The kid's eyes gave him away.

He couldn't pull the trigger.

Isaac's voice was shaky when he spoke. Bitter. Angry.

'You're mocking me, aren't you?' he spat.

Shit. If he lost the kid now, he'd never gain his trust.

'Just like the kids at school. Every girl I ever asked out on a date.' His voice was rising, eyes wet with tears he was trying hard to blink away.

This was bad. Very, very bad.

'I'm not mocking you,' said Harry gently. He kept his body relaxed, tone calm, even though his knees were smarting on the floor.

'Yes you are!' said Isaac, raising the gun and waving it carelessly at Harry.

Great move, Harry. Give the kid a fucking loaded gun, then piss him off.

Harry shook his head slowly. 'You know that's not what this is, Isaac.'

'Then why give me the gun? To prove I'm too chicken to use it?'

Harry shook his head and smiled. 'On the contrary. To show you that if you wanted to, you could. Right now. Right here.'

Isaac's eyes softened a little but the tremble in his hand remained.

'That shit Abu-Nazir preaches – words are easy,' Harry went on. 'He's like any other hate-preacher out there, a second-rate asshole who preys on people he thinks are sheep.'

Isaac opened his mouth to object. Harry raised his hand, slowly.

'You're not a sheep. If you were, you would have pulled the trigger by now because that's what sheep do. They follow. What I'm offering you, Isaac, is a chance to put that gun down, knowing you had all the power and yet decided to share it with me. We can leave this house together and find the people we need to end this. We could save hundreds, thousands of innocent people inside those mosques.'

Harry calmly, steadily got to his feet. 'Twelve hours from now, that is the stuff people will be talking about. The boy who rose against the hate to save Bradford.'

Isaac smiled. It didn't reach his eyes.

'Sounds like a speech from one of those crappy nineties movies.'

'It is,' said Harry smiling. 'Thing is, just because it isn't delivered by a Hollywood golden boy, doesn't mean you can't believe it. Listen to the sound of those helicopters in the distance. Does it get any bigger than this? What greater stage could you ask for to play the hero?'

Harry tapped his forehead. 'Think about it. Everyone is expecting you to be one thing. Surprise them.'

Isaac's hand was starting to lower.

'Heavy, isn't it?' said Harry.

Isaac nodded.

'Lower it then. I'm not taking it from you.'

Isaac let his hand fall to his side. 'What's a police officer like you doing with a gun like this?'

'I'm not your usual type of detective.'

'You're a criminal, you mean?' said Isaac, raising an eyebrow.

It was a question Harry had asked himself a thousand times.

'No. I mean I get shit done.'

'And you want me to turn on my friends and help you find them?'

'What makes you call them friends?'

Isaac grunted and shook his head. 'They look after me. Look out for me.'

'How so?'

Isaac thought about it. 'We . . . they . . . you know . . . teach me things. Help me be a better Muslim.'

'Can I give you my honest opinion?'

Isaac nodded.

'The videos I've seen of you guys? You look lost. They're not making you a better Muslim. They're preying on your vulnerability.'

Isaac made to protest but stopped himself.

Harry moved slowly and picked up a sketch pad from the table.

'I read somewhere that writers and artists always need to show you what's going on, never tell you. I thought that was pretty good advice. *Show, don't tell.* I made it my thing in life – showed my boss I work like a dog, never just telling her. I show my Muslim wife that I love her by buying her a new prayer mat every year when it's Ramadan and waiting to eat with her when she's fasting. And today, I showed you by giving you that gun that I'm not full of shit. Looking at the sketches in this book,' said Harry, waving it at him, 'you're showing me that, deep inside, you want to be a hero.'

Isaac smiled dismissively.

'No? Play it out with me then,' said Harry. 'The bomb goes off and a thousand innocent Muslim people die. What do you think the fallout from that will be? It will shape the future landscape of our country and God knows what the retaliation will look like. We live in an unstable world. This will turn everything to shit. It's the 9/11 of our times and we all know what happened there.'

'There's no way—'

'Turn on the TV. Have a look.' Harry was losing patience, painfully conscious of the time ticking by. He pulled his phone from his pocket, unlocked it and handed it to Isaac. 'Have a look at Twitter and tell me I'm wrong.'

Harry watched him, watched his eyes widen and his mouth drop.

'What do we have to do?' said Isaac.

THIRTY-ONE

FROST WAS ALONE IN the command room.

Of all the things Saima's exploration of the bomb could have revealed, he had not considered this.

A sleeper cell, clearly aligned to the Patriots, had run a diagnostic test on the bomb to ensure it had not been tampered with. A simple radio transmitter on the device was found to have a range of around a hundred metres. With the immediate area surrounding the mosque clear, only one option remained. The sleeper had to have been *inside* – a human sacrifice in case a special ops team entered the building intent on ending the siege. This was a failsafe that Frost could not counter remotely.

If a diagnostics test failed, the sleeper would know the bomb had been compromised and could then detonate the device. Bomb-disposal experts had suggested it could be triggered with a simple, battery-operated remote, something they could not use technology to nullify. The Patriots had thought of everything. This blocked almost every move Frost could make.

They had no way of knowing when the sleeper might run a test or what might cause the sleeper to activate the bomb. The Patriots had a wild card.

His mind was a mess. He ran a sweaty hand across his face, glad to be alone, even if it was only for a few minutes. The military commanders had been informed of the development and were assessing their own protocols.

Saima had removed herself from the basement and together with Hashim returned to the grand hall. He admired her courage. She hadn't panicked when many would have.

Strong woman. Determined.

She needed to be. One thing was clear – the sleeper could have been anybody.

Except her.

That much he was certain of.

Which meant his only ally in trying to figure out who the hostile party inside the mosque might be was Saima Virdee.

He'd asked a lot of her already but there was no other choice.

Frost dialled her number.

THIRTY-TWO

AARON SAT AT THE kitchen table eating his tea.

He hadn't stopped asking for Mummy and Daddy since he'd come inside. Joyti had been forced to tell him they were still at work. She had tried to call Harry but his phone had gone to voicemail and she didn't trust herself to leave a message.

He would call soon.

Joyti watched Aaron neatly breaking off pieces of the chapatti she had made him and dipping them into a chickpea curry. Joyti had been surprised. She knew Saima cooked Asian food at home, yet seeing Aaron happily eating her curry had buoyed her dwindling spirits.

Her thoughts constantly flitted from the little boy in front of her to his parents, out there amid the chaos.

Why did Saima have to be inside the Mehraj mosque?

What would happen to Harry if Saima didn't make it through this?

Her heart ached for her son. She would do anything to stop his pain.

Ranjit didn't know Saima was in danger. He had lain on the sofa, door pulled to, with his eyes closed, ever since he had come in from the garden. Even on an ordinary day her husband was usually slave to the news channels. The fact this was happening on their doorstep and he wasn't interested told her one thing.

Her risk had paid off.

She left Aaron at the table and hovered by the living-room door.

'Would you like some food?' she asked Ranjit, stepping inside.

When he didn't reply, she touched his bare feet, squeezing them gently.

'Close the door,' he replied without moving. 'Leave me alone.'

She hesitated.

She had known what she was doing when she sent Ranjit outside to face Aaron.

Joyti clearly remembered the first time she had seen the little boy. The sight of Aaron had unlocked all the memories she had fought to bury.

Hardeep as a child, running around their shop chasing customers.

Hardeep as a child, sitting on her knee crying after a fall.

Hardeep as a child, falling asleep in her arms when he had been suffering a raging fever.

Memories she could not hold on to in the wake of Ranjit's decision to disown their son.

Joyti suspected the same thing had happened to her husband this afternoon.

'Let me help you,' she whispered.

'You cannot,' he replied. 'Nobody can. Now please shut the door and leave me be.'

Back in the kitchen, Joyti found Aaron licking his plate.

'Do you do that at home?' she asked, shaking her head.

'Mummy shouts at me,' he said with a smile.

'It's not nice.'

'I like it.'

'What else do you like?'

'Ice cream. Grandma always gives me ice cream?'

It wasn't really a question. He knew he would get one. Joyti saw him once a week and in those few hours she spoiled him rotten.

'I got to have bath soon,' he said matter-of-factly.

Joyti reached for another ice cream from the freezer.

She knew it wasn't right to let him have another but there were far graver things to worry about today.

'Would you like Grandma to bathe you?'

He nodded, biting greedily into the ice cream.

'What about sleeping here? Do you want to sleep with Grandma?'

Aaron thought about his answer, smiled and coyly shook his head.

'I sleep in my bed. I got my Batman blanket and my Pooh bear. He . . . he . . . sleeps next to me.'

Joyti nodded.

'Come on, Hardeep,' she whispered. 'I need you.'

THIRTY-THREE

HARRY CHECKED HIS PHONE.

Eight missed calls, six from his mother, two from Saima.

No voicemails.

'Why don't you think about where Abu-Nazir might be hiding? I'll be a moment.'

Harry closed the living-room door and stepped out into the hallway, the most distance he could put between himself and Isaac. Saima answered immediately.

'Are you OK?'

'I am.'

'Where are you?'

'Imam Hashim's office.'

Her voice sounded shaky. Something wasn't right.

'What's happened, Saima?'

She told him what had happened with the bomb and of her follow-up call with Frost.

'A sleeper cell?' he said, amazed. 'Are you ... shit, I don't know ... "OK" seems like such a stupid word to use.'

'I'm OK. I mean, my life flashed before me but, to be honest, it's not the first time.'

She forced a laugh and Harry smiled. She was some woman.

'Frost asked me to . . . help.'

'You good with that?'

'You know I am. How's Aaron?'

Harry smiled again. *Typical Saima, all about her boy.*

'I told you, he's with my mother.'

'Why aren't you there with him? How can you leave him alone for so long?'

'I'm working, Saima. Everyone needs to play their part today.'

'You need to get to your parents and put him to bed, Harry. He won't sleep otherwise.'

'Saima – my mother has looked after—'

'—did you leave his Batman blanket there? His pyjamas? His Winnie-the-Pooh?'

Christ, this wasn't going to be easy.

'He'll be upset and confused, Harry. Today must have been awful for him.' Her voice cracked. Harry hated to hear her this way.

'I can deal with everything that's going on. The mosque, City Park, the bomb, the sleeper – all of it. What I absolutely cannot deal with is my four-year-old in a strange house, afraid. You will go to that damn house, Harry Virdee, and you will put my boy to bed – do you hear me?'

She was almost shouting now.

Harry took the breath he needed. 'Saima, he is my boy too. Do you think I would let him suffer? You have to trust my mother. I can't go and sit at home while this city burns around us and you're stuck in the mosque. What if something happens to you? What do I tell Aaron then?'

'You know I am not the priority here, Harry. Our son is the priority.'

'You are both my priority. Please, Saima—'

'Your father is there. God knows what he's said to Aaron. You know what he's capable of.'

It was the thing Harry had been trying not to think of. And now she'd said it aloud. Harry trusted his mother, but he also knew his father.

Was Aaron really safe there?

'If Mum needs me, I'll go back.'

It was a promise he knew he would be unable to fulfil.

'Saima, stop crying. I need you to hold it together.'

Harry glanced at the broken mirror, hanging clumsily next to the front door. He caught his reflection. The crack in the mirror distorted his image, cutting him in half right down the centre.

It was exactly how he felt right now.

'What did Frost say when he called? Did he give you any clues what to look for?'

Her voice steadied a little. 'He said to trust nobody.'

Harry wanted to give her some reassurance but didn't know what to say.

'I want to find who it is, Harry. It might . . . give us all a better chance.' She was right but the odds were against her: they were one in a thousand. 'How do I start?'

Harry told her the only thing he could think of. 'Try and find the calmest person in the room, Saima.' He paused then added, 'Or the one making the most noise.'

THIRTY-FOUR

ISAAC WOLFE COULD HEAR Harry on the phone in the hallway. The detective had taken the gun with him but that was OK.

Isaac put his hands across his chest and started to perform the Islamic nafl prayer, a quick form of worship that he used to charge his courage. Once finished, he remained on the floor, facing Mecca, eyes closed.

He had gained Harry Virdee's trust. It was a fragile allegiance but it was something.

The next few hours were about one thing.

Isaac Wolfe was going to reunite with his leader, Abu-Nazir, because he knew there was a much bigger nightmare to come.

One Harry Virdee would never see coming.

THIRTY-FIVE

HIS CALL TO SAIMA had barely disconnected when Harry phoned his mother.

She answered immediately and Harry heard in the background the one thing he absolutely didn't want to hear.

Aaron crying.

I should be there.

He closed his eyes, trying not to let his emotions overrule his head.

'Hardeep, are you coming?' she said, clearly leaving the room judging by the sound of Aaron's cries fading.

'I can't, Mum. I just . . . can't.'

She paused for only a moment. 'It's OK,' she replied, her voice resolute. 'It's OK.'

'Has he eaten?'

'Yes.'

'Properly?'

'He had chapatti and curry and a Magnum.'

'He'll fall asleep when he's tired from crying, Mum. There's a dummy and a Batman blanket in the blue bag. Give them to him and lie next to him in bed.'

'He doesn't have any pyjamas, Hardeep.'

'It's warm, Mum, just let him sleep in his underwear.' Harry sighed. 'Mum, I need you to help with this. I need to know you can cope with him overnight. How's everything . . . else?' He couldn't bring himself to ask the question directly.

Her voice was fierce. 'Nothing is happening to Aaron whilst I am alive. You don't worry.'

'I need to go, Mum,' he said, fear pooling in his stomach. He wanted to throw his phone against the wall and smash the house to pieces. How could he not be there for his boy?

He hung his head. 'My phone might be off for a while, Mum. If it's urgent, leave me a voicemail, but only if it is urgent.'

'And Saima? Is she OK, Hardeep?'

'She's fine, Mum.'

'Almukhtaroon – tell me how you got involved with them? It's new, right? You were locked up until fairly recently. How did it happen? Tell me everything,' said Harry, checking his phone for the time: 18.25. They needed to move.

He was back in the kitchen with Isaac, his head still cloudy for having spoken to his family. He knew this was the only thing he could do to protect them.

Isaac spoke hurriedly. His mother, Noori, was a second-generation Pakistani immigrant, born and raised in London. She'd been a shop assistant when she had become pregnant with Isaac. She and her boyfriend had moved to Bradford to escape their local community and the backlash for having a child out of wedlock.

The shame.

Isaac's father had died before he had been born. He knew almost nothing about him.

Noori had changed her surname from Hussain to Wolfe, afraid

her family would try to track her down. Afraid of what they might do if they found her.

'Why Wolfe?' asked Harry.

'She liked to read. Came across the name in a book. Plus, she thought it was safer to use a name nobody would think of.'

Isaac had worshipped his mother. She had worked two jobs to make sure he never wanted for anything. She had wanted him to become a doctor.

Harry thought about Isaac's stellar grades; the kid had been on his way.

Then, quite suddenly, his mother had been diagnosed with stage-four breast cancer. By the time she'd seen her GP it was already too late.

'Four months later, she was dead,' said Isaac.

Harry sighed; he still had Aaron's cries in his head.

'Just like that, she was gone,' said Isaac, his face blank. 'I was alone.'

They sat in silence for a moment.

'And the youth detention centre?' Harry ventured.

'Someone at school said something about her. I lost it.'

Isaac stopped. He didn't need to say any more. Harry imagined the rest.

The boy would have fallen on the wrong side of the government's Prevent programme, meant to tackle radicalization. Harry slouched in his seat, dismayed. Instead of helping Isaac, Prevent had put him on a darker path.

'Is that how you found Almukhtaroon?' asked Harry.

'Ironic, right?' Isaac allowed himself a smile. 'Abu-Nazir was visiting another kid inside. I asked some questions, he came to see me and, well . . . when I got out . . . he was there.'

Harry leaned back, scrubbing his palm across his stubble.

'He's a white guy,' said Harry, shaking his head. 'Didn't that strike you as weird?'

'It was because he was white that I listened. It felt like so much more of a statement coming from him.' Isaac glanced up at Harry but didn't stop talking. 'It felt like I had family again. The more Abu-Nazir taught me, the more I saw how unfair the world had become to the Muslim community.'

Harry struggled not to interrupt. This was textbook: lost Muslim kid falls victim to charismatic hate-preacher.

'How do we find the others?' Harry asked, voice firm. He wanted to find those fuckers now more than ever.

'First, I want to know what happens after that,' said Isaac.

'We negotiate with the Patriots.'

'They want us dead. That doesn't sound like a negotiation to me.'

Harry had been expecting the question. 'The Patriots will know that nobody is handing you over to be executed. If I were a betting man, I'd put my money on them asking you all to go on TV and stand down.'

Isaac slouched in his seat. 'Abu-Nazir would die first.'

Harry smiled. 'In my experience, when death actually stares you down, most men do what they can to stay alive.'

'I hope you're right.'

'What about Amelia? What is her role?'

'You've heard the stories, right?'

Harry had. She was known as the black widow, using her position as Abu-Nazir's partner to entice young, impressionable men to join the cause.

'Is she submissive to Abu-Nazir or are they equals?'

Isaac paused and just the fact that he did so gave Harry the answer. Abu-Nazir was not in charge.

'I got it. Let's move on to the muscle. Fahad-Bin-Azeez.'

Isaac's tone changed, now more serious.

'Nobody calls him that, just Azeez. And he is altogether different.'

Harry's leg started to twitch. He needed to get going but he couldn't rush this. Isaac had to be on his side, had to believe Harry was on his.

'He's the tough guy. I . . . I . . . don't really spend much time with him but Abu-Nazir says everyone's frustrations at how the Islamic world is perceived manifest differently, and that people like Azeez are necessary. Words get you so far, swords the rest of the way.'

'Those his words, are they? Abu-Nazir's?'

Isaac nodded. 'Azeez is huge. You're no match for him.'

'You just tell me everything you know about Azeez and let me worry how to take him down.'

THIRTY-SIX

JOYTI PUT HER PHONE away, wiped tears from her face and went back into the kitchen. Aaron was exactly as she'd left him. She hurried to him, ignoring his flailing arms trying to bat her away. Distressed, he called for his mummy. She held him close. His head was growing heavy with exhaustion and he nestled into her.

Her heart missed a beat.

She struggled to her feet, lifting Aaron with her. As she passed the living-room door, she saw Ranjit was not there. She went to the window by the front door. His car was gone.

Rage exploded inside her.

How could he hate Aaron for the sins of his father?

She gritted her teeth, pulled the chain across the lock and secured the top internal bolt. Her husband was not welcome any more.

Aaron continued to cry, tears from his warm face dampening her skin.

She took him upstairs, struggling with her hip, wincing in pain. She sat Aaron on her bed.

'We're going to sleep in here tonight, my boy. Just you and me.' She stroked his head to soothe him.

'No, I want my mummy,' he said, still crying.

'I know. But tonight you are going to stay here, with Grandma. Mummy and Daddy said so.'

Joyti handed Aaron his Batman comfort blanket and his dummy. His cries stopped for a moment.

'My blue 'jamas?' he asked hopefully.

Joyti grabbed a remote from the bedside cabinet and passed it to Aaron. She pressed a button and the bed moved underneath them, lowering them towards the floor. It was a specialist unit, for her hip.

Aaron took the remote, eyes lighting up.

'Do you want to sleep on this bed, tonight?'

He nodded. 'I keep this?' he said, shying away from her, afraid she might take the remote away.

'If you sleep in this bed, you can keep it.'

He nodded, sucking on his dummy, making it squeak. He really was the spitting image of Harry.

She jumped at the noise of the doorbell.

Ranjit.

'Grandma, somebody here?' said Aaron, still playing with the remote.

'It will go away soon.'

She could hear Ranjit's key in the door. The doorbell went again. And again.

'Grandma, I don't like that noise.'

'You stay here,' she said and started towards the stairs.

At the bottom, she unlocked the door, ready to tell Ranjit he was not welcome.

She didn't have to.

Her husband stood on the doorstep, face grave, a large carrier bag in each hand. He raised them to show her. It was children's clothing.

And on top of the first bag was a pair of blue pyjamas.

THIRTY-SEVEN

HARRY GRIPPED THE STEERING.

If you fail tonight, everything will fall apart.

He'd sailed through the nearly empty streets. Now, close to the city centre, there were helicopters hovering above, police cars, ambulances and fire engines everywhere.

This was the biggest test the city had ever faced. The biggest test Harry had ever faced.

He headed for the side streets.

'How certain are you Azeez lives here?' asked Harry.

'It's the last place I know he was staying.'

'Staying?' said Harry.

'He moves around a lot. He's paranoid he's being watched. Works hard to stay under the radar.'

Harry thought of the Police National Database he had searched. *NFA*. No fixed abode.

Intelligence reports linked him with addresses around Manningham, Leeds Road and Tong but this address on Back Lane hadn't been mentioned anywhere.

That needled Harry. He glanced at Isaac, the kid staring out the window. Could he really trust him?

'There,' said Isaac, pointing at the first house on the street: semi-detached, show-stopping front garden – red and yellow roses bordering a pristine lawn.

Harry drove past and parked further up.

Quarter past seven on the car's clock, and it was still daylight. This shit would have been so much easier in the dark.

'Are you sure this is the place?' asked Harry, not convinced. It was far from the shit-hole he had been expecting.

'Shared a taxi with him once. That's it.'

The garden was bothering Harry. Whoever lived there had poured a heck of a lot of time, effort and love into it. It wasn't the work of someone who drifted from place to place.

'Who else lives there?' he asked Isaac.

'I don't know. Family friend, he said.'

Harry stared at Isaac but saw nothing in his expression to make him think this was a set-up. His mind went to the gun Isaac had handed back to him.

'He wants to go back to Syria,' Isaac offered.

Harry thought of the recent headlines. Over a thousand young Muslim men had returned from Syria. Apparently, they were all on watch lists but, with resources badly stretched, those identified as 'low risk' had longer leashes.

With his connection to Almukhtaroon, it seemed unlikely Azeez would have been downgraded to low risk. Unless he had never been to Syria.

A dreamer, thought Harry. Azeez wanted the glory and camaraderie of combat but had been too chicken-shit to actually go there. He liked that theory. Maybe Azeez was nothing more than a playground bully.

Harry pulled a pair of handcuffs from the glove compartment and waved them at Isaac.

'You can't be serious?'

'I can't be scoping that place out worrying you might get a rush of blood to the head and do something stupid.'

'I'll come with you.'

'No.'

'I'm not wearing those.'

Harry sighed.

'You put a loaded gun in my hand and now you want to handcuff me in the car?'

Harry slapped the cuffs on Isaac, one across his right wrist, the other around the steering wheel. 'Finished with your speech?' he said.

Isaac looked despondent.

Harry got out of the car.

THIRTY-EIGHT

FROST HAD HIS EYE on the clock on the far wall: 19.30.

Two hours before darkness hit them. It would bring another complication. In this city, fading light usually brought fading hope. He was pleased Saima had sounded resilient when he'd asked her to help find the possible sleeper cell but Frost didn't have much hope. It was a one-in-a-thousand shot, a lottery.

One piece of positive news was that he had just received word there had been no fatalities from the blast in City Park. The twenty-minute evacuation order had been time enough for everyone to leave. Many people had been taken to hospital with minor injuries, most from the stampede to evacuate, some from flying debris. Bradford Royal Infirmary was in a state of emergency; other hospitals around Yorkshire were also receiving patients. A Gold Command had been set up for the NHS trusts. The medical service, like the police force, was bracing itself.

One thousand and nine people were at risk inside the mosque.

A line of communication had been set up between Frost's team and the Patriots. It was an international phone number, which had been traced to an area of no-man's-land in Russia. What was clear, however, was that this was not a Russian operation. From them, this would have been an act of war, and the Soviets were far too cute for that.

No, this was the Patriots situating themselves in a place where the West had no allies to call on. It was smart.

Tariq had wanted to speak with them but Frost had not allowed it. He didn't trust the politician.

His team had found nothing on the Patriots. There were several low-level criminal groups around the country who used the nickname, none of whom had the capabilities to pull this off. Cyber experts had not been able to take anything from the video clips. The Patriots had left nothing but smoke.

Frost pinched the bridge of his nose. They were six hours into this crisis with no concrete leads. They hadn't tracked a single leader of Almukhtaroon and nightfall would make that all the more difficult. Worse, it would bring the vampires on to the streets. Frost had been updated that social media was rife with groups of anarchy-seekers on the streets of Bradford supposedly hunting Abu-Nazir. The enormous police presence in and around the city centre and specifically now around the Mehraj mosque had detained dozens of locals, all seeking to stir up trouble. Maintaining civil order was becoming more challenging.

Even the brilliant Detective Superintendent Clare Conway, in charge of locating Almukhtaroon, could not bring Frost the good news he hoped for. She had many intelligence leads but, as yet, not a single member in safe custody.

The five hundred extra officers from Yorkshire and the North East had arrived and were now strategically positioned around Bradford, a bold, visible statement that the police were in charge. This thing was on a knife edge and if Bradford kicked off, they would have little hope of containing it.

He was waiting to hear from the detective superintendent responsible for evacuating the other hundred and four mosques but he had not yet checked in. Perhaps, Frost thought absentmindedly, there would be good news there. He couldn't sit about in his office waiting for the update.

Up on the second floor, Frost was searched by an armed military soldier.

Protocol.

Tariq Islam and special ops commander David Allen were standing in front of a large desk. Tariq's mobile phone was on the table, the line open to the government's COBRA committee.

Frost nodded for the men to start. The revelation of the sleeper cell had made what he was about to hear a more pressing matter.

'We plan to enter the mosque through a sewage tunnel that gives access to the basement,' Allen opened with confidence. The Patriots had destroyed nearby access points with their bomb in City Park – intentionally or unintentionally, they could not be sure – which was slowing the operation considerably. A special ops team had gained access to the sewer system further out of town and were now one mile from the main line that would take them to the basement of the mosque.

Commander Allen spoke with the ease of a man who thought this was nothing more than a routine day in the office. 'We've dispatched a small robot armed with several cameras to trawl the route, make sure there's no unwelcome surprise waiting for our men down there.'

It would take a couple of hours, Allen went on. If it showed nothing of concern, the special forces team would look to enter the mile-long stretch at 22.30 with a proposed entry to the basement of the mosque at 23.00, giving them seven hours before the Patriots' deadline expired to try to defuse the bomb.

'What about the sleeper cell inside the mosque?' asked Frost, stepping towards the phone on speaker. 'If our contact inside cannot give us a name, can the bomb-disposal team disable it without the sleeper knowing?'

Allen didn't mince his words. 'No. But if we gain access, we have a good chance of disabling the device.'

The Prime Minister's voice on the phone interrupted them.

'Commander Allen, please define "a good chance".'

'All I can say, Prime Minister, is that looking at the pictures and video footage made available to us, we feel confident of a favourable outcome.'

Frost wanted to smile; Allen was just as good as the PM at evading direct questions.

The PM asked the Home Secretary for an update. He should have asked Frost, but this didn't trouble Frost. He listened closely to ensure the information was accurate. Five minutes later, the PM gave Commander Allen authorization to proceed and the phone call ended as a knock sounded on the office door.

'You wanted an update as soon as I could get it to you.' The young DS looked at Frost. She stopped talking, her face troubled.

'What now?' he said, realizing another body blow was imminent.

'I'm afraid the other mosques within the city have not been evacuated.'

'Why?' asked Frost, unable to keep the surprise from his voice. *Why the fuck not?* he wanted to shout.

'Because, sir, they have refused to open their doors.'

THIRTY-NINE

SAIMA WAS SITTING ALONE in Imam Hashim's office.

Crying.

She couldn't help it. Much as she wanted to believe Aaron was OK, she needed it confirmed. She had tried to call Joyti, who hadn't answered. Saima didn't have the house telephone number, having never needed to call it.

How could she focus on what Frost had tasked her with – trying to locate the potential sleeper – when her mind would not focus on anything except images of her little boy crying, afraid, confused over why he was sleeping in a strange house without either of his parents.

The past six hours felt like a blur. The pace and adrenaline of first undertaking the search and then locating the bomb had made time fly. Now, sitting here, she finally had a moment to think of nothing but Aaron.

She called Joyti again. And again. But she did not answer. Saima wanted to throw her phone against the wall and scream. This was her little boy. Surely Joyti would have realized that Saima needed to speak to him before he went to bed? For her, leaving the mosque was far from certain and she'd be damned if she didn't hear Aaron's voice one more time. Perhaps she was being overly dramatic. She didn't care.

If she got her head clear, she could do as Frost had asked. She had been calm on the phone with him – resilient even. They were all in this together and everyone needed to play their part. Before she could take up that challenge she needed a clear head.

Saima tried to Facetime Joyti. They had done so before; her mother-in-law knew how it worked. The call connected on the fifth ring and Saima's heart felt like it might burst from her chest.

Joyti's face appeared on screen, smiling but also with a degree of concern she could not hide.

Saima started to cry, more out of relief than anything else. She asked desperately about Aaron.

Joyti spoke to her in Punjabi, a language Saima was fluent in. 'He is fine. I put him to bed and he is asleep.'

'Let me see him, Mum.'

Joyti asked how she was but Saima shook her head and again pleaded to see Aaron.

'If he hears you, he'll wake up, Saima,' said Joyti.

'I won't say a word, I promise. I just need to see him.'

Joyti moved from wherever she was, taking the phone with her. Saima had never been inside the house so she didn't have any bearings. Then the screen showed a bed, some distance away, as if Joyti were in the doorway. Saima could see Aaron's body, his head on a pillow.

She put her hand across her mouth, stifled her cries, then asked Joyti to go a little closer.

Now, with the phone right above Aaron, Saima saw him clearly. He had on some blue pyjamas she had never seen before, his dummy in his mouth, and looked to be sound asleep.

Saima cried hard, using her hand to absorb the noise, her whole body shaking. She just needed to get this out – be done with it.

Joyti slowly withdrew from the bedroom and made her way downstairs, arriving in the kitchen.

'Beti, are you OK? Tell me.'

Beti – daughter.

'I'm OK, Mum,' said Saima, not showing herself on the screen, simply speaking into the phone.

'I . . . I . . . am praying for you, Beti. Everything will be fine.'

Saima couldn't speak any more and remained silent. Joyti seemed to sense this and tried her hardest to put Saima at ease. 'He had all of his tea, Saima, no problems. Ranjit even went to the shops and bought him new clothes and a toy – you have nothing to worry about. Like I told Hardeep, your boy is now my boy and with my life I will protect and look after him.'

After the call Saima put the phone by her side, put her hands over her face and let it all out. Aaron had looked so peaceful asleep, not a care in the world. Just as it should be.

Hearing Joyti's calm voice, speaking as perhaps only another mother could, had made Saima want to speak to her own mother, something simply not possible. Instead, she reached for her phone and dialled her sister, Nadia. She answered immediately and was alarmed to hear Saima sounding so upset.

'I'm OK, I just, you know, being away from Aaron and trapped inside this place is getting to me.'

Nadia asked what was happening and Saima told her she didn't know, that as far as she was concerned, it was just a waiting game. Then she got down to the real reason for the call.

'Listen, Nads, if . . . you know, things should not go so well in here, if the worst happens, Harry is going to need your support. You're the only family I've got.'

Nadia tried to be positive and told Saima she was being silly – that everything would be OK. It was the only thing she could say.

'I know all that, Nads, but still, should it not happen that way, promise me you'll be there for Harry. That you'll do what you can.'

Nadia gave Saima her word, swore on her life.

Finally, Saima asked her for one more thing. Something she had never done before. She asked Nadia to call their mother in Pakistan and to tell her that Saima still loved her and that she was sorry for all the heartache she had caused everyone by marrying Harry. And that, if this situation resolved itself, she wanted to try and reconnect.

Nadia fell silent and Saima knew it was because what she was asking would perhaps not be met with the response she wanted.

'I don't care if it is not received well, Nadia. Just promise me you will do it.'

Nadia said she would.

Having disconnected the call, Saima wiped her face and took a few minutes to compose herself, mind now cleared.

Saima Virdee had work to do.

FORTY

THIS IS TREVOR HOLMES reporting for ITV news from Forster Square in Bradford where just behind me you can see the iconic Mehraj mosque, confirmed to be the location of a second explosive device inside a city already devastated by a major blast earlier in the day. As you can see, there is a dramatic police presence around the mosque with the cordon having been extended in the past hour. We have been forced almost a quarter-mile away.

The breaking news we have just received is that the other hundred and four mosques within the city have not evacuated, in spite of being allowed to do so by the terrorist organization calling themselves the Patriots. We understand that the very young and elderly have left these sites but the majority of the worshippers have remained in situ.

With thousands of police officers throughout the city and indeed around those mosques, this breaking development seems to go against the advice of the security services who, we understand, are in urgent talks with the imams of those mosques to find out what exactly is going on. One thing remains certain: with darkness approaching, Bradford has a very long night ahead of it.

FORTY-ONE

HARRY APPROACHED THE REAR of the property.

There were clothes on the clothesline but he couldn't see anyone in the house itself. Harry opened the rear gate and hurried down the path to the house.

The back garden was as perfectly tended as the front, not a blade of grass out of place.

Must take hours.

He was about to peer through the window next to the back door when he saw the handle move and the door flung open in front of him. A short, thin, black guy appeared in the doorway, a rucksack over one shoulder, heavy carrier bags weighing down both hands.

Couldn't have been Azeez; this guy hadn't seen a gym in his life.

He stopped, face aghast at seeing Harry in his doorway. Before Harry could react, the man charged at him, catching him off guard. Harry stumbled as the man flew past him, still carrying all three bags.

All Harry could think as he leapt after the stranger was how ridiculous he looked running for freedom carrying two cheap carrier bags, both ready to split any second.

Harry reached him in four powerful strides. He grabbed him, one arm around his neck, the other snaking around his torso.

'Police.'

The man whimpered and dropped the bags then, to Harry's astonishment, burst out crying.

The skinny black guy had identified himself as Roderick Manuel Alfonso. His driving licence said he was forty-two and it was registered to this address.

He continued to cry as Harry secured him to a kitchen cabinet door with a second pair of handcuffs.

The rest of the house was empty. Azeez wasn't here.

'What's your deal?' said Harry, opening Roderick's rucksack.

Clothes. Toiletries. A few hundred quid in cash.

The carrier bags each contained a laptop, which confused Harry. Surely the laptops would have been better in the rucksack and the clothes in the cheap plastic bags? This guy wasn't thinking straight. He was frightened.

'Azeez? You know him?' asked Harry.

Roderick continued to cry. It was starting to piss Harry off.

'You sick? Crazy? Or you in mourning?'

Everything about this bloke was off. His T-shirt was on back to front, his belt undone, one of his socks blue, the other red. Harry prodded him with his finger.

'You want to dial that shit down?'

Roderick didn't.

Exasperated, Harry grabbed the key from the back door and told Roderick he'd be back.

'Never seen him before,' said Isaac, looking as perplexed as Harry.

'Didn't think this was our guy,' replied Harry. 'I'm gonna take a proper look around. You see if you can calm him down.'

Harry locked the back door, taking the key with him. As he passed the staircase, he also checked the front door was secure. He didn't think Isaac was going to bolt but wasn't willing to take the risk.

The house was pristine. Rows of tiny porcelain ornaments were perfectly aligned on the mantelpiece in the living room. Plumped cushions on the sofa made a diamond formation. More of a show home than one where people lived. Upstairs was just as bad. Harry hurriedly searched both bedrooms.

The second had a wardrobe full of clothes for a man much bigger than Roderick.

Thirty-six-inch jeans.

Seventeen-inch collars.

Everything else either XL or XXL.

Seemed Azeez might have been here after all.

He was halfway down the stairs when he stopped. He could still hear Roderick crying.

Something wasn't right.

Surely not?

He went back upstairs. Back in Azeez's bedroom, he went for the bed. Duvet tucked tightly under the mattress, pillows snug underneath the duvet – more like a hotel than a home.

Harry pulled the duvet free. Dust swirled around his face. He backed off, coughing, blinking it out of his eyes.

Harry went to the other bedroom and did the same thing. No dust this time. He examined the pillows. Both well worn.

Harry frowned. He gave the room a little more focus. Blackout blinds on the windows, wires hanging loose behind the TV – a USB-to-HDMI cable. He found a mini-tripod down the back of the TV cabinet. Whichever camera it had once held had been connected to the TV screen. Amateur video at its best.

He opened the first bedside cabinet.

Empty.

Harry moved around the bed to the second and pulled it open. There it was.

FORTY-TWO

RODERICK ALFONSO CONTINUED TO cry like a baby in his kitchen.

Harry grabbed a chair and sat down opposite him.

'Stop that,' said Harry, showing him his police ID. 'I'm Detective Virdee from the Homicide and Major Enquiry Team.'

'Oh shit, oh Jesus! Honestly, I didn't know he was going to do it. I tried to stop him!'

Harry held up a hand. He couldn't show his alarm at the man's response.

'Do what?' said Harry. 'Who are we talking about here? Let's start at the beginning.'

Harry saw the shift in the man's demeanour, the narrowing of his eyes and the realization that Harry might not know what he was talking about.

He wiped his eyes with his free hand and shook his head. 'Nothing.'

Harry wasn't about to let him get away with that.

'What do you do?'

'Huh?'

'Job?'

Roderick shook his head. 'I'm on disability.'

'You ran away from me pretty quickly.'

'I . . . er . . . took my painkillers just before you arrived. They . . . help.'

'Who do you live here with?'

'I live alone.'

'I don't think so.'

'I do.'

Harry slapped him. He didn't have time for this shit.

Roderick didn't cry this time. He sat there, stunned.

'I really hope I don't have to do that again,' said Harry, leaning a little closer and dropping his voice.

'You . . . you . . . can't do that as a police officer!' said Roderick.

Harry slapped him again. Harder.

'If I have to do that a third time, Roderick, something in your face is going to break.'

Roderick's eyes seemed to darken.

Isaac hung back behind Harry.

'He was right,' said Roderick quietly. 'This country *is* diseased. Infected.'

Harry said nothing.

When the silence hit a minute, Harry reached into his pocket and removed the items he had found in Roderick's bedside cabinet.

A handful of Viagra tablets, a gimp mask and a nipple clamp.

He dropped them one by one on the floor in front of Roderick.

'They're going to have a right old time with you in prison, aren't they? So is it you or Azeez who gets to wear the mask?'

Roderick didn't need to reply. Harry saw the answer in his face.

Harry pointed to the laptops stuffed inside the carrier bags, the ones Roderick had been running with. 'Bet there's a lot of saucy shit on those. Saw the leads hanging from the TV. No video camera, mind.'

Roderick glanced at his rucksack, realized his involuntary

mistake then looked away. Harry opened it and dumped the contents on the floor. A silver Sony camcorder clattered on to the tiles.

'I don't really give a shit about your sex life, Roderick. I want to know where Azeez is. You tell me that and you can get back to running wherever it was you were going.'

Harry waved the camera at him, placed it on the table.

Roderick looked at the dustbin.

'Something in there you don't want me to find? Something worse than what's on that camera?'

Suddenly Roderick stood, pulling open a drawer beneath the cabinet he was cuffed to and brandishing a knife.

Isaac stepped back, just out of reach, eyes searching for Harry's, who ignored him and folded his arms across his chest.

'Really?' he said, frowning.

Roderick was waving the knife wildly at Harry, eyes glazed over, face twisted into a frightening snarl. Gone was the cry-baby.

Harry picked up the chair he had been sitting on. 'This only ends one way,' he said, raising it to throw at him.

Roderick shook his head. He was frightened and angry. Maybe the guy was mad.

Harry tightened his grip on the chair. Once he threw it, Roderick would have to drop the knife to use his hand to defend himself. Harry would put him down with a swift kick to the balls and then, well, he'd be forced to play a little dirtier.

Harry never got the chance.

Before he could do anything, Roderick started laughing, shouting something incoherent in what sounded like Arabic before closing his eyes and putting the knife to his neck. Then, without hesitation, he cut his own throat, eyes wide and crazy.

Isaac stood frozen in disbelief.

Harry stood there, chair still raised, stunned, blood haemorrhaging everywhere as Roderick collapsed to his knees, wavering slightly before slumping to the floor.

FORTY-THREE

JOYTI VIRDEE ALWAYS FOUND the act of making Indian tea soothing. Allowing water to boil, adding loose tea, cardamom and fennel
seeds, then a generous amount of milk, and allowing it to simmer.
The longer it simmered, the richer the tea. Her mind was on Saima.
Trapped inside the mosque.

Alone.

At least she had seen that Aaron was asleep. Not that it had been
easy. Aaron had cried incessantly, exhaustion finally taking over.
Joyti doubted he would wake until morning.

Today she allowed the tea to simmer for a quarter-hour longer
than usual, her mind now going to Ranjit.

He had been to the supermarket, bought Aaron clothes and a
toy. Nothing from the usual range, everything from the premium
line. A small detail but an important one, she felt.

Joyti turned off the stove, poured two cups through a tea strainer
and carried them into the living room along with a packet of Ranjit's favourite, custard creams.

Her husband was sitting quietly at the table by the window,
staring outside, the brightness of the day starting to fade. She left

the door wide open; if Aaron started to cry she needed to hear him. Joyti doubted he would. She had rarely seen a little boy as tired as he had been.

She placed the cups on the table and sat down opposite Ranjit. He didn't look up.

'Tea,' she said softly, jolting him from his thoughts. He looked in her direction, momentarily confused. She nodded towards the table. He hadn't eaten anything all day.

The silence lingered.

Joyti blew gently into her cup, the heat rising from the tea.

'You know, when our son bought us this house, I was so pleased,' said Ranjit finally, taking his tea, leaving the biscuits.

'It's a lovely house,' she replied.

'I liked the view. The hills in the distance. It reminded me of the place I grew up in Punjab after my family had been forced to leave Lahore.' Ranjit looked down into his teacup. 'When I was a child, I wished I could run over the hills because I had heard stories there was gold on the other side.'

Joyti listened quietly, unsure why Ranjit was telling her this. She knew how the partition of India had affected her husband's family. One day they had woken up to find themselves living in the newly formed Pakistan. It had taken only three days before the looting had started. The British had fled, leaving Sikhs and Muslims to engage in a bloody conflict on both sides of the border.

'We left our home on a Friday. I always remember it because I could hear the mosques sounding their call-to-prayer.'

He laughed uncomfortably and took a sip of his tea.

'My mother was carrying my younger brother' – Ranjit paused – 'Charanjit.'

Joyti had never heard the name, had never known her husband had a younger brother.

'You—'

'He was my mother's favourite.' Ranjit spoke over her. 'Youngest always is.'

She smiled. Even Ronnie knew that Harry had always been her favourite.

'Charanjit was my favourite too. He used to sleep in my bed at night and when it got too hot I would fan him until he slept.' Ranjit wiped his eyes. 'We left Lahore on this Friday. We had heard from our neighbours, a Muslim family called Baig, that we were not safe any more. They were good people. We used to go to their house for Eid dinner and they would come to ours when it was Vaisakhi. This Friday, though, they told us to leave because we were in danger. And we did, in the baking heat. My father, two older brothers and my mother. My mother carried Charanjit until she became too tired. Then I carried him.'

He wasn't drinking his tea any longer, but he gripped the cup as if the room had grown cold.

'He was so heavy,' said Ranjit, his voice now just a whisper.

The expression on her husband's face was one Joyti had never seen before.

'There were thousands walking with us. We heard whispers that vandals were coming – to rape the women, kill the children, and the heat . . .' Ranjit shook his head. 'It felt like we were walking through fire.'

He got up from his chair and moved towards the dark corner of the room, as if the pale light from the window was burning his eyes. His voice had changed. Was it pain? Or fear?

'Charanjit stopped moving in my arms on the eighth day.' He placed his hands on the wall as if the wind had been knocked from him and he could no longer stand.

Joyti went to him but she didn't embrace him. She didn't know how. Why had she never heard this story before? In all their years of marriage?

'We . . . wanted to cremate him but there was no wood. Nothing to make a fire. So . . . so . . .' Ranjit broke down. 'We laid him down by the road – next to other children – and covered his body with leaves . . .' His voice trailed off.

Joyti wrapped her arms around her husband.

'We left him there! He was such a pure, innocent child. He should have been cremated so his spirit could have returned in the next life as something worthy! We could not do this for him. We . . . had to keep walking!'

He smashed his fists against the wall. 'What kind of God could allow that to happen?'

Another crack of his fists on the wall.

'My father kept pushing us to walk – he never cried. He just kept us moving. My mother, a part of her died that day. She was never the same again.'

Joyti hugged him as tightly as she could, feeling his body starting to shake, her tears soaking into his shirt.

'Those bastard Muslims took Charanjit's life. They took my mother from me! They ruined us. Homeless, penniless and now incomplete.'

Joyti heard a wheeze inside his chest, a sound she knew only too well. She moved to the shelf above the mantelpiece and snatched his inhaler, pushing it into his hands.

Ranjit put it to his lips and inhaled deeply, repeating it several times, keeping his body in the corner as if afraid to step out from the shadow.

'Charanjit had a birthmark behind his right shoulder. A perfectly formed circle.'

Joyti felt her head swim.

'That . . . that . . . child upstairs,' he said, continuing to cry.

She looked at him, pained.

Ranjit pointed upstairs. 'That boy, I swear to you, Joyti . . .' He balled his hands into fists. Not bitterness but pain. He stared at his wife, disbelief on his face.

'That boy upstairs has the same birthmark as Charanjit. I want more than anything to take him in my arms, kiss him, inhale the sweetness from his skin and never let him go! But I cannot.'

FORTY-FOUR

SAIMA WALKED UP AND down the grand hall, pushing a cart filled with food – the one thing the Mehraj mosque was not short of. As people ate, the edginess that had existed inside the room seemed to settle.

Saima had not offered to help cook in the kitchen, instead volunteering to distribute food. It gave her the chance to walk among the worshippers.

A sleeper cell? What did that even mean? Everyone she had so far seen appeared to be perfectly normal. A few faces she recognized; most, however, she did not.

The room had fragmented into four clear groups. The elderly, men, women, and youngsters. The differences between them were stark. Saima was concerned about the last group – the young boys looked anything but passive. Tensions were rising – boredom, too much social media and, the most worrying aspect, anger. The older men seemed to be on it – watchful.

Saima had been drawn towards the women in full burkas first, but then questioned it. Trying to be objective, was it not too obvious for the sleeper to be wearing a burka? There were half-a-dozen women dressed in the outfits. Saima had approached them, spoken with them and left, unfazed.

Imam Hashim entered the room, pushing a cart full of drinks. He caught her attention: smiling, embracing those who needed it. He was the epitome of a man in control.

Christ, she was being cynical but Harry's words filtered into her mind:

Look for the calmest person in the room . . .

Hashim was certainly that.

She thought back to her attempts at analysing the bomb, Hashim by her side. He had been the perfect example of calm.

Finished with the food cart, Saima made her way back to Hashim's office, located at the right-hand side of the stage. She had left her phone on charge inside.

Having double-checked he was still at the other end of the grand hall, Saima sat down at his desk. She opened the drawers and found nothing more than religious texts. The computer was on and she moved the mouse, bringing the screen to life. Saima clicked on the email icon and scanned a few of the most recent emails.

She frowned. They were in Arabic, which Saima couldn't understand. She glanced at the keyboard – also Arabic. She took a few moments to figure out which the Send button was, then forwarded the last five emails to herself. Saima unplugged her phone, checked the emails had landed then deleted them from Hashim's Sent folder.

Nothing to it.

She moved to the couch and used Google translate on her phone to decipher the emails. It took a short while to figure them all out. Once she had, she could hardly believe her own eyes.

Imam Hashim.

Saima stood up, alarmed, the phone shaky in her hand. She tried to call Harry but it went to voicemail. Saima needed to tell someone what she had found.

Frost.

She scrolled to his number and was about to hit Call when the office door opened and Hashim strode in.

He closed the door then turned to look at her, clearly annoyed.

'Put your phone down, Saima.'

She stared at him, uncertain.

He pointed to the corner of the room.

Saima turned to see a small, dome-shaped CCTV camera, fixed in the ceiling. She hadn't realized it was there.

Hashim showed her his phone: real-time footage of them both.

Saima's thumb was poised to call Frost. Hashim closed the gap.

'Give me your phone, Saima.'

'I won't.'

'Let me explain.'

She pointed at him, outraged. 'You cannot do this, Hashim. I will not let you.'

FORTY-FIVE

NEITHER HARRY NOR ISAAC moved.

Blood pooled around Roderick's body, the knife by his side. Harry couldn't stop replaying how quickly and unhesitatingly it had happened. What the hell had made Roderick so afraid that he had slit his own throat?

Harry looked away. In his experience, only a very specific type of fear or mental illness could make a man do such a thing.

'You OK?' said Harry, looking to Isaac.

'I'm not the one who just slit my own throat,' replied Isaac, voice surprisingly calm. Harry didn't like what he saw in Isaac's eyes. Something dark surfaced then disappeared.

'Most people react after they've witnessed something like that.'

Harry wanted to add, *Especially ones who take medication for anxiety.*

Isaac met Harry's gaze. 'I don't know what you want me to say. I'm not sure what just happened.'

'Makes two of us.'

'Aren't you going to check his pulse?'

Roderick's arm was dangling awkwardly, still cuffed to a cabinet door. Harry unfastened the cuffs and put them in his pocket. 'He's as dead as anyone I've ever seen.'

'So, what now?'

'Why are you so calm about this?' Harry grabbed Isaac by the arm.

'I don't know what you expect. I'm supposed to cry? Faint?'

'All that and more.'

'Sorry to disappoint.' Isaac shook him off.

'He did that because he was afraid,' said Harry. He stepped around the blood, still pooling on the floor.

'Are you going to call an ambulance?' said Isaac.

'No.'

'Are you really a police officer?'

'Yes.'

'You don't act like one.'

Roderick had been staring at the bin just before he killed himself. Harry removed the lid. He couldn't see anything except the black bin bag. He carried it into the living room, away from the blood, Isaac following behind.

Harry emptied the contents on the floor.

Four pieces of cardboard, four plastic sheaths.

'Shit,' whispered Isaac.

'We need to move quickly,' said Harry, alarmed.

This time, he was comforted by Isaac's tone. If the kid hadn't reacted to what they were looking at, Harry wasn't sure he could have continued to work alongside him.

'You start down here. I'll do upstairs. Tear the place apart,' said Harry.

Isaac was still mesmerized by the contents of the bin: four empty packages that had each clearly contained a large kitchen knife. 'What am I looking for?'

'Azeez has a location in mind. He's dreamt of this, obsessed about it, and most importantly coveted the location. We only covet areas we know well. In this house is a clue to where the sick fuck is headed. We need to find it, Isaac. *Fast.'*

Isaac could hear Harry tearing the house apart upstairs. He was doing the same down here. They needed to find Azeez. Without him, Isaac couldn't get to Nazir, to safety.

He was angry at himself for letting the detective notice his reaction to Roderick's suicide.

Isaac knew Harry didn't trust him.

What he also knew, though, what he had experience of, was that desperation often left a man exposed. Vulnerable.

He wasn't about to underestimate Harry Virdee.

Isaac was banking on the fact that Harry would underestimate him.

Upstairs, Harry ransacked both bedrooms, not completely focused. It was distracting, having part of his brain focused on Isaac downstairs. Harry had always had a sixth sense when it came to people. The kid wasn't toxic, but there was something deeper going on that Harry didn't like.

For now the only question Harry needed an answer to was: could he trust Isaac not to have a pop at him?

For now.

Harry discovered a few photos of Azeez. Vanity snaps of him on a beach. Nothing that gave him any clues to where Azeez might be headed.

Wherever Azeez was going, he intended to kill.

He should call this in. What would he say? How the fuck had he got here and what about Isaac?

The bastard had to be local. Probably close enough to go on foot. Someplace small yet with enough people to cause headline-grabbing casualties.

Isaac's voice startled Harry from his thoughts and he hurried downstairs.

'Found something?' said Harry, rushing into the living room.

'Payslips.'

Harry took them from him. The last three months. Each was for four hundred pounds, for part-time employment.

Harry checked the front, found the address.

'Oh, Jesus,' he said, stuffing them into his pocket. 'Come on.'

Harry grabbed Isaac and together they headed for the back door, stepping past Roderick's body.

Outside they ran for the car, Harry praying they were not too late.

Quebec Nursing Home, Dementia Specialists.

FORTY-SIX

QUIET.

What happened now?

'Why didn't you tell me?' Joyti asked finally. They were sitting back at the table.

'Poured dirt in the grave,' he replied. It was an old Indian saying. When bad things occurred, you simply buried the facts and never spoke of it again.

Joyti's heart broke for her husband.

'When I first saw the boy,' said Ranjit, pointing upstairs, 'I thought I was seeing things.'

Ranjit reached for his now cold tea.

'When I heard him crying, my chest started to ache.'

'We've shared so many burdens, Ranjit. Why not this one?'

'I didn't want to believe it had happened. I didn't want to remember.'

'How old were you?' she asked.

'Eight,' he replied. 'I was too young to know loss like that. And I saw it every day in my mother's eyes.' Ranjit looked at Joyti. 'You and her share the same look of sorrow. The day Hardeep left, your eyes became like hers.'

Joyti winced. She wanted to ask him why, then, had he not understood her pain? Why had he banished their son? It wasn't the right time.

'How could I do to you the very thing that was forced upon my mother?'

Joyti looked away. He had understood what she was thinking.

'I must be a real tyrant,' he said, 'not to have afforded you the opportunity my mother never had – just to be a mother to your child, to protect him and love him, no matter what.'

Joyti wiped a tear from her face.

'I saw what the Muslims could bring – the pain, the loss' – he paused – 'the suffering.'

Joyti opened her mouth but Ranjit raised his hand.

'On the day terrorists descend on Bradford to ruin this city we call home, a boy arrives in my house to torment what little life I have left.'

'Torment?'

Ranjit nodded. 'Until I stared at his little face, I thought I had suffered all I had to suffer.'

Joyti leaned forward and put her hand on his.

'So, nothing changes?' she said softly.

'I want to go upstairs and crawl into bed with him, Joyti,' said Ranjit, starting to cry again. 'I want to wake him up, take him into the garden and fly a kite with him, like I used to do with Charanjit.'

'Then do it!' said Joyti, putting her hands together as if in prayer.

Ranjit slammed his hand on the table, making tea spill from both their cups. 'I cannot, woman!' he cried.

Joyti allowed her tears to soak her face.

'What kind of sick man must I be that I cannot go upstairs and embrace that boy? My heart and mind are working against each other. I wish I were dead, Joyti—'

She got up to go to him but he stormed past her, hesitating by the living-room door, hammering his fist into his chest, the sound sickening.

'My bones are too old, my mind too stubborn and my heart too weak to do what you ask. I am,' he said coldly, 'dead inside.'

FORTY-SEVEN

HARRY SCREECHED HIS CAR to a stop outside Quebec Nursing Home, yelling for Isaac to follow as he got out.

It wasn't a small place. At least thirty rooms, he thought. Thirty vulnerable targets.

It appeared peaceful but Harry knew better than to feel relieved yet.

'Shouldn't we call for backup?' said Isaac.

'Not until we actually have a problem.'

If Azeez was here and had not yet carried out his attack, Harry needed to detain him himself. But if he found a knife-wielding lunatic in there, he'd be forced to call this in.

Tariq Islam's voice boomed loud in his ear.

The government does not negotiate with terrorists and that policy will not change simply because thousands of lives are at risk.

They looped around the side of the nursing home, Isaac on Harry's heels. He wasn't sure what use, if any, Isaac would be. Or if Azeez was even here. He could never really be sure in his job, but two decades of policing told Harry Azeez would be inside. He had to try.

Thirty vulnerable elderly patients. It'd be a tragedy of the worst kind.

The back entrance, like the front, had automatic double doors and a window either side: four panels of glass. Curtains were drawn across the first two. Peering through the third panel, Harry saw a brutish figure, tall, broad, skin dark against his white vest. He was tying up a member of staff, the last of five. Harry spied a knife in his hand, another down the back of his jeans, handle sticking out. The room was full of elderly residents, most looking bemused. A few appeared to be shouting at Azeez.

He grabbed Isaac, put his fingers to his lips and nodded for him to have a look.

'Azeez?' said Harry, giving Isaac a few seconds even though he knew the answer.

'Yes,' replied Isaac, mouth dropping open.

Harry tried the door but it was locked for the night.

'We need to hurry,' said Isaac, panic clear in his voice.

In the rush to get here, Harry had left everything in his car.

He was unarmed.

Harry returned to the window. Azeez was still with the staff. A car pulling up behind drew his attention and he turned to see a blue Ford Focus parking in the rear carpark. A young woman in a yellow healthcare uniform got out.

Nursing home staff.

Isaac moved with Harry, both of them rushing towards her. She saw them coming, tensed and turned to run.

'Wait!' called Isaac, but she was on the move, sprinting. And now screaming in panic.

Harry flew past Isaac, reached the girl and threw one arm around her, putting his other hand across her mouth.

She bit down, her teeth puncturing his skin.

Harry cried out in pain as she bit harder, shaking her head from side to side like a pit-bull. Then the girl moved her head backwards, butting Harry in the nose.

He let go, stumbling, as she ran for her car. Isaac came towards Harry, who waved him away.

'Go after her!' he snapped at the boy.

Harry blinked away tears and touched his nose.

No blood.

Back in her car, the young nurse reversed wildly.

Harry hurried in front of the car, struggling to get his police ID from his jacket with his injured hand.

He heard the gear change, no doubt from reverse into first.

Isaac moved out of the way but Harry stood firm, waving a pair of handcuffs and his identification in desperation, hoping Azeez had not seen any of this out of the window. Hoping they had not triggered his attack.

Harry saw something in the young woman's eyes shift.

She wasn't bluffing.

As the car came at him, Harry dived out of the way. He felt a gust of air brush by him, the car closer than he wanted it to be.

She was gone.

Harry, on the floor, groaned. He'd fucked it up.

He heard Isaac approach, offer his hand, which Harry ignored.

In his other hand, he waved a set of keys at Harry. 'She dropped these. Want to bet one of them opens that back door?'

FORTY-EIGHT

THEY ENTERED A KITCHEN, a lingering smell of cooked onions. He saw what appeared to be three empty trays of shepherd's pie on a worktop, waiting to be washed up.

Harry could hear Azeez's voice from the room next door, loud and angry.

'Weapon,' whispered Harry to Isaac, pointing for the kid to have a look and gesturing for him to be discreet.

Isaac pulled the kitchen drawers open on one side, Harry on the other. The bite the nurse had inflicted on his hand was bleeding. It hurt like a bitch. Harry grabbed a cloth and pressed it firmly against the wound, wiping blood clear. He'd been bitten before, a drug addict several years before. A fleeting memory of seeing Saima in A&E, of antibiotics and a dressing, flickered across his mind. He focused on the task. Surely there must be a knife around here.

Had Azeez been in here and secured them all?

'Come on, come on,' he whispered, hearing Azeez in the other room. He was becoming increasingly irate. He crept to the door and nudged it with his foot, thankful it didn't creak.

Azeez was about twenty feet away, muscles taut, sweating heavily in the heat. He was now standing proud in front of the residents, a knife in each hand. The cook, judging by her apron, was on her knees at his feet, eyes fixed on the floor.

The sight angered Harry, white hot fury rose in his chest.

These innocent people.

Azeez gesticulated wildly as he shouted. Harry couldn't hear his words, he was too focused on the knives in his hands. Every few seconds, one of them would find its way to the blonde curls of the cook cowering on her knees.

Azeez was enjoying this – his moment of glory, his time to exert control and feel all-powerful. Harry clenched his teeth; he was going to tear this bastard apart.

'Harry, we should call for backup,' Isaac said, fear in his voice.

The residents' faces were a mixture of bemusement, fear and blankness. Some looked unfazed and Harry was momentarily grateful that they might be too unwell to realize what was happening.

Azeez grabbed the cook's hair suddenly and yanked her head back, raising a knife.

'Shit,' whispered Harry. He turned to Isaac. 'This goes bad, don't be a hero. Call 999.'

'Let me help you.'

'No. He can't know you're here.'

'Why?'

'No time,' said Harry impatiently, 'just do it. You hear me?'

Isaac nodded.

Harry was ready to enter when something on the counter caught his attention. He flipped the lid of a small pot and stared at the contents.

That could be useful.

Harry put the container in his pocket.

He stepped into the corridor.

Azeez's head snapped up at the noise. He glared at Harry, pointed a knife at him, eyes cold with rage.

Harry walked towards Azeez, lifting an empty chair on the way.

'I am Detective Chief Inspector Harry Virdee. Hello, Azeez.' He stopped about ten feet away, poised to throw the chair, nothing more than a distraction technique.

Azeez waved a knife at Harry. 'Drop it.'

Harry glanced at the cook; she was unharmed. He replaced the chair on the floor.

Harry and Azeez held each other's gaze, their eyes burning, both motionless.

Then Harry smiled and started to laugh.

FORTY-NINE

'DO YOU WANT TO tell me what this is about?' Hashim asked Saima.

She didn't know what to say. Her face was flushing and she couldn't meet his gaze. He didn't know there was a sleeper cell. Frost had told her to keep that vital piece of intel to herself. All she had told Hashim was that the bomb had been too complex to disable. She thought she had delivered the lie well enough.

Hashim sat at his desk, calm as you like. 'These are extraordinary times we find ourselves in,' he said, clicking a few buttons on his keyboard, then turning his computer screen to face her. Sky News – live footage of the Mehraj mosque. Her eyes narrowed as she saw the enormous police presence.

Saima knew they might be planning a break-in to try to save the worshippers, to try to defuse the bomb. Frost had hinted to her it might be coming but knew he couldn't confirm it.

'With all this going on, I find you acting like some sort of spy? Did what happened in the basement not build some trust between us?' He sounded genuinely wounded, looking at her with a critical eye. 'Are you something far removed from what you appear to be, Saima Virdee? A spy for these Patriots; someone I should detain?'

He was really turning this on her? Saima was outraged. 'You are so full of shit.'

She regretted the profanity and glanced at the canvas of Mecca on the wall behind Hashim. Saima grabbed her ears and whispered, 'Toba astaghfar.'

I seek forgiveness from Allah.

'Assume it has been given, Saima. Now, I'd like an answer to my question,' said Hashim.

She sighed. 'I wanted to send an email. My mobile has no reception, but I couldn't use your keyboard, it's in Arabic.'

Hashim gave her a menacing smile.

Saima knew she'd been rumbled.

'How long should we play this game?'

She nodded at the computer, still streaming the live feed from outside the mosque. 'You're very calm, considering what's happening out there.'

He didn't respond.

Saima couldn't stop thinking about the emails she had read. It was time to confront him. 'I know what is going to happen in a few hours. You cannot! Think about what you and the other mosques are doing!'

'You do not know anything, Saima.' His words were delivered with real anger.

Saima came across to him, determined. Frost had told her the sleeper cell would have a simple device no larger than a car-key-sized remote.

'I wonder, would you turn out your pockets if I asked you to?' she said.

'Are you asking?'

'I am, unless you have something to hide, Imam.'

Hashim shook his head in dismay.

'Fine,' he said, standing up and emptying his pockets.

A mobile phone. A wad of twenty-pound notes. Rosary beads.

Saima stared at him, waiting.

Hashim smiled and turned his pockets inside out, showing her they were indeed empty.

'Do you intend to frisk me? Inside a mosque?' he said, bemused.

She didn't reply. Her eyes never left his.

'Really, Saima, this is very improper,' he said, raising his arms. 'Do what you must. We are not leaving until we both understand each other.'

She couldn't frisk him. It was a step too far. He'd called her bluff.

Saima backed away, retaking her seat.

Hashim reclaimed the contents of his pockets and sat down, waiting.

'Who else knows why the other mosques have not evacuated?' she asked him.

He stared at her hard enough that she was forced to drop her gaze.

'You're looking for a sleeper cell,' he said. It wasn't a question.

Saima didn't reply.

'You are not the only one with influential contacts outside this mosque. I know just as much as you. But it is right that they trusted you.'

'How did you know?' she said, looking at him.

'Like you, I have people on the outside whom I trust. And they trust me to find such a person.'

Saima saw what he was contemplating. 'You think it might be me?' she said incredulously.

'You're snooping around my office.'

'With good reason. I saw your emails – care to explain them?'

'No.'

'And you say you have nothing to hide.'

Hashim's face hardened. 'Do not meddle in things you have no knowledge of.'

'Or you'll what?'

'First, tell me what you have learned about the sleeper cell.'

'Nothing. I'm looking for a needle in a haystack.'

'As am I. And since we seem to be the only two aware of this, it would be far wiser to tackle it together.'

Saima pointed at his computer, her anger palpable. 'I don't trust you.'

Hashim shook his head. 'Fine. I will tell you something you do not know but only if, right here and now, you swear to keep it secret.' He pointed to the canvas of Mecca behind him. 'With God as your witness, swear that what we speak of in this room will go no further.'

'If it does not put anyone's life at risk.'

'Nobody inside *this* mosque.'

Hashim didn't say any more.

Saima glanced at the painting of Mecca. She swore an oath of secrecy.

Hashim stood up and made his way to her, perching on the desk.

'You're a brave woman, Saima. Lots of heart. Guts. Determination. I saw that in the basement. Clearly, important people outside trust you and I will too.'

Hashim told her about the emails.

She was about to protest when he raised his hand then pointed to the canvas behind him. 'Have faith,' he said, simply.

Saima struggled, went to say something but stopped. *This was too much.*

'How do we find this sleeper, so that the things I have told you do not come to pass?' Hashim retook his seat. 'I know everyone inside this mosque.'

'Everyone?'

He nodded. 'Some for many years. Some more recent.'

'Nobody new?'

'No.'

'Are you sure?'

'Why do you think I have been moving through the crowd so often? Why I am handing out food and drinks and engaging in prayer circles?'

'Could someone be hiding in the building?'

'They could. We have swept it twice. Another search is under way.'

'Have you told anyone about the sleeper?'

'There is nobody to trust.' Hashim pointed towards the grand hall. 'Somewhere down there is our shaitan, Saima. In plain view.'

Shaitan – devil.

'It's time we worked this through together because soon what I have confided in you will come to pass.'

FIFTY

AZEEZ TIGHTENED HIS GRIP on the cook, shaking her head a little as he lowered the other hand to her throat, blade only inches from her skin.

'Don't come any closer,' said Azeez.

'You're quite something, aren't you,' said Harry, calming his laughter so he could speak. He reduced the distance between them.

'You cannot stop me,' said Azeez.

'Sure I can.'

Harry focused on the cook. From near the front of the hall, a few elderly residents, those still with their marbles, shouted for Azeez to put down the knives.

'What's your name?' he asked.

'Ellie,' she said.

'Everything's going to be fine, Ellie.'

'Hey!' snapped Azeez. 'Are you fucking stupid?'

Harry nodded. 'Clearly,' he said, before facing the elderly audience. 'This will all be over in just a few minutes, folks,' he said calmly. He turned back to Azeez and started laughing again.

Azeez looked angry and confused.

Harry searched for the words, something to injure Azeez, the more offensive the better. He needed Azeez to come for him.

'Ellie, he's not going to kill you. I doubt this gay boy can do anything except bend over.'

A shift in Azeez's eyes. Slight, but Harry saw it.

'Oh yeah, I know all about you. Got your boyfriend in custody. He likes to talk. In fact,' said Harry, stepping even closer, 'he showed us some footage on his laptop and that cute little camcorder.'

He stopped talking for a moment, allowing the silence to fill in the details in Azeez's mind.

'Radical Islamic warrior likes to take it up the arse. I'm guessing you're not banking on a one-way ticket to the promised land?'

He saw Azeez's grip on the cook's hair slacken.

'I'm going to upload the shit I've seen to the net. I reckon we could go viral. What do you think?' Harry put both his hands inside his pockets, making himself as unthreatening as possible.

Azeez lowered the knife a fraction.

'I've got my hands in my pockets and *still* you're afraid to come at me?' Harry got on his knees, taking the piss. 'All those muscles. All that rage and you're afraid? Try it. Let's see just how tough you are.' Harry paused, hesitated, then forced himself to add, 'Faggot.'

What happened next was quick but Harry felt like it occurred in slow motion.

Azeez let go of Ellie, who fell to the floor at his feet. He stepped past her, face contorted, spit spraying from his lips as he cried out.

Harry clenched his fist around the pot of chilli powder in his pocket and flipped open the lid with his thumb.

Azeez was on top of Harry, knife raised, ready to strike. Harry closed his eyes and threw the powder forcefully into Azeez's face before rolling quickly away.

Azeez screamed.

Harry had learned this technique at his corner shop, seeing his father defend himself against at least three armed robbers this way. Chilli powder in a corner shop couldn't be classed as an offensive weapon, but it worked.

Harry got to his feet and watched Azeez drop both knives, hands clawing at his face.

He waited until Azeez had done all the damage he could, powder rubbed firmly into his eyes, his nose, his mouth, then picked up the knives from the floor as Isaac emerged from the kitchen.

'You OK, kid?' said Harry to Ellie, helping her up and inspecting her neck.

No wounds.

She muttered something incoherent, moving away from Harry towards the crowd of elderly residents.

Harry turned to Isaac and held up a finger. He didn't want Azeez to know Isaac was here.

There was only one way he could do this.

He picked up a chair and swung it at Azeez's head. One swift crack and he was out cold.

'He'll be fine,' Harry said in response to Isaac's concerned expression.

Harry had two of the Almukhtaroon leaders in his custody.

And ten hours to find the others.

FIFTY-ONE

HARRY PULLED THE CAR round to the rear entrance of the nursing home and opened his boot. The wound on his hand was pulsing and he thought that by now the nurse who had bitten him would have reached a police officer. It wasn't a pressing concern. She wouldn't have known the altercation was related to Almukhtaroon. Officers would record it as an opportunistic assault and with everything else happening in Bradford right now, it would be low priority.

His altercation with Azeez had happened so quickly that Isaac had not had the chance to call 999. For now, they were still in the game.

Azeez would know the location of the other two leaders of Almukhtaroon but the bastard was unlikely to crack. Harry didn't believe the 'Saviour of God' would respond well to pain. It would simply harden his resolve to die as a martyr.

'Everything calm?' Harry asked Isaac as he went back inside.

Isaac nodded. 'I can't believe he was ready to kill all those people.'

The boy appeared shell-shocked, as if the capabilities of the Almukhtaroon were only now dawning on him.

Harry put his hand on Isaac's shoulder and squeezed it. 'Now you see why we need to keep going and find the others.' They locked eyes and Isaac nodded firmly.

Isaac handed Harry a green first-aid box, nodding at his hand. 'That nurse took a chunk out of you, didn't she?'

'Hell hath no fury like a woman scared,' replied Harry, smiling, taking the box from him.

'The cook is throwing up in the other room. Support staff are with her – care workers.'

Harry sighed and opened the box. 'Is there CCTV in this place?'

Isaac shrugged.

Harry nodded for him to go check. 'Ask the staff.'

Isaac hesitated. The sound of retching coming from down the hall.

'She's throwing up, not dying,' said Harry, waving him away.

The first-aid box proved useful, some antiseptic and a bandage. 'Bingo,' whispered Harry, opening the bottle of TCP and moving to the sink. He poured it over his injured hand, wincing.

Isaac re-entered the room. 'No CCTV,' he said.

'Good,' said Harry, grimacing.

'That hurt?'

'No shit, Sherlock.'

'There's some paracetamol in there, too.'

'Take it with you.'

Harry pointed to a small cardboard container. 'What are those? Plastic gloves?'

Isaac nodded.

Harry lifted out a pair and shoved them in his pocket.

For later.

He held out his hand and instructed Isaac how to dress it, thinking of the numerous times he'd seen Saima do this.

Saima.

He had to get her out of there.

'Pull it tighter,' said Harry as Isaac reached the end of the bandage.

Azeez was where Harry had left him, cuffed to a radiator and unconscious. He'd been out for a while now. There was a chance Harry had misjudged the blow and seriously injured him. He should have used his elbow. Harry had searched him and found no more weapons but had found a small version of the Koran in English stuffed inside Azeez's back pocket. Harry had put it in his car. He had an idea for later on.

'Here,' said Harry, struggling. 'Help me.'

Together, they lifted Azeez into the boot of his car.

Back inside, Harry went to the room where the staff were holed up. They were all young girls and all of them foreign nationals. They hadn't registered who Azeez was. They had tried to call 999 when Azeez had first become violent, shouting and screaming incoherently, but he had stopped them. Harry assured them he would call this in but explained that, with what was happening in the city, officers might not respond until tomorrow.

Harry drove fast past police vans with flashing lights, officers in full riot gear. He tried to call Saima but his phone was showing no reception. The networks must be down again.

He saw a phone box and pulled over, killing the lights but leaving the engine running.

'What is it?' asked Isaac, looking concerned.

Ordinarily, Harry would have headed to Queensbury Tunnel, but there would be road blocks in his way. He couldn't risk it, not with Azeez in the boot. He might wake up any moment. And Harry hadn't taped his mouth shut. He needed to confirm he wasn't injured from the blow before restricting his oxygen supply.

Harry needed a secure location.

He needed Tariq Islam to pull some strings.

Tariq . . . He'd been at Bradford City football stadium earlier. The place had been evacuated. Locked down.

Harry smiled.

'Wait here,' said Harry, turning the engine off and exiting his car, heading towards the phone box.

Isaac sat quietly, watching Harry. He closed his eyes, steadied his breathing.

Watching Harry take down Azeez had been quite something.

There was a determination inside of Harry Virdee. It meant Isaac could not, even for a second, risk underestimating him. He'd been worried that Virdee wouldn't be able to pull this off, but they would soon be on their way to Abu-Nazir and Amelia. Using Harry as a vehicle to get to Abu-Nazir was his only shot and with Azeez now secure, Isaac knew that all that stood between him and his leader was his ability to pretend he wanted to help Harry.

He could do that.

Harry checked the time: 20.30.

Nine and a half hours to go.

He searched his contact list, pulling up a familiar name. Ben Mitchell, Bradford City FC.

He stuck 50p in the phone booth and dialled.

Dead tone.

'Shit,' whispered Harry and tried again.

He was about to try a third time when he stopped. 'Idiot,' he hissed. The mobile networks were down. If Harry's phone wasn't working, then neither was Ben's.

Harry went back to his mobile, this time looking for the land-line number.

Six rings.

Eleven.

'Hello?' said a voice.

'Ben?'

'Who's asking?'

'Harry Virdee.'

'Jesus, Harry, what's going on?' Ben sounded more angry than scared.

'Arma-fucking-geddon.'

'Tell me about it. World's gone crazy.'

'How's it where you are? Armed police? Squad cars? Is the stadium on lockdown?'

'No, Harry, it's a wasteland out here. No one about. I mean, we had the evacuation alert a few hours back, like, got everyone out, but since then I've been told to pretty much lock everything up and piss off home.'

'So, why haven't you?'

'You think I'm leaving my stadium to hooligans who think they can take the piss while the police are busy elsewhere?'

That was Ben all right. Bradford City Football Club first, everything else second.

'Are you alone?' said Harry.

'Yeah. Why?'

'I need a favour.'

'Heard that before.' Ben sounded tired but also as though he was smiling.

'Can you open up the delivery entrance for me? I need to drive my car inside. I'll explain when I get there.'

Harry looked back to the car, mood darkening.

It was time to find out what was really happening inside Isaac Wolfe's head.

FIFTY-TWO

HARRY PULLED INTO THE delivery bay of Bradford City football stadium. He watched the massive metal gates closing in his rear-view mirror, plunging the car into an eerie darkness.

'You a football fan?'

Isaac shook his head.

'Welcome to the best football club in England,' said Harry.

'Isn't this dangerous?' Isaac asked. 'We're less than a mile from City Park.' He unfastened his seatbelt.

'This place has already been evacuated, swept and signed off. Nobody is coming back here any time soon,' said Harry, switching off the ignition and waiting.

Lights flickered overhead as a stocky old-timer appeared in the doorway through to the main building.

'Come on,' said Harry. 'This is us.'

Harry walked towards Ben. He was now in his sixties and he'd once owned the bakery next to Harry's dad's corner shop. It had been Harry's first paid summer job, cracking eggs, mixing cake batter and – the worst part – making the filling for the meat pies. Ben pulled him into a firm embrace.

'Weird to be here when it's dead,' Harry said.

'Not for me. Open up, lock up. This is how I like it.'

Ben stepped to the side of Harry and stared at the passenger seat of the car. 'Who's the kid?'

'Helping me with enquiries about what's going down in the city.'

Harry was banking on the fact Ben wouldn't recognize Isaac. He might have seen fleeting images on the news but at least his age group didn't obsess over social media like the younger generations. Besides, the images on the news were of Isaac wearing traditional Islamic robes. He looked vastly different in Western clothing.

'Usual cop shop not good enough?'

Harry dropped his voice. 'I could do with this staying between us.'

Ben nodded and held up his hand, all five fingers spread wide, and folded his little finger and his thumb across his palm. 'I owed you five favours. We're down to three.'

'Who's counting?' said Harry, slapping him on the shoulder.

'Me. How's my boy getting on?'

Harry had got Ben's son a job on the force. He wasn't exactly cut out for police work but he was trying.

'Gareth's doing fine, I hear,' said Harry. He'd heard the opposite but there was no point hurting the old man's feelings.

Harry watched Ben's expression as Isaac got out of the car. Ben nodded at the boy, no sign he registered who he was.

Harry told Isaac to stay put and moved to the boot with Ben.

'Got a parcel in here, Ben. Don't want to freak you out so, ahead of time, I'm going to let you know this' – he pointed at the boot – 'is one of the assholes these guys who call themselves the Patriots want.'

Ben raised his eyebrows, mouth dropping open a little. He said nothing.

'We good?' said Harry.

Ben nodded. 'I trust you,' he said. 'You do whatever you need to bring this home.'

He was about to open the boot when Ben said, 'Truth be told, can't say I much disagree with what the Patriots are doing.'

Harry paused. He didn't look at Ben, afraid his face would show that he hadn't liked what he'd just heard.

'I think there's a lot of innocent people at risk,' said Harry.

He waited for a response and got none.

Harry popped the trunk.

Azeez's feet came screaming towards him and hit Harry firmly in the chest, knocking him to the ground.

Harry fell backwards and hit the floor hard, seeing Azeez trying to flip his body out of the trunk. Isaac didn't move but Ben did. He grabbed the lid of the boot and slammed it shut, the sharp edging hammering into Azeez's thighs.

There was a piercing cry but Azeez didn't stop.

Rookie mistake, Harry – should have seen that coming.

Ben hammered the boot into Azeez again but he kept coming. Ben started to retreat.

Azeez couldn't see – eyes shut tight, presumably still burning from the chilli powder. Blind and cuffed he was hardly a threat, apart from his flailing limbs.

Harry got up and brushed himself down. 'There's an easy way and a hard way,' he said calmly. Isaac remained by the passenger-side door. Harry raised his finger to his lips, glaring for Isaac to get back in the car. He didn't want Azeez to know he was there. Harry had plans for them both.

'Fuck you,' spat Azeez, his head moving side to side, eyes still closed.

'You can walk or be carried,' said Harry, stepping closer. He touched Azeez on the arm and moved swiftly to the side as Azeez tried to headbutt him. Harry dodged it and moved behind Azeez, grabbing him around the neck with one arm, his other snaking around his body to grab his balls. Harry squeezed.

'Like I said, walk or be carried.' The potency of chilli powder made Harry's eyes water. He could only imagine the pain Azeez was in.

He felt Azeez's body relax. He had given in.

Harry went back to his boot and got the Koran he had found on Azeez from his laptop bag. He saw his Rolex, thoughts momentarily going to his mother and Aaron.

Focus, Harry.

Harry secured Isaac in the car using handcuffs, ignoring the kid's protests. He didn't want to burden Ben with babysitting him and, moreover, Harry needed a clear head for what he was about to do.

Bradford City Football Club had a small prison cell inside the stadium, used in times gone by when fans became out of control and stewards had needed somewhere to hold them, waiting either for the match to end or the police to arrive. It was now used to store pallets of plastic water bottles.

Ben opened it up for Harry and wandered off, clearly not wanting to know more than he already did.

Harry shoved Azeez to the floor, leaving the handcuffs in place, and pulled a bottle of water from one of the cases. He poured the contents across Azeez's face using his other hand to clean the chilli powder from his eyes. He told Azeez to open one eye at a time. Harry gently poured water over it.

'Blink as fast as you can,' he said.

It took around five minutes and at least five bottles of water before Azeez could keep his eyes open. The whites of his eyes were red raw – almost like they were bleeding. He looked like some kind of demon.

'Can you see?'

Azeez nodded. He was breathing heavily, Harry thought more from tiredness than anything else. The anger was still there but Azeez knew he wasn't about to escape.

'Painful, no?'

'Fuck you.'

Harry put his hand in his pocket and pulled out the pot of red powder. 'Heard a story once,' said Harry, crouching by Azeez and keeping the chilli powder in sight. 'My old man told it to me. When he lived in India, this thief broke into his home and tried to steal some money. My grandad – head of the village – was pretty well stocked. He had a rifle and a handgun. He collared this prick but he didn't shoot him.'

Azeez stared at the chilli powder.

'They didn't put in his eyes. They stripped him bare and rubbed it into the crack of his arse and all around his cock.' Harry laughed. 'Sadistic, right? They sat him down and hauled a massive paving slab on his lap so he couldn't move. No squirming or jumping up and down on the spot.'

Harry moved to a broken slab of rock in the corner of the room and placed the pot of chilli on it so Azeez could see it. 'Something like that anyway.' He tugged the disposable gloves he had taken from the nursing home from his other pocket and put them on the ground.

He really hoped he wouldn't need them.

Harry whistled. 'Apparently, he screamed for over three hours before he passed out.'

'Who are you?' Azeez grunted.

'I told you. A cop.'

'Cops don't act like you.'

Harry leaned back and relaxed. 'Guess I'm a little different.'

'So, you approve of what is happening in Bradford then?'

'Do you want to leave this place?' Harry ignored his question. 'I'll make you a deal.'

Azeez spat on the floor. 'I'd rather die.'

'I know. Die a martyr, all for the cause. I'm not asking you to help me find your mates.' Harry held his gaze. 'Cards on the table? I've always wanted to have a one to one with someone like you.'

Azeez raised his eyebrows.

'An extremist nutter.'

'You are so ill-informed. I pity you.'

Harry reached for Azeez's Koran and placed it on his lap.

'This is very simple. You tell me which page, section, chapter states that you can kill innocent people, like you were going to do back at the nursing home, and on my life I'll release you.'

FIFTY-THREE

SAIMA HAD MOVED AWAY from the grand hall into the foyer, her head throbbing.

Finding the sleeper cell was not something she was going to manage. The more she looked, the more she convinced herself she was seeing things that were not there.

Darkness was starting to set in across the city now and Imam Hashim had told the congregation he had been advised to close the shutters outside the windows. The mechanical noise of steel slowly descending across the glass was startling. Once they were closed, they would no longer be able to see what was happening outside. Saima imagined an increase in police personnel, flood-lights erected and, somewhere in the darkness, plans being finalized for a full-out tactical assault should the Patriots' demands not have been realized.

Saima watched the view she was looking at slowly vanish. With a final clang of metal Bradford disappeared. A momentary feeling of claustrophobia hit her and she hoped the finality of seeing the windows black out did not push the congregation inside the grand hall into a panic.

She was spinning her phone in her hands, thinking of Imam Hashim's emails and his explanation for them. She believed him, no question there, but was struggling with keeping it from Frost. He needed to be warned.

Could he stop it from happening?

Saima doubted it. The police were surely already at breaking point.

Harry wasn't answering his phone, no doubt up to his neck in part of the investigation. She had hoped that with her life at risk, his priority would have been keeping himself out of harm's way, focusing on being there for Aaron if this all went to hell.

She knew it was unlikely. He didn't have it in him to stand down.

Downstairs four men continued to guard the front doors. She moved into the corner of the foyer, back against the wall so she could see if she had company, and called Frost.

He answered immediately, her calls no doubt being prioritized. She spoke softly and quickly, confirming there had been no progress on the sleeper cell.

Then Saima told him why the other hundred and four mosques had not emptied.

And why Frost had less than three hours to counter it.

FIFTY-FOUR

THE JAIL CELL WAS a claustrophobic, nightmarish space. The air was close and suffocating, sweat dripping down Harry's face. He waited.

When another minute trickled by and Azeez had still said nothing, Harry took the Koran back.

'Funny that. You can't tell me where it says you can kill a room full of innocent elderly people.'

Harry held the book high and spoke a couple of lines that Saima frequently quoted to him. *'And do not kill one another, for God is indeed merciful unto you.'*

'My wife is Muslim. She recites those lines to me, usually when people like you, terrorists, do something like the shit you tried tonight.'

Harry tried again. *'The first cases to be decided among the people on the day of judgement will be those of bloodshed.'*

Azeez raised his head.

'Oh, you've read that bit?' said Harry.

'The bloodshed has been that of our people for many years.'

'Your people? And who are those? Homosexuals? Refugees?'

Azeez smiled. 'I know the voice of the shaitan and it is yours.'

Harry sighed. 'Profound of you. So, this devil of yours, is it him that inspires you to kill the innocent?'

'Fuck you.'

'There I was, trying to be respectful and not use bad language in the presence of your holy book. My wife would have my tongue if I disrespected it that way at home.'

'She's not a Muslim if she is married to a kaffir like you. She's a fucking slut.'

Kaffir – disbeliever.

Harry calmly placed the Koran on a stack of water. Usually he'd have knocked Azeez's teeth out for the remark but he couldn't show this weakness. Azeez would never stop if he saw it. He grabbed a bottle of water, opened it and took a long gulp, wincing that it was warm, like the humid air they were trying to breathe, the two men cramped together in that tiny space.

'Homosexuality?' said Harry, replacing the Koran in Azeez's lap. 'That allowed?'

Azeez was looking at the Koran. He remained silent.

'Not like you can hide that sort of thing, is it? I mean, the Almighty knows everything, right? So, when you're filming your best moves with your boyfriend, he knows about it.'

Harry pointed at Azeez. 'Shall I go and fetch the laptops we got from your place? Play you a few clips? Jog your memory?'

Azeez was starting to breathe heavily. He tensed as if he were about to charge but Harry pointed to the chilli powder in the corner of the room.

'Be a good little boy and settle down.'

'What do you want?'

'To know where Abu-Nazir and Amelia are.'

'I don't know.'

'Sure you do.'

'Even if I did, I would never tell you.'

'So, you do know and you're not telling me?'

'I know my rights. I don't have to talk to you.'

'Your rights?' said Harry bemused, unable to hide the smirk on his face. 'Now you want to talk about rights.'

'I want my fucking lawyer.'

Harry removed the Koran from Azeez's lap and walked out of the cell, placing it in the hallway out of view. It was Saima's influence, not his own superstition.

Back in the cell, he pulled the plastic gloves over his hands and grabbed the chilli powder. He moved quickly over to Azeez and tried to yank his jeans down. Azeez started to thrash. He was strong, his torso thick with muscle.

Harry couldn't manhandle him and backed off.

'I warned you. Unless you want another blast of this in your eyes, you better calm down and let this happen. If you start talking, we stop.'

Azeez was grunting with rage. Harry came closer with the pot of chilli powder. Azeez turned his face away and stopped kicking out.

Harry pulled Azeez's jeans down, then his boxers. Quickly, he flipped him over, kneeling into his back, pinning the big man to the floor. This wasn't going to be easy.

He poured chilli powder into his gloved hands.

'Last chance. Either tell me where Abu-Nazir is or I'm going to light you up from the insides.'

Harry yanked Azeez's head off the floor and got a barrage of abuse. He let go.

'Have it your way. I'm not going to lie to you – this is going to *burn*.'

FIFTY-FIVE

JOYTI CHECKED ON AARON for the third time in an hour. She was sure he would sleep right through the night but couldn't help herself checking.

She entered the living room where Ranjit was sitting on the floor, in a dressing gown, hair loose on his shoulders. He hadn't eaten much, spoken even less and spent over an hour in the shower. When he had emerged, he had asked Joyti to do something she had not done for years. Massage his head with coconut oil and comb his hair.

Joyti sat behind him, his head in her lap, and poured oil into her palms, rubbing them together, then started to massage Ranjit's scalp. He relaxed, eyes closed.

The house was eerily quiet.

After a moment he said, 'How much of your life have I taken from you?'

'Don't say such things,' she replied, tutting.

'I have though, haven't I?'

'No.'

'You've always served my needs. Always listened to what I said. You never fought me. Even when I banished Hardeep.'

She hesitated. Joyti couldn't remember the last time her husband had said her son's name without despair or hate.

'Why ask these questions of me now?' she said, pouring more oil into her hands.

'I'm just a man, Joyti,' he said sighing.

'I don't know what you mean.'

'I'm not as strong as you. Women have always been stronger. Stronger will. Bigger hearts. You never stop giving and men never stop taking.'

'Stop this foolish talk,' she said. 'You gave a lot to this family.'

She couldn't find a better reply.

'I ask you again, how much of your life have I taken from you? Be honest.'

Joyti thought back to the years of not having seen Hardeep. Of missing her grandchild being born. Of feeling . . . incomplete.

Ranjit grasped her hand. 'Your silence tells me I am right. Do you know what I was thinking about in the shower?'

Joyti moved her husband's face to the side and continued to massage his scalp, stroking the skin on the side of his wrinkled face. 'What?' she said.

'I was thinking why I didn't die last year when I had my heart attack.'

She tutted again. 'What has gotten into you?'

'I should have. My heart stopped for more than a minute. Until she saved my life.'

She.

Saima. He still couldn't say her name.

'She did her job,' said Joyti.

'She did more than that. She' – he paused, eyes closed – 'showed me her spirit.'

Joyti's hands stopped.

'What you saw, was it –' Now she had to think carefully about her words. '– a good thing?'

Ranjit took a moment replying. 'It was,' he said.

Joyti's lip quivered. Something had changed today.

'You have stopped,' said Ranjit.

'I . . . need some more oil,' she replied, lifting the bottle.

'What is she like?' asked Ranjit. Joyti blinked back tears. Her answer had to be the right one or she might end a conversation she had never thought she would have with her husband.

'She is like Harry.'

'Go on.'

'Big heart. Loving. Tough.'

'Tough?'

'Mmm.'

'I suppose they have loved together and lost together. They would be similar.'

Ranjit raised his hands, putting them on top of his wife's, holding them where they were on his head. 'Sum her up for me in one sentence.'

'Why?' she said, feeling him squeeze her hands.

'Humour me.'

'Why only one sentence?'

'My father always told me that if you cannot sum up another person in one sentence – often one word – then that person is not to be trusted.'

Joyti thought hard. 'I will if you will do the same for me first.'

Ranjit laughed, a tired, empty sound. 'That's a good answer.'

They kept their hands holding each other's.

'I can give you one word or one sentence,' he finally said.

'You choose.'

He nodded, squeezed her hand a little harder and said, 'Pure.'

She smiled, glad he couldn't see her crying behind him. 'Charmer,' she said.

'I haven't heard you say that in a long time.'

'Because you haven't been.'

'True.'

'My turn, is it?'

He nodded.

Joyti thought of Saima. She had only really known her for the past year, their relationship still felt so new. She knew what she was made of, what Saima was capable of. She saw that in Harry's eyes when he talked of her.

'Sacrifice,' she said finally, letting go of Ranjit's hands and resting hers on his temple, stroking it. 'Is it a good word?'

Ranjit nodded.

FIFTY-SIX

HARRY TOOK ISAAC OUT to the centre of the football pitch, a lone floodlight highlighting the stand. His eyes were drawn upwards. He could hear helicopters continuing to circle in the distance. His thoughts turned to Saima. Daylight had faded, leaving vivid streaks of purple in the sky. On any other day it would have been something to savour. Now he only wondered if the darkness would bring further complications inside the mosque.

In the far corner of the field, a solitary light was on in Ben's office, visible through the vast windows. He was busy deleting the last sixty minutes of CCTV recordings and then disabling the system. Harry had made sure of it.

Isaac appeared sullen.

'Azeez didn't tell me anything,' said Harry.

'I told you he wouldn't. Beating him up won't help.'

'I hardly touched him.'

Isaac looked at Harry and raised an eyebrow.

'I've given him something to think about but I doubt he will talk,' said Harry, resigned.

'What now then?'

'Plan B. You.'

Isaac looked confused.

'He trusts you, right?' Harry asked.

Isaac nodded.

'I'm going to throw you in the cell, hands and feet taped, but I'll leave a little slack between your wrists. You can't ask him straight out where Abu-Nazir is because he'll get suspicious. Instead, ask him for a safe location for you guys to escape to. Get *him* to offer up the information. By that time, you'll have worked your hands free, you can loosen his restraints and make a break for it.'

'You said he's in a locked jail cell.'

'I'll leave the keys in the outside of the door. One twist and you're both out. Soon as I hear the lock, I'll head in and drag you outside to teach you a lesson. From there, we'll go wherever Azeez wanted you to go.'

Isaac was nodding, his demeanour a little softer.

Harry sighed and shook his head. 'I . . . can't have you going into that cell looking as you are.'

'Huh?'

'Unmarked.'

It took a few seconds for the penny to drop.

'You see that you cannot go in unharmed?' Harry pressed his point.

Isaac shrugged. Harry didn't take his eyes off him, making it uncomfortable. Finally, Isaac nodded, reluctantly.

'You see that door over there?' said Harry, pointing past the boy. As soon as he turned to look, Harry punched him in the face.

FIFTY-SEVEN

HARRY BUNDLED ISAAC INTO the cell and shoved him to the floor, next to Azeez who was still handcuffed and gagged. The boy's nose was bleeding, his T-shirt stained heavily. He'd been angry, outraged, when Harry hadn't even allowed him to tend to the wound.

'Got another of your mates, Azeez,' said Harry, kicking out at Isaac and just missing. 'You don't look so good. Feel like talking yet?'

Azeez's face was pouring with sweat, the chilli no doubt now fully absorbed into his body.

Harry held up a bag of ice he had lifted from one of the freezers in the food concourse. Azeez's eyes lit up and he mumbled something incoherent into the gag around his mouth.

Harry placed the ice on the floor, inches from Azeez, and lowered the gag, pulling back just in time to avoid being bitten.

'You fucking pig!' Azeez spat.

'I bet your ass is hotter than the sun right about now. You remembered where Abu-Nazir might be yet?' asked Harry.

Azeez swore every profanity Harry had ever heard, eyes bulging with fury. Harry could not even imagine what damage the chilli was doing to his insides. He opened the packet of ice, pulled out an ice cube and popped it in his mouth, holding it between his teeth so Azeez could see it. Harry spat it on the floor.

'Such a waste,' he said.

Harry removed another, repeated what he had done.

Azeez was panting heavily, the lower half of his body wriggling on the floor.

'You see this, Isaac,' said Harry, standing up and gesturing at Azeez. 'This is what you've got to look forward to. I'm popping out, going to buy some extra-hot chilli powder.'

Harry exited the cell and secured the door.

'Twenty minutes,' he smiled.

Isaac waited for Harry's footsteps to recede.

Alone now with Azeez, he stared at the ceiling.

He was doing the right thing.

He was sure of it.

But Isaac was tired.

He started to struggle with the tape securing his hands. There was plenty of give. Blood continued to drip from his nose.

He'd been pissed off when Harry had struck him, even more irate when he'd tripped over his own feet and hit the ground.

Whatever it took to get back to Abu-Nazir.

Azeez continued groaning like a dying man. After witnessing what Azeez had been about to do at the nursing home, Isaac found it hard to feel sorry for him.

'I'm getting us out of here,' said Isaac, playing along with Harry's instructions. 'Do you know where we will be safe?'

Azeez wasn't listening. Sweat poured down his face. He looked delirious.

It took only a few minutes for Isaac to get his hands free. He wiped the blood from his face and pinched the bridge of his nose, squeezing hard, then turned to Azeez.

'How . . . how did you?' said Azeez, momentarily sobering.

Isaac couldn't free Azeez's hands but he did, for the sake of keeping this charade alive, loosen the tape around his feet.

'Ice,' said Azeez desperately, nodding towards it.

Isaac grabbed the bag.

'You need to help me,' Azeez whispered, head bent low.

Isaac was unsure. 'How?'

'Take my jeans down, open the ice and let me sit on it.'

'Do you know where Abu-Nazir is? We need to get out of here and get somewhere safe.'

Azeez shook his head. 'Don't know.' He nodded at the bag of ice. 'Open it. Help me. Quickly.'

Isaac opened the bag of ice and pulled at Azeez's jeans, hesitating at his underwear.

'My boxers. Pull them down.'

He watched as Azeez lowered himself on to the ice, letting out a sigh of relief.

'Please,' he said, nodding towards his crotch.

Isaac scooped several cubes of ice which had fallen from the bag to the floor and threw them into Azeez's lap, who sighed in satisfaction.

'Well, look at you two.' Harry's voice interrupted them.

Isaac flinched as Harry entered the cell, grabbed him by his hair and dragged him to his feet.

'Slippery little bastard, aren't you? Getting out of your binding.' He threw Isaac out of the cell. 'Stay put or you know what you've got coming.'

Harry turned back to Azeez, who had his eyes closed. He seemed hardly conscious of what was going on around him.

Harry kicked at the bag of ice. 'Shall I take that with me?' he said.

Azeez opened his eyes. He looked far worse than Harry would have expected. Desperate.

It was enough.

'Well?' he asked when they were out of earshot.

'Saville Tower, Dewsbury,' Isaac said confidently.

'What?'

'That's what Azeez said.' Isaac held his gaze.

'There's no way,' replied Harry.

'That's what he said. Come to think of it, I've heard that location mentioned before.'

'Everyone knows Saville Tower. I'm not buying it. The bastard is lying. Sending us to our deaths.'

Isaac shook his head. 'He gave me a number. Said we can call Abu-Nazir once we're free to check he's still there.'

Harry punched the number into his phone. 'You remembered it in one go?

'077 is standard. Next six are a mixture of mine and my mother's dates of birth and the last two are the year I left school. Easy.'

Harry was impressed.

'It's how smart people remember information; align it with something personal. There's books written on it.'

'All right, all right. Don't get too clever.'

He wanted to trust Isaac but something here didn't add up, he could feel it.

'Saville Tower makes no sense. Even the Yorkshire police officers don't go without armed backup. I don't get it. A notorious Far Right tower block – the one location Abu-Nazir would stick out like a whore in a nunnery.'

Isaac shrugged. 'I don't get it either.'

Harry went to his car and removed the burner phone Tariq had given him earlier. He handed it to Isaac.

'I need you to confirm he's there,' said Harry.

'You don't think me calling him is going to be suspicious?'

Harry shook his head. 'You're alone. Scared. You need a secure location until all of this dies down.'

The cheap handset didn't have a speaker function. Harry dialled the number Isaac had told him before handing it over, staying close and trying to listen, but he couldn't even hear the dial tone. He made Isaac hold the phone away from his ear so he could listen.

The call connected. The timer started to count down.

'It's Isaac. I need help.'

'Where are you?' came the muffled reply.

Harry had listened to Abu-Nazir's videos on YouTube but truthfully it could have been anyone on the other end of the line.

'Near the football stadium. I . . . need to get out of Bradford. Everyone is looking for me.'

'Are you alone?'

'Yes.'

'Azeez?'

'I'm not sure.'

'Saville Tower. Call when you arrive.'

The line went dead.

Isaac handed the phone back to Harry.

Abu-Nazir hadn't given a location in the tower, but he wasn't stupid. He'd have eyes watching. If Isaac did arrive, his identification would be confirmed before the number of a flat was given.

It's exactly what Harry would have done.

Saville Tower? Harry kicked the wall in frustration. Something wasn't right.

But it was all he had.

FIFTY-EIGHT

POTS AND PANS.

The worst job in the kitchen but one Saima was happy to do now.

For the past hour she and Imam Hashim had been working together to check the worshippers in the mosque, desperately trying to find the sleeper cell, neither with any real notion of what to look for.

Everyone had to contribute to the night's efforts and she was happy to play her part. It brought some welcome respite from the searching. But her mind wouldn't ease.

There were several women with Saima, all of them strangers. They cleaned in silence, everyone's minds clearly elsewhere. Saima wiped sweat from her brow. At home, Harry did the washing-up. Said it gave him time to think calmly about his day. She'd never argued – having a dishwasher husband was more than most of her friends could say.

Friends.

Her mind wandered again.

Before marrying Harry, she'd had a lot of friends. They'd grown up together, taken Koranic lessons, dodged the vicious auntie at the mosque.

After she'd married Harry, the shame had been too much for her friends and family. It had seemed easier to let everyone go.

Now, apart from her sister, Saima had mostly white friends who had no clue about everything she and Harry had been through. She wondered if Nadia had called their mother and told her what Saima had said about being sorry. Guilt was something Saima had got used to carrying but her current predicament had made it feel heavier than ever. If this siege ended badly, she wanted her conscience clear. She wanted her parents to know she had tried.

Saima said goodbye to two women who had finished their cleaning, leaving just her and one other. She hurried up. The last thing she wanted was to be left alone here. She squeezed some more washing-up liquid on to her scourer, turned the hot water on and kept scrubbing.

God only knew what Harry was doing in Bradford. He'd sacrificed so much to be with her. She worried he'd be cracking skulls trying to bring this standoff to an end, to get her out of here alive. There had been a time when she'd known nothing of Harry's willingness to bend the rules, of his complex relationship with his brother Ronnie, of what Ronnie did.

Maybe ignorance really was bliss.

Her stomach was tied in knots. All she wanted was for Harry to be safe. With Aaron.

Distracted, her hand found its way directly underneath the hot tap. 'Shit!' she cursed, retracting it. Skin red raw. Heat spreading up her wrist.

The lone woman left with her called out, asking if she was all right.

Saima didn't reply, instead turning off the hot water, turning the cold on and pushing her hand under it: standard scalding protocol. At times like this she was glad to be a nurse.

Fifteen minutes was protocol but she wasn't standing down here that long. Five would have to do. She timed herself: 22.25.

The woman came over to see if she was all right.

Saima didn't recognize her.

'Are you OK?' said the woman. She was wearing a burka but with her face uncovered. Wisps of black hair escaped her headscarf. Her complexion was so fair it made Saima think she might be a convert.

Saima nodded. 'Took my eye off the hot water. Just a minor scald,' she said. 'I'm Saima.'

'Maria.'

'Are you all done?'

'Thankfully.'

Maria started on Saima's remaining two pans.

'You don't have to do that,' Saima said.

'Can't leave you. Imam said not to stay alone.'

Saima was pleased. The enormous kitchen was now a ghostly space, all shadows and secrets. 'Thanks.'

'Shit day, isn't it?'

'And the rest. Do you have family outside?'

'Yes. They're freaking out.' Maria's smile was kind as she scrubbed.

Saima adjusted her hand under the tap. 'Kids?'

'Not yet. You?'

Saima couldn't stand the iciness of the water any longer and withdrew her numb hand. 'A four-year-old boy, Aaron.'

'Precious,' said Maria, turning the tap off. She grabbed a towel from the side and started drying her hands, the sleeves of her burka inching up.

Saima frowned, noticing something unusual on Maria's wrist. She stared at her a little harder. Burka. Hair covered. No visible jewellery. Saima focused again at her wrist. Maria noticed where she was looking.

'Can you pass me that towel, please?' said Saima.

Maria didn't move, a momentary thing, nothing more.

'Sure,' she then said, handing it to Saima.

Saima took the towel, drying her hands. She was thinking fast. 'Couldn't do me a favour, could you?'

'Sure,' said Maria, watching Saima intently.

'Could you grab one of those bigger dishcloths and wrap it around my hand like a makeshift bandage? The heat from this burn is going to needle me all night.'

A pause.

'I work in A&E. I don't want the skin to break and scar.'

Saima had to know if she'd been mistaken.

'Sure,' Maria replied, grabbing the dishcloth.

Saima raised her hand and turned her palm up.

As Maria started to dress it, Saima manoeuvred her hand so that Maria's wrist turned with hers, her sleeve moving up just enough.

'What the hell are you doing?' snapped Maria, forcefully shrugging Saima's hand away.

A whole sleeve of tattoos.

Forbidden in Islam.

Sometimes girls got a small one somewhere discreet, on the hip or back, but Saima couldn't think of anyone she knew who had a full sleeve.

'Sorry! I love tattoos but I've never had the courage to get one,' said Saima.

Maria pulled her sleeve firmly back over her wrist.

'Don't worry about the bandage,' said Saima, turning to leave. She needed to get to Imam Hashim, needed to tell him she'd potentially found their sleeper cell. 'It won't stay on long anyway.'

She felt a firm grip on her arm.

'Very clever, Saima Virdee.'

How did she know her surname?

'But you should have left this well alone.'

FIFTY-NINE

THIS IS GEMMA WILES reporting live for BBC news from the Mehraj mosque in Bradford. Darkness has been banished by several large floodlights erected around the perimeter of the mosque. The police presence here is, as you would expect, considerable, and within the last ninety minutes it has greatly expanded. Our sources tell us this is in preparation for an influx of Islamic worshippers from the other hundred and four mosques within the city, who have not officially evacuated their places of worship but intend to amass here, in Forster Square retail park, to hold a midnight vigil in a show of solidarity with the people trapped inside the Mehraj mosque. We understand senior police officials are in urgent talks with the mosques, concerned that such a large gathering could stretch police resources beyond their limit as well as provide a clear target for Far Right supporters. Social media appears rife with examples of clashes between the Far Right and Bradford's Asian population, which, as yet, have not ignited something larger. With no leaders of Almukhtaroon in custody and a growing feel of despair inside the city, Bradford has a difficult night ahead . . .

SIXTY

HARRY KEPT AWAY FROM the city centre, taking the route through Clayton towards Wibsey. From there he'd go via Cleckheaton towards Dewsbury. He had left Azeez bound and secured in the stadium's prison cell. Ben would be there all night but he didn't want him involved.

Harry's injured left hand was throbbing, the bite the nurse had inflicted on him starting to sing. The wound hadn't clotted yet, blood still fresh. Damn thing was too deep and needed stitches. He'd retied the bandage, pulling it tighter.

This side of Bradford seemed calm, a world away from the chaos of City Park. No flashing lights. No helicopters, armed police or tactical units. Just . . . Bradford.

'Are you OK, Harry? You don't look good.' Isaac fidgeted nervously.

'We're going to attempt to lift Abu-Nazir and hopefully Amelia from Saville Tower. If I felt OK about that, I'd be a fool.'

'Maybe we shouldn't go. Call in the real police?'

Harry snorted. 'Real police? What the hell do you think I am?'

'I don't know, but I do know you don't act like a policeman.'

'I get the job done. That's why they asked me to round you lot up.'

Harry regretted the slip of the tongue immediately.

'Us lot?' said Isaac, contempt in his voice.

'I didn't mean it like that.'

'Yes you did.'

'Really? That's what you're going to take issue with right now?'

'"You lot." That's everything that's wrong with how the world sees Muslims.'

'Fuck off. I married one.'

'Doesn't stop you lumping us all together, though, does it?'

Harry pulled the car over, tyres screeching, and grabbed hold of Isaac.

'What the fuck do you know about how I see the world? You think I enjoy putting my life on the line knowing that if it goes south, my son might wake up tomorrow without a mother or a father?'

Harry shoved him roughly into the passenger door.

'I'm doing this so a thousand innocent Muslims don't get incinerated, one of them my wife. I'm doing this because if that bomb goes off we'd see a new generation of nutters, all inspired to seek revenge. Do me a fucking favour and park your sanctimonious, everyone's-against-the-Muslims crap.'

Harry pulled the car back on to the road, his blood pumping.

None of this was about Isaac. It was Saima. He had no idea what was happening inside the Mehraj mosque. Harry hadn't called her, afraid it would derail his focus.

And Aaron. Was his boy OK in that house? He couldn't let himself think about it. It was too much to contemplate.

Abu-Nazir and Amelia. They were his best shot at ending this. Christ, he hoped the bitch was there with him.

The atmosphere in the car was thick.

He pulled the car over again and switched off the engine. Both of them sat in silence.

'I shouldn't have done that,' said Harry.

'It's fine,' Isaac whispered.

'We're about to enter the most dangerous estate in the north of England. This isn't the time for us to fall out.'

Isaac nodded.

Harry restarted the car and continued on their route, the atmosphere still strained.

He needed a plan. They could not just rock up at the tower.

He wished he could call in Ronnie's men. What Harry could have done with that kind of backup! But they'd never do anything without his brother's say-so. And he still couldn't get through to him.

They entered Dewsbury in silence, Saville Tower visible ahead. Harry drove past, circled around and stopped fifty yards from the entrance to the cul-de-sac.

One way in.

One way out.

'What now?' said Isaac.

Harry switched on the burner phone Tariq had given him and handed it to Isaac. 'Call Abu-Nazir. Ask him which flat he is in.'

The conversation was short. Isaac confirmed he was a mile away and Abu-Nazir simply said, 'Flat 420,' and hung up.

Only two words spoken – impossible to say whether it had been Abu-Nazir or not. Harry pulled out his own phone, the battery dying, and Googled Saville Tower and flat 420.

It was on the top floor, meaning it afforded a sweeping view of the area.

'Stay here,' said Harry, dismayed. He removed the keys from the ignition.

'Where are you going?' said Isaac.

'For a walk.'

Outside, the day's heat continued to radiate from the tarmac as Harry walked on the road past the entrance. Saville Tower loomed large.

Harry loitered on the far side of the pavement, casually looking over at the entrance, searching for ideas.

He had once been involved in an armed raid on Saville Tower after a body had been thrown from the top floor. The operation hadn't gone well – more lives had been lost and the IPCC investigation was still ongoing.

The raid had, however, thrown up something Harry had since forgotten.

S.S. Singh Convenience.

How did an Asian-owned corner shop exist in the most Far Right block in the north?

The lights were still on. The closing time on the fascia was listed as 00.00.

Bingo.

SIXTY-ONE

ONE HOUR TO GO before the other hundred and four mosques in Bradford emptied for a planned midnight vigil near the Mehraj mosque. The game of tactical chess was on a knife edge. Frost could not stop the approximately ten thousand worshippers from convening in Forster Square, and he didn't have the manpower or resources to control such a crowd. For now, it was in the hands of police and community-liaison teams, while here, on the second floor, Frost was in a secure room with a military escort outside. With him were Tariq Islam and Commander Allen, everyone focused on a laptop computer screen.

This was it: the special ops' attempt to use the sewer systems to gain access to the basement of the Mehraj mosque. The robot had not revealed anything suspicious about the access route. Neither had two police dogs. Frost wasn't overly reassured by the canines. Water in the tunnels was what reduced the operation's probability of success. But they were ready to give it a go.

Two teams of six men were deployed. One team would enter the basement, the other would remain on standby in the tunnels.

Frost watched the computer monitor showing the dark,

confusing footage of the special ops team navigating the murky sewage tunnels underneath the city. His eyes were focused on them but his mind was running wild. It was 23.10. In fifty minutes' time, Bradford would have the sort of march on its hands that could result in chaos. His officers were strategically placed to ensure a smooth passage and stop a growing Far Right element from intervening.

He hated what was happening, but conceded it was a smart move by the Islamic community. A worldwide audience would see them unified and peacefully supporting their fellow worshippers, trapped in the worst of all nightmares. However, if the Far Right got to them, the police would lose control.

Frost didn't have any of the four leaders of Almukhtaroon in safe custody.

Saima had not been in touch with any progress from the inside.

The monitor showed the special forces team making slow, measured progress. Frost was about to ask Allen how far out they were when a loud explosion on-screen almost made his heart stop.

The visual went blank.

Commander Allen, with a radio in his ear, stepped away asking for an urgent update.

Frost held his breath as Allen listened carefully before removing the device and turning to face him.

'The Patriots just blew the tunnel.'

SIXTY-TWO

HARRY, HEART IN MOUTH, watched Isaac enter the estate. If the kid was playing him and wanted to escape, this was his chance.

He was relieved when the boy entered the corner shop. Harry waited a couple of minutes then exited his car, heading towards the store.

The entrance to the estate had graffiti sprayed on the wall. *Christ was a white man.* It summed up the estate perfectly – too stupid to realize Christ had been Middle Eastern with a skin colour more closely aligned to Harry's.

He went to check the time, realized his watch was in the car and momentarily paused.

You've got a five-grand Rolex in your boot in the worst area in Yorkshire.

Too late for that now. He checked his phone instead: 23.03. Nothing from Saima or his mother.

Harry entered the corner shop and saw Isaac on the far side, looking at the sweets.

Sweets at the back? This place was all wrong, not least the bizarre midnight closing hour. Shelves of booze, right next to the exit. On this estate? It was an invitation to steal it. Coffee, deodorant – all the things people bought regularly were near the door, at eye level.

Harry had been raised in a corner shop; this shit was second nature.

What kind of amateur was running this place?

Mr Singh looked no older than Harry, sitting behind the counter, bright orange turban, neatly trimmed beard. No protective glass between him and the customers. Nothing to stop anyone jumping over the counter to rob him.

All wrong.

'Hey,' said Harry, taking a closer look around the store.

No CCTV cameras.

What the fuck?

Singh didn't take his attention off his mobile phone. In Harry's experience, the half-hour prior to business end was critical – prime-time for robberies. Singh didn't give a shit.

'What do you need?' asked Singh.

His voice was pure Yorkshire, just like Harry's.

'A word,' said Harry.

Isaac loitered near Harry, in the periphery of his view.

'A word? The fuck I look like to you? Citizens' advice? You're either buying or not. If not, piss off. It's late.'

As Harry got closer to the counter, prepared to push Singh a little harder, he saw why the shop didn't have CCTV and probably why he wasn't concerned with anyone attempting to shoplift.

Two powerful-looking Alsatian dogs were sitting on the floor beside him.

Harry smiled. Smart move. One dog to chase anyone who dared to steal, one always by Singh's side.

There were many threats Harry Virdee could negotiate. Big bastard dogs were not one of them.

'Either buy something or, like I said, piss off,' said Singh, focus still on his mobile phone.

'Can you close up?' said Harry.

That got Singh's attention. He glanced at Harry. Then at Isaac. Then at his dogs. The message was clear: Harry had no control here.

'I'm Detective Harry Virdee.'

'Then you definitely ain't welcome on this estate. What are you? Stupid?' Singh stood up. The dogs stood up with him. 'You ain't got backup because it's all in Bradford, sorting out that Paki shit-storm. Anyway, if you were a detective, you'd know cops don't come into this estate without armed backup.'

The dogs started to growl.

Harry put his hand in his pocket for his identification.

'Don't bother with ID,' said Singh. 'On this estate, you can get passports so realistic, you and I could piss off to Syria without any-one giving us a second look.'

Harry folded his arms across his chest.

The dogs growled a little more.

In his periphery, Harry saw Isaac back away.

'I'm going to count to three,' said Singh. The dogs stood tall, ears raised, mouths hanging open.

Alone with Singh, Harry would have bent him in half and dropkicked him out of the store.

'One,' said Singh.

But he couldn't find a way to argue with the dogs. He turned to see Isaac almost by the front door. Clearly the kid was afraid.

'Two.'

Harry let the pause linger. He didn't think Singh was bluffing. Not on this estate.

Just as Singh opened his mouth to say 'Three', Harry leaned a fraction closer, dropped his voice and said, 'Bet the Q5 moves on this estate. What are you shifting? A thousand £10-wraps a week?'

Singh stayed silent.

'I'd hate to put a call in to Enzo and tell him you've been unhelp-ful. That shit finds its way to the top of the food chain, and well' – Harry glanced towards Saville Tower – 'plenty of middle-men who could run this operation. Maybe even this store. Where would you be without a supplier?'

Enzo was Ronnie's number two and a name known to only very few people. He handled the streets while Ronnie handled the business: distribution, pricing and management of heroin.

Q5 was the latest code for the pure-heroin wraps Ronnie distributed.

Singh's eyes darted around the store, panicked now.

'You think I'm bluffing? You want me to call Enzo?' said Harry, removing his phone.

'You a cop?'

Harry nodded. 'You think this shit gets moved without someone on the inside knowing?'

Singh placed one hand on each of his dogs. Both of them stopped growling.

'What the fuck are you doing here?' said Singh, still not quite sure how to proceed.

'I need your help.'

'I don't help pigs, connected or otherwise.'

'I'll get you ten per cent off your next delivery.'

Singh sniggered. 'Like you have the power to make those decisions.'

'You want to try me? I can discount it or I can hike it. And if you really piss me off, I'll cut it completely. You've got sole distribution here and you want to chance all that for your fucking ego?'

Singh didn't reply.

'Close the fucking store, lock the dogs out back and let's do what needs to be done here.'

Singh nodded towards Isaac.

Harry beckoned him over and said, 'He's with me.'

SIXTY-THREE

THEY WERE ALONE IN the kitchens.

Just as Saima had been ready to strike, Maria had pulled a small, simple-looking electronic device from her pocket and waved it at her, ordering her to sit down.

The remote was just as Frost had said it would look. Hard to believe that little thing could detonate a bomb.

Saima had followed instructions.

Maria didn't amount to much: slight, and shorter than Saima. But if Harry had taught Saima anything, it was that underestimating people was one of the most foolish things you could do.

'How did you know my surname?' asked Saima, sitting on the floor, back against the wall. Maria was standing in front of her, out of reach.

'It doesn't matter, does it?'

Saima shrugged. It was obvious there was a leak somewhere in Frost's unit. 'So, what now?'

Maria stood a little taller. 'I'll tell you when you need to know. If you choose to play games, this will all end sooner than anyone wants.' She waved the remote at Saima.

'I don't believe killing a thousand innocent Muslims is going to help you and the Patriots make your point.' Saima knew her best bet was to keep talking and to keep listening. Imam Hashim would notice soon enough that she hadn't returned from the kitchens.

'Sacrifice, especially on a scale like this, will mean what we stand for cannot be ignored. Things will change.' Maria's eyes were cold.

'And what things are those?'

'Taking back control of our country.'

Saima tapped the back of her head against the wall, beating a steady rhythm to keep her brain focused. 'If we're all going to die, doesn't hurt to tell me a little bit about yourself, does it?'

'I don't think so.'

'So, what then? We just stay down here in silence?'

Saima stopped tapping her head against the wall and focused on Maria.

'In a little while, once I'm sure you understand what's at stake, we are going to go back upstairs to rejoin the crowds, and you and I are going to be close. Like sisters, arms linked, inseparable. If you go to the toilet, I'll be handing you paper to wipe. Got it?'

Of course she did. She nodded at the remote in Maria's hand. 'You're in control here.'

'I know. And if you force my hand, I will do what I was sent here for, without hesitation.' Maria pulled a mobile phone from her pocket and waved it at Saima. 'I text every thirty minutes, code words. If anything happens to me, they will know. So don't get any stupid ideas.'

'And if you do not get the leaders of Almukhtaroon?'

Maria raised her hand, pointing upstairs. 'Then a higher power will decide our fate.'

Saima forced a laugh. 'You are threatening to kill a thousand innocent people yet you believe in God?'

'The fight for the survival of every religion on the planet has involved far more bloodshed than this. Do not be so foolish as to kid yourself into thinking death does not play a part in creating a new world order.'

Saima got to her feet slowly. 'A new world order? Is that what you're about?'

'Yes.'

'And you achieve that by persecuting Islam?'

Maria shook her head and smiled. 'You are so naive. This has nothing to do with religion. Today is simply the biggest calling card we could have created.'

Saima shoved her hands in her pockets. 'Since you seem to know everything about me, you'll know that I need to call my husband and check in.'

'Nice try.' Maria stooped, removed Saima's phone from her pocket, dropped it on the floor and stamped on it, hard enough that it shattered.

Saima let out a wounded cry.

Aaron.

Harry.

'Since we are sisters now, Saima Virdee, the only person you need to talk to is me.'

SIXTY-FOUR

HARRY AND SINGH WENT out to the storeroom, full of newspapers and stock, leaving Isaac alone in the shop. Harry was painfully aware midnight wasn't far away, leaving just over six hours to bring this thing home. He felt the pressure starting to weigh on his mind.

'I deal with Enzo,' said Singh. 'Don't know shit about you. What do you want anyway?'

'Access to the tower.'

'What the fuck for?'

'Need to lift someone.'

'Who?'

'None of your business.'

Singh moved an outer of detergent off a wooden stool and sat down, one dog sitting obediently next to him. The other had stayed in the shop with Isaac.

'You know how hard it is to live on this estate as a brown man? I've earned my place. Got the locals' trust, built a business—'

'—based on drugs.'

'Fine. But I still created this place the hard way.'

'Bullshit,' said Harry, more forcefully than he intended. The Alsatian growled. Harry softened his tone. 'No one here's buying newspapers from you. Your booze display is mostly cheap cider. Fag sales are way down. The drugs are your lifeline. And I can take it away.'

'Get Enzo on the phone,' said Singh, his tone sharp. The dog growled a little louder, stood up.

'He's busy.'

'Then you best return when he's not.'

Harry was getting annoyed. 'If I walk out of your shop without the help I need, I promise you – I give you my fucking kasam, your business is over.'

'What do you need to know?' said Singh reluctantly.

'Not everyone can know you're a dealer or some fucker would have snitched on you by now. So how do you exist here?'

'Done time. Ain't a Paki. The tower knows the difference between me and them.'

'You mean Muslims?'

Singh smiled.

Harry didn't bite.

'If I walk out there, to the tower, how long will I last before they come for me?' said Harry.

Singh shook his head slowly. 'Which flat?'

'Four twenty.'

'Top floor. That's a lot of eyes to pass.'

'Can it be done?' said Harry impatiently.

Singh nodded. He was studying Harry closely.

'When I do a drop-off, I wear my yellow turban. It's bright enough anyone can see it. And I take one of the dogs with me. They all give me space, no fucker messes about. If I go for a walk with a blue turban, people scatter, hide or flush their drugs – means we've got cops on the estate.'

'Genius,' said Harry, genuinely impressed.

'I'll give you the yellow turban. Take one of the dogs. That will

give you your shot. Thing is, if it gets ugly, dog's not going to protect you. Just as likely to take you down. Their loyalty is to me.'

'Come with me then,' said Harry.

Singh shook his head. 'Two of us is unusual. They'd smell a rat.'

Harry sighed heavily and nodded towards Isaac. 'That mean I
can't take the kid with me?'

'You can take him. Young white kid with me wouldn't be a red
flag.' Harry was thankful Isaac was fair enough to pass for white.

Harry glanced at the dog. 'He going to come without ripping me
to pieces?'

'If I hand him over to you. Make it clear you're friendly.'

'Can I take him inside the tower?'

Singh shook his head. 'He won't go inside with you but he will
get you there. When you've reached the tower, take his lead off and
push him back in the direction of the store and say my name forcefully. He'll come home. You're on your own when you come out.'

'They'll think I'm you, though, right?'

'I never walk around here without my dogs. They might notice.
They ain't academic these lot but they're street smart and razor
sharp with it.'

Harry covered his face with both hands and rubbed it wildly,
mind throbbing, feeling tired and irritable.

'If I can make your life easier, what's it worth?' said Singh.

Harry lowered his hands. 'Easier?'

'You can get to the top floor without even entering the tower.'

'How?'

'Fire escape.'

Harry stared at him, waiting for the catch.

'There's a security code for the bottom gate that gives you
access.'

Singh stopped talking.

'How much?' said Harry.

'Five grand.'

Harry laughed. 'You best try again.'

Singh stood up suddenly and pushed Harry hard enough that he hit the shelving behind him with some force. Tins of food fell to the floor and the dog barked noisily, the other running through from the shop.

Harry saw Isaac peering around the counter, alarmed. He looked apt to do a runner.

Fear invaded Harry's body. The dogs were ready to tear him to pieces.

Singh yelled for them to stand down.

'You want to rock up in here, throw Enzo's name around to get an audience with me, then ask for my help – shit that puts everything I've built here at risk. And when I want payment, you try to tell me I'm taking the piss?' Singh jabbed a finger hard into Harry's chest. 'Don't take the fucking mick with me, Harry Virdee. Either cough up five grand cash in used notes or' – he pointed towards his front door – 'get the fuck out.'

Harry was annoyed at himself. He should have seen this coming.

He could get five grand from Ronnie once this was over. He held up his hands, apologetically. 'You're right—'

'Price just went up to ten.'

Harry wanted to react, mood souring. Singh was taking the piss but Harry would give this man everything he had to get Saima home safely from the Mehraj mosque.

'Fine,' he said, coolly.

'I don't do credit.'

'You think I carry ten grand around with me?'

'I don't give a fuck if you do or don't.'

The dogs growled again at Singh's raised voice.

'Look, I give you my word—'

'Your word isn't worth ten grand to me.'

If the dogs hadn't been there, Harry would have been making a very different type of deal with Singh.

'I can give you a five-grand deposit now,' said Harry. 'My watch. In the car. Rolex. Brand new.'

Singh looked unsure.

'It's legit. You can Google its value.'

Singh nodded. 'Thing is, Harry, I know something about watches, so it better not be some Kirkgate-market rip-off or our deal is off and you can forget about Saville Tower.'

SIXTY-FIVE

KESH – UNCUT HAIR.

   Kara – steel bracelet.

   Kanga – the comb.

   Kaccha – cotton underwear.

   Kirpan – steel sword.

Ranjit Virdee had observed the five Ks of Sikhism. He had lived as good a life as he thought possible.

He had drunk alcohol, smoked cigarettes and allowed his faith to lapse when he had first arrived in England, desperate to make a new home for his family. The memories of partition had never allowed him to forget his bitterness towards the Muslims who had hurt him. There wasn't a single day when he didn't think about his baby brother, Charanjit. That last kiss on his cheek, feeling his skin wet with Ranjit's own tears before walking away. Was it his mother screaming or had it been him?

He couldn't remember.

Ranjit stared at the items on the dining table, blinking away tears.

Upstairs in Ranjit's home slept a little boy with the same innocence as Charanjit. The same birthmark.

The same ability to warm the coldest souls.

He raised his hands and covered his face, letting the tears come, body shaking.

What kind of a man could not embrace a four-year-old child?

What kind of monster had he become?

He was tired, so very, very tired. Ranjit didn't want to live this way any more. Was he a good Sikh or simply a bitter, twisted old man who had given priority to his 'standing' within the community rather than his role as a father?

Hatred was wrong in Sikhism. The scriptures said it, explicitly. And yet . . .

He didn't deserve life.

He didn't want it any more.

For over seven decades he had hidden the memory of Charanjit lying still and beautiful by the side of the road so deep in his soul that at times he had hoped it was nothing more than a vivid dream. He could no longer pretend.

Ranjit ran his hands through his hair, the oil Joyti had massaged into his scalp soothing. He lifted his sword from the table, his sacred kirpan, turned the blade towards his chest, then used both hands to steady it.

He didn't want this life any more. Didn't deserve it.

Whatever he was, man or monster, he was already dead inside. This was simply progression of that.

Hardeep may have betrayed him but Ranjit had inflicted that hurt on Joyti. She was a good woman, undeserving of the type of man he had become. Without him, she could live freely.

She loved their grandson, their daughter-in-law. Ranjit thought back to when he had met Saima, when she had cared for him in hospital. She had asked him for forgiveness for marrying his son. She had stretched out her hands, wanting to touch his feet and say she was sorry.

He pushed the tip of the sword against the skin of his naked chest, the steel cold.

'If you touch my feet, with your hands, I will be forced to cut them off . . .'

How could he have said such a thing when she had saved his life?

He bowed his head, closed his eyes.

Monster.

She would never forgive him. He could not ask her to.

With hands shaking, Ranjit knew this was a sin but he had already committed so many.

Tomorrow, he would not awaken.

Finally, he would be at peace.

The sound of Joyti's voice stopped him. He felt her body brushing against his shoulder as she came to his side.

'Walk away, Joyti,' he said quietly. 'You do not need to see this.'

'Open your eyes,' she replied, the touch of her hand on his head.

'I have seen all I ever want to see in this lifetime.'

'Open them, Ranjit. Now.'

Her tone stopped him. He turned to look at her.

Ranjit dropped the blade.

SIXTY-SIX

CRUNCH TIME.

Harry still couldn't be sure that Isaac was trustworthy. He might have gone along with him because he genuinely wanted to help capture Abu-Nazir and Amelia, or he might have had something else in mind altogether. At this point, Harry didn't have much choice but to trust him. He was only one step away from having the leverage Tariq Islam needed.

What happened once he delivered all four leaders of the Almukhtaroon to Tariq?

Harry didn't know.

Handing over his Rolex to Singh had not been easy. He'd made it abundantly clear to Singh that he intended to come back for it.

Singh secured his yellow turban to Harry's head. It didn't feel natural. He may have been born into a traditional Sikh family but wearing the turban felt alien.

Harry glanced at his reflection in a small, dirty mirror in the storeroom. His breath caught in his throat.

He'd always thought he looked like his mother, yet now, with the turban, he was struck by how much he looked like his father.

'Here,' said Singh, handing Harry a yellow high-visibility jacket. 'Part of the programme.'

Harry slipped it on.

'This better be how it's done,' he said, aware how easy it would be for Singh to set him up. They'd be dead men.

'It is,' said Singh flatly.

'Spotters?'

'Few and far between at this time.'

Singh grabbed Harry's hand and placed it on the dog, telling the dog firmly that Harry was going to take him for a walk. He spoke to the dog as if he were a child on a naughty step.

He clipped a lead on Oscar and handed it to Harry.

'Oscar needs to know you are in charge. There is a hierarchy with dogs. You've heard of the expression top dog?'

Harry nodded.

'Dogs are subservient only if they know who is top dog. That needs to be you. No need to fuck around and yell at him. You speak firmly, if needed, but he shouldn't need obvious command. As long as he feels you are in control and not afraid, you'll have no issue. Got it?'

Harry nodded.

'Don't nod like a frightened schoolgirl.'

'I got it,' said Harry firmly. He pulled a little on the lead, feeling the weight and power of the dog.

'It's five hundred yards to the tower. They'll be watching. You might hear some whistling. Four short, sharp blasts. If that happens, raise your left hand high, then lower it. Keep your fucking head down. Got it?'

'Yes,' said Harry, trying his best not to show his nerves at having Oscar on a lead. He wasn't a dog-lover. Didn't mind them but didn't trust them not to take a chunk out of his body. He'd been there several times on the job.

'When you reach the tower, take the lead off Oscar, command him to go home and make your way to the fire escape. The code is 0666, sign of the devil.'

Singh smiled. It wasn't a warm expression.

Harry didn't find it funny.

They moved into the shop, the dog pulling, its weight considerable. Harry tightened his grip on the lead. Isaac jumped out of the way, clearly also not a dog-lover.

'One thing,' said Singh, putting a firm hand on Harry's shoulder.

'What?' said Harry, turning to look at him.

'Shit goes bad in there? Don't come back here for help. Doors are locked until morning. Got it?'

Harry walked away. 'Come on, Isaac. We're done here.'

Five hundred yards to Saville Tower.

The night was still warm, meaning the youngsters from the estate were likely to be out wandering the streets.

They walked with intent, the dog on Harry's right, Isaac on his left. Oscar seemed to know exactly where he was going, head high, pace brisk.

Harry had taken his crowbar from the car and stuffed it down the front of his trousers, the lip sticking out of his waistband but easily concealed by the high-vis jacket.

The houses they passed were in a sorry state. The rendered walls were decaying, slates missing from roofs, gardens unkempt and full of rubbish. As consistent was the area's fierce allegiance to the flag of St George. There were also National Front banners: a fascist group from the eighties.

Harry spotted a used syringe lying in the gutter.

Nice place.

'Kids up ahead,' whispered Isaac.

'Head down. We walk straight past them.'

'They'll see you're not the corner-shop keeper,' said Isaac urgently.

'You give them too much credit. Singh and I are two brown men with turbans and stubble. We all look the same.'

They approached the group of teenagers, cigarettes in mouths, bottles of cider in hands, the smell of marijuana in the air.

Harry and Isaac passed them without incident. He wasn't sure if it was the presence of the dog or if Singh strolling towards the tower was just a routine occurrence. Harry imagined it was a little of both.

He relaxed as they approached the building. It loomed in front of them.

As Singh had promised, Harry heard the whistle. Four sharp blasts. He raised his left hand high then lowered it.

'You OK?' he asked Isaac. The boy nodded, clearly uneasy. Harry stooped and unfastened Oscar's lead, commanding him firmly, 'Home.'

The dog immediately ran away leaving Harry and Isaac to hurry towards the metal staircase.

Harry punched in the code. 0666.

This better work.

He hit the green button and the metal gate clicked open.

'Come on,' said Harry, pulling Isaac in behind him.

They closed the gate and climbed the stairs, the sound of their feet echoing on the steel treads.

When they reached the first floor, Harry stopped, turned to Isaac and raised his finger to his lips. He slowed his ascent, gentler footsteps, taking them two at a time.

They were more than halfway up before they hit their first obstacle.

A young lad, maybe eighteen, pissed up and smelling strongly of marijuana, was sitting in their way, cider in hand, spliff burning on the step by his side.

'Yo, Big Singhy. Late-night fix? Someone must need that shit baaaaaaad,' he said, smiling at Harry, completely unaware he wasn't Singh.

We all look the same.

'Something like that,' said Harry, pushing past the boy, who let them pass.

They arrived quickly and without incident at the top of the tower block. Harry could hardly believe his luck.

No incidents. No drama.

The gate at the top wasn't locked. Harry nodded for Isaac to follow him and together they crept along the walkway. Harry glanced down at the estate. No one had come after them.

The door to flat 420 was unlocked.

A lapse or a trap?

They knew Isaac was coming.

Abu-Nazir was the most hunted man on the planet right now. He wasn't leaving his door unlocked. Harry tried to calm the panic rising in his chest.

'You go in first,' he said to Isaac.

The boy looked afraid and didn't move.

'They're expecting you.' Harry pulled him close. 'I'm right behind you.'

He nudged Isaac towards the door, pulling his crowbar from his jeans.

Harry followed him in, keeping close.

Two doors either side of him, both open.

Bedrooms. Empty, unlived in. Harry didn't like this. Didn't feel right.

He heard a television playing in the living room. Sky News. They were reporting, live from Bradford. And voices.

Harry grabbed Isaac and stopped him entering.

He pointed back the way they had come but Isaac didn't listen. Before Harry could stop him, he opened the living-room door and disappeared inside.

'Shit,' cursed Harry and went after him.

Two men were sitting on a couple of shitty couches. Not a care in the world.

'Isaac.' A sickly-white man stood. Ginger hair, blond beard.

Abu-Nazir.

He was dressed in Western clothing, which made sense. No way he got inside Saville Tower dressed in traditional Islamic robes.

The other man got to his feet. In his hand was a stun gun.

The weapon was not the most alarming thing.

Tyler Sudworth. Founder of the Far Right group the Pure English Society. In a room with Abu-Nazir? What the fuck was going on? Where was Amelia Rose?

'Come.' Abu-Nazir held out his arms to Isaac.

Isaac stepped into the embrace.

Sudworth slapped Isaac on the back and raised the stun gun at Harry.

Harry's eyes went wide but his feet wouldn't move. He couldn't believe what he was seeing.

'No,' said Isaac firmly and lowered Sudworth's arm.

Harry breathed a sigh of relief.

Isaac took the weapon from Sudworth.

The boy turned to face him and simply said, 'Harry Virdee, I'd like you to meet my father, Abu-Nazir.'

If Harry's jaw could have hit the floor it would have.

How the hell had he not seen it?

And Tyler Sudworth?

'You lose, Harry,' said Isaac, shooting 50,000 volts into the detective's body.

SIXTY-SEVEN

JOYTI VIRDEE HAD AARON in her arms, asleep.

Ranjit couldn't help but stare at the birthmark on Aaron's shoulder. Everything about the boy reminded him of Charanjit.

Joyti moved quickly, not allowing him to speak, lowering the sleeping boy into Ranjit's lap, who was forced to cradle him, protectively.

Ranjit had started to recoil but as soon as Aaron's warm body touched his skin, everything changed. He held his breath, afraid Aaron would wake up and start crying. He did no such thing.

Ranjit kissed the boy's forehead, then his cheek, before turning his face to stop his tears from hitting the boy.

Joyti wrapped her arms around his body, her lips on his face, whispering in his ear, 'Let it go, Ranjit. Let it go.'

He gritted his teeth, confused.

Ranjit Singh Virdee felt – alive.

Aaron was the very reincarnation of Charanjit.

Ranjit kissed his forehead again. He didn't want to let Aaron go.

Joyti sat beside him, took his face in her hands. 'Let it go,' she said again, crying silently.

'How do I do that?'

Joyti pointed to the five items on the table, touched the sword and said, 'Embrace your faith.'

'My faith got me here.'

'Foolish man,' she said bitterly.

He shook his head in disagreement.

'Who laid the very first stone of our holiest site, the Golden Temple? Do you even remember?' said Joyti.

Ranjit thought about his answer. 'It was a Muslim saint, Sai Mian Mir.' The story came back to Ranjit, whose eyes widened in realization.

'Our holy book, the Guru Granth Sahib, contains the work of two Muslim saints, Sheikh Fareedji and Bhagat Kabir Ji. Partition does not change these indisputable facts, yet for so long you have focused all your pain on what happened with your family, and the wider implications of partition. Was it any easier for the Muslims making their way into the newly formed Pakistan? How many of their women laid their children to rest by the side of the road?'

This was a conversation Joyti had wanted to have with her husband for many years. Once Harry had married Saima, she had gone back to the roots of their faith. Historically, Sikhism and Islam were more closely linked than most people realized.

'Do you remember who our very first guru, Guru Nanak's best friend was? Who accompanied him on his travels across the world?'

Ranjit shook his head but Joyti saw in his face that he knew the answer.

'Bhai Mardana Ji – a Muslim.'

Ranjit's face started to crack and she saw him desperately trying not to break down. Her play was bold, the truth hurtful, the history unquestionable.

Truth was something Ranjit had been cowering from for years.

Everything Joyti said was true but the world had changed. It was true that Sikhism's and Islam's origins were not steeped in hatred but had been polluted by, first, the partition of India and, second, the current hysteria surrounding Islam. When Ranjit had arrived in this country, he had Muslim friends. They had worked together, eaten together and gone out together. The war in Kashmir, a disputed territory between Pakistan and India, had strained their relationships but they had all allowed themselves to become that way.

'I'm lost, Joyti. I don't know who I am any more.'

'You are the man I married.'

'I don't know who he is.'

'I do. A strong man who sacrificed for his family. Worked hard. Loyal. Disciplined. And now . . . lost.'

'I want to go to sleep and never awaken.'

'Look at the boy in your arms.'

'I cannot take my eyes off him. I want to wake him up. I want him to hug me, call me Grandad and put his hands on my face.'

'You can have all of those things.'

He was crying again, wiping his eyes frequently.

'She will not forgive me.'

'Say her name, Ranjit.'

'I cannot.'

'Why?'

'I just cannot,' he said, starting to lose it.

Joyti took her grandson from him, allowing Ranjit to place his head in his hands. He cried hard and painfully.

'I gave her nothing but hate. And I did hate her, Joyti, I . . . do.'

'No. You hate yourself.'

He didn't reply.

'The community shame. Honour. What people would have said. All of that created the hate. Not Saima. Tell me I am wrong.'

Still crying, he relented. 'You are right.'

'Is it better to take your own life than finally show just how strong a man you can be? It will take everything you have to create a new chapter in our lives, with this little boy at its centre. That is what our faith will give you.'

He wiped his face, eyes red, spirit broken. 'I don't know how.'

Joyti pointed to the knife on the table. 'If having a Muslim friend was good enough for the Guru, if a Muslim laid the first stone that made our holiest site, why can a Muslim not save your life, tonight?'

He stared at her.

'That's right,' she said, kissing the side of Aaron's face. 'Our grandchild is half Muslim, half Sikh, but he is all ours. You can look on him as a true message, one steeped in history and legend. A boy to close a gap so large nobody thought it could be done. Why does he have the same birthmark as your brother had? Why does his face reduce your hate to nothing more than a memory?'

She saw the realization in his face.

He shook his head. 'I don't know what to do.'

'Do you trust me?'

'Always.'

'Come with me.'

'Where?'

'Just come.'

She walked away and Ranjit followed her.

Upstairs Joyti laid Aaron on her bed and lay down next to him, leaving a large enough gap for Ranjit.

'You have to choose. If you lie on this bed, you leave the hate and the past standing where it is. If you turn around and leave, then tomorrow morning, even if I do not find your body slumped at that table, you will forever be dead to me because right here, right now, a choice must be made.'

Joyti stroked Aaron's face, then looked at Ranjit.

'Choose,' she said.

SIXTY-EIGHT

THE EXPLOSION IN THE sewage tunnel had put a stop to special forces' plans to enter the mosque. No one had been injured. The tunnel had collapsed a few hundred yards in front of them. It had been a measured device, just enough force to block the route but not enough to have attracted attention or caused damage above ground. It had proved one thing. The Patriots were way ahead in this game. They'd clearly had a long time to plan this and knew every move the security services would be making.

Frost was back in the command room, getting updates on the ten-thousand-strong Muslim crowd heading for Forster Square retail park. As they'd promised, the mosques had begun to empty, everyone heading for one enormous stand of solidarity in Bradford with the world's media watching. Frost had no choice but to allow the peaceful demonstration to take place.

Limited CCTV had now been restored so he had real-time feeds coming in, showing a slow procession of Islamic worshippers holding candles, happy to take up position in the retail park the police had cleared for them.

Community leaders had tried to dissuade them from marching but to no avail.

Frost wondered how hard they'd really tried. He had spoken at length with several imams, advising them that this demonstration would use police resources desperately needed elsewhere, but they knew they had extra men in from all over Yorkshire. No, this was going to happen.

He'd left Counter-Terrorism ACC Peter Weetwood and Commander Allen speaking with COBRA downstairs. They had one final tactical option left to them.

A full-out assault on the mosque.

If the clock ran down too far and the powers-that-be made the call, they would storm the building. It was risky. There were many unknowns to factor in, not least the as yet unidentified sleeper cell inside the mosque. The easiest thing was to open the doors and allow the worshippers to run. That seldom went well. With only six hours remaining and none of the leaders of Almukhtaroon in custody, Frost and other senior members of this operation, Tariq Islam included, were forced to plan for an interception that might only have a 50/50 chance at success.

Frost was hoping for one thing.

That Saima Virdee came through for him.

SIXTY-NINE

HARRY CAME TO, HANDS cuffed behind him, feet tied and what felt like masking tape across his mouth. The skin on his chest burned where Isaac had Tasered him and his brain was foggy. The throb in his hand from where the nurse had bitten him was no longer the most painful injury he had.

The living room was empty, just a small lamp in the corner throwing shadows across the floor.

A clock on the wall said 01.00.

He'd been out cold for half an hour.

Isaac had double-crossed him. He must have been planning this all along.

And Abu-Nazir was his father?

Harry had been completely blind-sided. Or had his mind been so preoccupied by Saima, Aaron and the scale of everything unravelling in Bradford that he had simply missed all the signs?

Where the fuck were they all now? If they'd left, this was over. The thought spurred him to life and he tried to move, only to find his hands cuffed to the radiator.

What about Amelia Rose – where was she?

The fog lifted from Harry's head. And what the hell had Far Right activist Tyler Sudworth been doing here with Islamic extremists? He tried to focus.

The room was bland. Two shitty grey couches, a withered armchair and a small dining table with only two chairs. The TV was an old box unit, cased in a wooden frame. No pictures on the walls. Nothing personal.

This wasn't a home, this was a meeting point.

For what, an extremist reunion? In fucking Saville Tower?

Harry dropped his chin on to his chest, waiting for an idea.

At home, he often sat on the floor, as he was now, talking to his son at eye-level. Usually it was Aaron telling Harry off for not playing right.

Harry closed his eyes, but he couldn't think of his son. It was too hard.

Of course, his brain went straight to his wife. Saima was resilient, not the type to be cowering in the corner crying or praying for salvation. He smiled. It was one of the reasons he'd married her. She possessed a fierce type of determination – never the victim, always the fighter. God, he hoped she was all right.

The handcuffs seemed to have been threaded behind a metal pipe creeping out of the floor, connecting the radiator. There was about a foot of space, giving him a little slack. Harry wrapped his hands around the pipe and pulled at it.

Solid.

He leaned forward, using his weight.

No give at all.

He opened his eyes and looked for what was in reach but there was nothing. Just a loose socket. Electricity. He wasn't fucking around with that.

He hated the sensation of helplessness, blood pressure rising, sweat breaking across his body. Panic wasn't his thing. Harry moved his hands away from the pipe, to the radiator itself, just enough slack to get his hands behind it.

He leaned forwards and pulled.

Movement.

Harry tasted the bitter, acidic glue from the masking tape, grimaced and pulled harder. He gritted his teeth, adjusted his body and pulled again, leaning into the radiator, groaning. The handcuffs dug painfully into his skin, metal cutting sharply. Harry applied as much force as he could for as long as he could, feeling the radiator give a little before he ran out of steam.

Panting, he leaned back against the wall, light-headed. Then he adjusted his position, scrambling on to his knees and moving his feet behind him so they were touching the wall.

He pulled at the side of the radiator with everything he had, feet pushing off the wall. The cuffs screamed at his skin. His thoughts were of home: Aaron and Saima – their faces, their smiles, the feeling of Saima lying next to him.

A burst of energy, like an electrical current, charged through his muscles and Harry screamed into the masking tape. His body collapsed forwards. He turned and saw the radiator had come off its brackets. But there was a robust metal bolt pinning the radiator to the pipe. There was no way the cuffs were going to slide away past it. All he had done was create a mess.

His thoughts were disturbed by the sound of the front door closing.

Abu-Nazir entered the room. 'Having fun, I see.' He squatted in front of Harry and tore the tape from Harry's mouth.

Harry spat at him. Abu-Nazir simply wiped it from his face before slapping Harry, much like his father might have done. 'That was rude,' he said. Abu-Nazir retreated two paces.

'They'll be coming for me,' said Harry. 'The world and his dog.'

Abu-Nazir laughed. 'Such hollow threats. Isaac told me everything. You don't know if you're a cop or a renegade. I'll tell you what you are: you're a sacrifice to try and save Bradford.'

He brought a chair over to Harry, placed it in front of him and sat down, this time remaining out of spitting distance.

'You came here to take me in so that, if it came down to it, you could take my life to save all the people in that mosque – including your wife, I hear.'

Harry stared at him, surprised.

'The British government does not negotiate with terrorists but then they also cannot allow a thousand people to die while the four of us go free.' Nazir laughed. 'Got to love the laws in this country. If I walked into a police station right now, I'd be the safest person in the world. Make sure enough people see me, put it out there on social media and just . . . wait. What's your gut saying? I'd be safe or traded in?'

Harry didn't answer. The government wouldn't condemn four men to death, not even if it meant saving a thousand. Tariq Islam had been right – even Abu-Nazir knew it.

'I reckon an angry ethnic mob would tear the police station apart until they got us. That might be interesting.'

'What about Tyler Sudworth?' said Harry.

Nazir's face changed, not angry, just different. 'It was unfortunate you had to see that.'

'Not like you were hiding him. You knew we were coming.'

'I knew Isaac was.'

'Isaac knows about Tyler?'

'Of course. He's my son – he knows everything.'

Harry was confused. It must have been clear on his face.

'You still don't get it, do you, Harry?'

'Why don't you explain it to me?' Harry felt anger rising inside his chest. He pulled on the handcuffs again but in vain. 'How does the most hated religious preacher in the north get a flat in Saville Tower?'

Abu-Nazir sniggered. 'People are such fools.'

Something sparked inside of Harry, a thought so ludicrous he dismissed it before it gained traction.

'Have you read the Bible?' said Abu-Nazir.

'What?'

243

'Let's see how clever you really are, Detective Virdee. Tenacious, no doubt, but smart? I'm not so sure. So, to my question: have you read it?'

'No.'

'Heard of the devil?'

'Of course.'

'Could he exist if God didn't?'

Of all the conversations Harry had envisaged, this had not been one of them.

'Simple enough question, Harry. Is the existence of the devil based on the assumption of a God?'

'What?'

Abu-Nazir sniggered. 'You really are just as thick as everyone else.'

Harry glared at Abu-Nazir, confused.

'Yin and Yang. Good and bad. Two sides of the same coin or opposing forces? I guess it depends on where you stand.'

Harry frowned.

'The Far Right have a clear mandate in this country, one which exists because of Islamic fundamentalism. Without them, we would have little purpose. Little way of ensuring our message held meaning.'

Couldn't be. 'Get the fuck out,' said Harry. 'You're bluffing.'

'People so easily believe that a man with a beard and a basic grasp of Arabic who rants and raves about infidels and martyrdom could be a fundamentalist. The fact I'm white makes people take notice and want to follow me, but more importantly it keeps the Far Right strong because one of their own has crossed over to the dark side. Quite above all that, it brings in more money than you could ever imagine.'

Harry swallowed hard. 'You're telling me, that you, Abu-Nazir, leader of the Almukhtaroon Islamic fundamentalist group, are in fact a member of the Far Right?'

'Is it so hard to believe?'

'You had a child with an Asian woman.'

'The bitch was hot and I was young and stupid. When I found out she was knocked up I tried to make it work. But her family? Shit, those people are from the dark ages. Opened my eyes. Put me on the right path.'

'You are some piece of work, aren't you? And the boy? Your son?'

Abu-Nazir smiled. 'Blood is thicker than water.'

SEVENTY

THE LIGHTS IN THE grand hall had been turned off, leaving only dim lamps around the perimeter. Most people were lying down but many were still awake, sitting in small huddles, talking.

Hardly any mobile phone screens lit the darkness. Saima assumed most people's batteries were dead.

Maria was close by her side. They'd been escorted from the kitchen by two committee members sweeping the building. They hadn't noticed anything unusual.

As they passed the worshippers looking for a small, private area to rest, Saima heard the whispers from a group of men crowded around a mobile phone. The remaining hundred and four mosques in Bradford had emptied at midnight, their congregations heading for Forster Square, a few hundred metres from the Mehraj mosque. It would be one of the largest peaceful protests ever organized by the Muslim community in England, as many as ten thousand. As Hashim himself had told Saima in his office, this was an opportunity on a global scale to show how united the Muslim community within Bradford were, and furthermore the images of thousands of Muslims in candlelit silence would be a far more powerful image to relay across the world than a mosque surrounded by military. That needed to be the defining image of this siege – not fear and isolation but hope.

Saima followed Maria to a small empty space on the floor adjacent to the female washrooms.

'You should try and get some sleep,' said Maria.

'You're kidding, aren't you?'

'Hardly. You look exhausted.'

'Keeping secrets is exhausting.'

Maria ignored the jibe and sat down, her back against the wall. Saima took a place next to her.

'Don't you have a soul? Don't you fear God?' Saima whispered, staring into the crowd.

'I'm not here to have a theological debate with you. Either go to sleep or sit in silence.'

'Or what? You'll detonate the device?'

Maria didn't reply.

Saima pointed to a nearby group of four elderly women. 'I see them in Bradford Royal every week – the cancer department. They are not suffering, they come to give comfort to those who are. Make them tea, talk to them while they undergo chemotherapy.'

Again, nothing from Maria.

'And those,' said Saima, pointing to another group. 'They teach young women in Bradford how to sew and mend garments.'

Maria remained quiet and perfectly still, as if she were in a trance, eyes open, breathing calm. Saima thought she looked like someone about to enter a state of deep meditation.

'There are so many good people in this room. They don't deserve what you are threatening to do to them.'

They sat in silence for a while until Imam Hashim made his way over to them. Maria grasped Saima's arm, squeezing it tightly.

'Saima, I wonder if you might do me a favour?' he said, kneeling by her side.

'Of course,' she said, trying to shift her position but unable to because of Maria's grip.

'A lady needs an insulin shot. She missed her dose earlier. Could you help? She's a little confused.'

Maria tightened her hold on her arm.

'Of course,' said Saima. She looked at Maria and smiled. 'It would be weird if a nurse didn't help someone in need.'

She delivered the statement with enough bite that Maria relaxed her grip. 'I'll come with you, Saima. I can't get comfortable here.'

Saima stood up, thinking fast.

How could she tell Hashim about Maria?

The two women followed him to his office. Maria had hold of Saima's arm again. Leaning closer as they approached the door, she hissed, 'Be smart.'

Inside the office, an elderly woman was sitting on a couch, holding an insulin pen. Saima spoke to her in Urdu.

Was this her chance?

Surely Maria wouldn't understand the language?

She glanced at Maria. She had the greatest poker-face Saima had ever seen.

Saima took the insulin pen from the woman and asked what dose she took. The old dear said she didn't know, her son always took care of it for her.

The pen contained a long-acting insulin. Saima dialled it down to a low dose and administered it. She could always give her more if needed. She sat beside her and told Maria she had to wait a few minutes to ensure the woman was all right, something she'd made up to buy time.

'I hear the gathering of the other mosques is under way,' said Saima to Hashim.

He nodded. 'Roughly ten thousand worshippers holding candles in Forster Square. Faith will see us through this dark night.'

Saima nodded, racking her brains for an idea.

'Will you get some sleep?' she asked him, with emphasis on the word 'sleep'. It was clumsy but all she could think of.

Maria made her way towards Saima.

'This looks pretty comfortable,' she said, tapping the back of the couch. 'Why don't you sleep here for a while? You must be exhausted,' she said pleasantly to Hashim.

He shook his head. 'I'm responsible here. I fear when the clock enters the final two hours, things may well become unstable.'

The elderly woman beside Saima thanked her, kissed her cheek like her mother would have done and stood up to leave. Hashim escorted her to the door, keeping it open for the other women to follow. As they left, Hashim turned to Saima and said, 'Do we need to talk about anything?'

Maria arrived by Saima's side, within earshot of a reply. Saima sighed and said, 'No. Nothing to discuss.'

She went to leave the room, paused and had a last shot at trying to relay Maria was the sleeper by turning to Hashim and speaking in Urdu. 'Do you think the white people of this city will be with us tonight or against us?'

It was the most measured thing she could think of in the circumstances.

Maria, though, beat Hashim to a response, taking Saima gently by the arm and replying in perfect Urdu, 'This white woman is with you and that, my friend, is all that counts.'

SEVENTY-ONE

AFTER EVERYTHING THAT HAD happened, it all came down to money.

Harry thought of the documentary he had watched of Tyler Sudworth and Abu-Nazir. They'd seemed friendly, joking about their positions – one the saviour of the Islamic world, the other of the Western world.

Like yin and yang, they were opposites. One could not exist without the other. Abu-Nazir had jump-started Tyler Sudworth's political career. And without Tyler, Abu-Nazir would not have half the media focus.

The bastards had played the system perfectly and become wealthy in the process. Membership fees for Almukhtaroon, 'donations' from sympathizers around the world. As for Tyler, he was paid huge fees for public-speaking engagements highlighting the dangers of, among others, Almukhtaroon.

Saville Tower was a place Tyler was known to frequent, home to a lawless brotherhood who would never speak to the police or media. Tyler Sudworth's very own kingdom.

'This is Tyler's place, isn't it?' said Harry.

Abu-Nazir smiled.

'When things get hot, this is your safe haven. The last place anyone would look.'

'The thing about a brilliant illusion, Harry, is that you never see it coming or figure out how it happened.'

'I don't buy it.'

'We don't need you to. Your belief doesn't pay the bills.'

'Is that what this is about?'

'That's what everything is about.'

'Bullshit.'

Abu-Nazir snapped his gaze up at Harry. 'Are you really this naive?' His tone was disdainful. 'Money makes the world go around. Religion's a close second. Wars line the coffers of governments and, on the streets, identity politics pay our wages. Tyler fights for the white people of this country, and me' – he paused – 'I fight for the persecuted.'

'You don't talk for the majority. Neither of you do.'

'We don't need to. He gets money from foreign agencies. Don't you know? Nationalism is in. Big business. He clears seven figures propelling hate speech. Not a bad way to make a living, opening your mouth.'

'You twisted son-of-a-bitch.'

'Why? Because I make a living out of filling a void?'

'You're playing with people's lives.'

'No, governments play with people's lives. I've been there. Iraq. Afghanistan. Syria. Human lives have a value, I've seen it. And it's not as much as you think.'

Harry was beginning to see just what kind of monster Abu-Nazir truly was.

Far from stupid.

Far from textbook.

Harry found a flaw in the argument and told Abu-Nazir what he had stopped Azeez from doing at the care home. 'What about that? Azeez's hatred seemed pure. Didn't seem at all like he was playing a part to me.'

'Oh, he isn't,' said Abu-Nazir, getting off this chair and walking around the room. 'The man is angry, always has been. Combine that with his confusion about his sexuality—'

'—you knew about that?'

'—of course. It fuelled his anger. I knew he'd come in handy when the time arrived. Today was that moment. He was a pawn protecting the king. He had no idea what we truly stand for.'

'You're some piece of work. How does killing a care home full of pensioners serve any purpose?'

'It would have strengthened Tyler. In turn, that strengthens me, because the backlash against all Muslims would have been profound, not just the extremists. Those disillusioned turn to me. Between us we talk to millions of people—'

'Millions? You arrogant prick.'

Abu-Nazir waved away Harry's remark. 'Social media, the news and our hallowed freedom-of-speech laws take care of it. This, Detective Virdee, is how you play the game these days.'

'What about the innocent people inside the mosque in Bradford?'

'A thousand Muslims die every day in other parts of the world, usually fighting each other. If that happens in Bradford in a few hours' time, I'll view it as a good day for this city.'

'You twisted fuck!' Harry lunged forward, straining at the chains of his handcuffs.

Abu-Nazir retook his seat and removed the stun gun from his pocket. 'I wonder how many times I'll need to knock you out with this before it's all over.'

'This is over for you. Now that I know, soon everyone will.'

Abu-Nazir leaned a little closer and changed the tone of his voice to mimic a news headline. 'Abu-Nazir and Tyler in secret pact!' He chuckled. 'Your claims would disappear into the bottom-less news canyon. Do you have proof of these wild allegations?

Because one million YouTube subscribers say I'm right and you're wrong. Fake news is everywhere, don't you know? No proof. No credibility.'

Abu-Nazir had him.

'You need to let me bring you in,' said Harry. He saw no other way out of this. 'Like you said, you'll be safe there.'

'Don't be stupid.' Nazir pointed the stun gun at Harry. 'Time to go to sleep, there's work to be done.'

Harry could do nothing except brace himself.

'Wait,' said Isaac, entering the room and joining Abu-Nazir. 'Let me do it. I owe him a lot more than just one shot.'

Abu-Nazir handed him the gun, beaming. 'Boy's a chip off the old block.'

'Isaac, think about what you're doing,' said Harry, desperate.

Isaac smiled, crossing the room to bend low over Harry.

'You read my sketches but you didn't understand them, did you?' he whispered.

His brow was furrowed in anger. Harry recoiled.

'Isiah, my hero, you think he's me?'

Harry nodded, confused.

'His nemesis – what is he called?'

Harry thought back to the sketches. 'The Undertaker.'

Isaac dropped his voice a little more, leaned closer. 'And what was Abu-Nazir's name before he converted to Islam?'

Harry thought back to the police database, the news reports, anything.

Kade Turner.

An anagram for 'Undertaker'.

'And what's the Undertaker's weakness? His Kryptonite?'

Electricity.

Harry finally understood. He thought of Isaac's bedroom – the posters of superheroes, the detailed sketches of 'Isiah' saving the world. Of his wardrobe, with Isaac's Western clothing safely tucked away – not discarded but something to come back to at some point. Harry saw who the kid really was.

Isaac smiled, winked at Harry and got to his feet. He turned around, raised the stun gun and, this time, sent 50,000 volts into Abu-Nazir.

SEVENTY-TWO

THIS IS DOMINIC BELL, reporting live for Sky News from Bradford, where thousands of Muslims have amassed in Forster Square retail park, holding candles and chanting prayers for their fellow worshippers inside the Mehraj mosque. We are in the twelfth hour of this hostage situation, with no obvious breakthrough to report. We cannot show you live footage of the mosque but I can tell you that the police presence here continues to grow and I've seen at least four military vehicles in the area. I can tell our viewers that while skirmishes have been reported and arrests made, the feared large-scale disturbances between the Far Right and the approximately ten-thousand-strong crowd of peaceful Muslim worshippers have not, as yet, materialized. As this siege looks to enter its final few hours, we can only hope that a peaceful resolution awaits us all.

SEVENTY-THREE

HARRY STARED AT THE body of Abu-Nazir, unconscious on the floor, Isaac standing over him.

He was no stranger to fraught relationships between a father and a son but there was nothing Harry could say here.

Isaac pulled a set of keys from his father's pocket, set the stun gun on the floor and came to Harry, unable to make eye contact. He simply unlocked the cuffs and stood.

Harry scrambled to his feet as Isaac hammered several brutal kicks into Abu-Nazir's side. After the third strike, Harry made to intervene but Isaac pushed him away.

Another kick.

This time, Harry wrapped his arms around the boy and pulled him back, hard enough to lift him clean off the floor.

Isaac was crying.

Harry sat him on the chair and went across to Nazir. Satisfied he was still alive, Harry handcuffed him to the radiator where he had been, then quickly searched the rest of the house.

The first bedroom told him everything.

Earlier it had been empty but now he found an unconscious

blonde woman in jeans and T-shirt on the bed, hands and feet bound with tape. She must have entered the place after they did. Perhaps a lookout, outside the flat. Harry checked her pulse. She looked a lot like the images of Amelia Rose he'd seen online. He returned to the living room, where Isaac was once again kicking the hell out of Abu-Nazir.

'Hey, hey, hey,' said Harry, pulling the kid away. 'I get it, you want him dead, but that's not how this is going to go.'

Isaac didn't resist Harry's intervention and went thundering into a chair next to a table on the other side of the room.

'I got the headlines. You want to give me some of the fine print?' said Harry.

Isaac's eyes didn't leave Abu-Nazir. Whatever this was, it ran deep.

Harry thought back to Isaac's file and to what Abu-Nazir had told him.

'Let me have a stab at this. Your father fucked off as soon as your mother got pregnant. He had no contact with you until recently. What I need are the details that connect what just happened here.'

Isaac's body suddenly relaxed. He leaned forward, put his hands on the table, head on top of them. 'I don't know what happens now. I never thought about that part.'

Harry went to the window, peered outside. Even though the hour was late, Saville Tower was still alive.

Isaac started talking behind him. 'He's an awful human being. My mother said he always was, that's why she lied and told me he was dead. I didn't know his identity until she got cancer. Then she told me everything: how she'd moved to Bradford to get away from her community and the sense of shame, but also to escape him. He was a shit.'

Harry turned to face the boy. Isaac lifted his head from the table.

'He told me he stayed in London. Joined the army but was dishonourably discharged after a few years. The rest, well – it is what it is.'

Harry sat beside the boy. He spoke softly. 'Do you know what he was discharged for?'

'Being a coward.'

'How so?'

'Didn't tell me. Gave me some bullshit about being wounded in battle. Not a chance – there's more to it than that. And that bitch in there, Amelia, she knows. She's just like him. The fucking Rose and Fred West of identity politics.' Isaac smiled ruefully. 'You know, he told me I'd got my artistic streak from him. Said he used to sketch. I started the Kade Turner / Undertaker thing soon after realizing exactly what he was. Showed him my drawings. He was too stupid to figure it out.'

He hadn't been the only one. Admittedly, it had been well hidden, but now all the drawings Harry had seen made perfect sense.

'When did you realize he was working with Tyler Sudworth?'

'Six, maybe seven months ago. He told me to sell my mum's house and give him the money so we could grow Almukhtaroon, and I agreed. I put it on the market. All he wanted was the money. I fooled him. I devoted myself to his every word, gained his trust. I always knew there would come an opportunity. You gave me that tonight.'

There was so much Harry felt he needed to say to the boy, so much Isaac probably needed to work out. That was a problem for another time. Four and a half hours until the Patriots' deadline. *Time to see this out.*

'What now?' said Isaac, going to the window, parting the curtains slightly and staring out over the feral estate.

Harry joined him. Five hundred yards to freedom.

'Now, Isaac Wolfe, we get the fuck off this estate,' he said.

SEVENTY-FOUR

HARRY HAD PUT ABU-NAZIR and Amelia on the couch in the living room. They had both come around now, their mouths gagged to stop them from screaming, hands tied in front of them. Isaac was in the kitchen. Harry needed to keep father and son apart. The less conflicted Isaac was, the better.

What mattered now was getting the hell out of Saville Tower. Harry was conscious that Tyler Sudworth might return at any point. He also wanted to call Saima and give her some hope that things might be changing, but the best thing he could do for her was to get Abu-Nazir and Amelia Rose to Tariq Islam – from there, he didn't know what would happen.

Harry had to get Abu-Nazir and Amelia to walk out of the tower without drawing attention to themselves, and to do that he needed to put one of their lives on the line.

Which one?

Harry went to the kitchen, closed the door behind him.

'How long have Nazir and Amelia been together?' he asked.

'Why?' Isaac was clearly surprised at the question.

'Do they love each other? Or are they just fucking?'

'He told me they've been together for years.' Isaac shrugged.

'So, they're solid?'

'Pretty much. Why?'

'We need to get out of here but they obviously won't come willingly. This estate will tear us to pieces if we're seen. If we put our heads down, walk hard, we are five hundred yards from freedom. At this hour, we'll pass maybe a handful of kids, all probably pissed or high.'

'Let's go then.'

Harry shook his head and nodded back towards the living room. 'I need to . . . encourage them.' He grimaced.

'Tell me, Harry.'

He told him.

'Jesus,' Isaac said, shaking his head. 'That's . . . I don't even know the right word.'

Harry nodded. He simply didn't have any other choice. Had there been only one of them, he could have thrown them over his shoulder and made a run for it – five hundred agonizing yards. But with two people and time desperately short, this was crisis mode.

'Which one?' asked Isaac.

Harry grimaced again. 'Can't do that to a woman. Does she care enough about him to put his life first?'

'I think so.'

'Really?'

'She loves him. No question.' Isaac stopped talking but Harry could tell he had something else to say. 'What if . . . you go too far? We need them . . . in one piece for later.'

It was a possibility. 'I'll play it as safe as I can.'

'Do it.'

Harry paused. 'He's your father. You sure . . . about this?'

Isaac opened a kitchen drawer, rummaged through it and handed Harry a large kitchen knife. He said nothing. Didn't need to. His face said it all.

Back in the living room, Harry crouched in front of Abu-Nazir and Amelia. He was focused, building his rage, and his courage.

Saima inside the mosque.

His son alone.

City Park reduced to ruins.

One thousand innocent lives.

The couple stared at him, clearly unsure what was happening. It wasn't just the knife Harry was twisting in his hand but the blood that rushed to his head and his short and heavy breathing, as if his chest were on fire. Harry Virdee was angry.

These two were afraid of him. Exactly what he needed.

'You guys love each other?' he asked, mood souring.

Amelia made to speak, the gag muting her. Nazir too. Harry wasn't interested in conversation. The longer he knew as little as possible about them, the better. Hard decisions were coming his way. He didn't want to see the human side of either of them if he could help it.

'We're going for a walk. Out of here, down the fire escape, then across the yard to my car. Quickly and orderly. I don't intend to fail, not when I'm so close, but logic dictates you'll both try and stop me. Create a commotion. Try to run.'

Harry focused on Amelia.

'Do you love him?' he said, pointing the knife at Nazir.

She nodded. Tears streaming down her face.

Harry believed her.

'Only way I guarantee neither of you try to fuck with me is to put a clock on one of your lives. I'll give you the choice, Nazir.'

Harry brought the blade to his own face, stroking his stubble with it, eyes burning with anger.

'You want to take this for team Almukhtaroon or should she?'

His muted response sounded like he was offering himself up.

'Just a nod or a shake of the head.'

Abu-Nazir nodded.

'I'm going to cut you, Nazir. Badly. It'll need attention and if we don't reach my car quickly, you'll die.'

Harry held up a cloth and waved it at him. 'I'll wrap a tourniquet around the wound; give you a borrowed lease of life. It's a few hours until the Patriots' deadline expires. You won't die in that timeframe. If you fuck me around and we don't get off this estate, the last thing I'll do is rip that tourniquet off you so you don't make it either.'

Harry turned to Amelia. 'You best follow my orders. Don't think I'm not capable of doing the same to you. My wife's inside the Mehraj mosque. I'll be damned if my kid's growing up without his mother.'

Harry grabbed Abu-Nazir, who started to struggle.

Harry flashed the blade towards Amelia. 'Should I pick her instead?' he snapped.

Abu-Nazir stopped fighting it.

Then, to the sound of Amelia's muted screams, Harry raised the knife, took aim and plunged it hard into Nazir's flesh.

SEVENTY-FIVE

SAIMA WAS FIGHTING OFF sleep.

Like so many of the congregation around her, she was determined to see this through.

Maria was still by her side. Saima had watched as she typed out a message and pressed Send.

'I check in every thirty minutes, Saima. Do. Not. Test. Me.'

Saima had no way of overpowering her without the people Maria was working with finding out. Who knew what might happen then?

Saima needed to get her identity to Frost or, at least, inform Imam Hashim. She could not let the identity of the sleeper go unknown.

But she had no phone. And she couldn't get anything out of Maria. She was guarded, controlled and focused.

Her head hurt. Every idea she conjured turned out to be a dead end.

'I need the loo,' said Saima, unable to sit still any longer. Maria pocketed her phone and got to her feet.

The washrooms were generously proportioned to allow for

worshippers to wash before prayer. There were four rows of toilets, each a dozen long. The doors were all closed. Maria nodded Saima towards the row nearest the sinks.

'Keep the door open,' she whispered.

'I can't pee with you watching me,' replied Saima.

'Door open,' repeated Maria and shoved Saima towards a cubicle.

Saima didn't really need to pee. She entered the cubicle and turned to face Maria, who had both hands in her pockets, no doubt one on her mobile, the other on the device which would remote-detonate the bomb. Saima couldn't read her face, it was blank.

The two women held each other's gaze for a moment. When Saima didn't back down, Maria said, 'Fine. Door closed. You don't open it in ninety seconds, I'm coming in.'

Saima moved to close it. Just as she did, there was the sound of breaking glass at the far end of the toilets.

Maria's eyes darted to her right as Saima ran from the cubicle.

There it was again. Quieter this time.

Saima's mind went into overdrive. Either this was a rescue attempt or it was someone trying to escape. Either way, with Maria here, one hand on her remote, she didn't like it.

At the end of the last row of cubicles, Saima stopped and saw a teenage boy holding a small marble ornament, standing on the toilet to reach the small window. Unlike so many of the larger windows, it did not have a shutter.

'No! Stop!' said Saima.

At the sound of her voice, the boy panicked and began to squeeze himself through the tiny gap, catching his bag and his clothes on the remaining glass. Saima reached out for him, jumping on to the toilet seat and managing to grab his foot.

'You can't!' she shouted. 'What about the rest of us!'

He kicked out at Saima, catching her in the chest. She fell from the toilet seat, crashing into Maria, both women hitting the floor. They landed hard. Saima's head cracked on the marble and the world started to spin. Maria gathered herself immediately, phone to her ear.

She said one word, calmly and clearly: 'Breach.'

SEVENTY-SIX

FOR ACC FROST, THOSE eight seconds after the mosque window was smashed would forever be etched on his memory.

He was called to the CCTV banks immediately, in time to hear the voice of one of the snipers over the radio.

Frost watched as a young man ran from the mosque, full-pelt towards the police cordon, head down, arms pumping furiously by his side.

He heard the voices shouting, urgent, ordering him to stop.

Frost saw the bag in his hand.

The guy kept running. He didn't hesitate.

They had clear protocols for this.

Eighty metres.

Sixty metres.

Despite their shouts, the guy wasn't stopping.

'Target acquired.'

At the sound of the sniper's warning, Frost's blood ran cold. His eyes never left the screen. If he was a hostile, if he reached the police cordon, if that resulted in any loss of life . . .

Fifty metres.

That was a lot of 'ifs'.

Forty.

More voices ordering him to stop.

Thirty.

Frost could hardly breathe, then he heard the words no Gold Commander ever wanted to hear.

'Shots fired. Man down.'

SEVENTY-SEVEN

THE HUMIDITY HIT HARRY as soon as they stepped out on to the dark walkway on the top floor of Saville Tower. Abu-Nazir went first, Harry just behind him, then Amelia escorted by Isaac.

Harry had tied a tourniquet around Abu-Nazir's arm to stem the bleeding. Neither were gagged – it would draw too much attention. The wound on Abu-Nazir's arm was enough to keep them both compliant. The sooner they got out of here, the sooner it got tended to. Harry had the knife in his pocket. He'd warned them both that if they tried anything cute, he'd end this for them right now. Looking at the fear in their faces, he knew they believed he would do it.

With the yellow turban back on his head, Harry was alert to everything around him as they headed towards the fire escape.

His heart was racing.

He didn't trust Abu-Nazir or Amelia not to try something. Harry paused. Should he have gagged them? He still had time. He glanced down at the estate. The night was dark but there were signs of life on the street below. The red tip of a cigarette on the street corner, the glow of a mobile phone, the interior light in a car.

No, gagging them was an obvious red flag. Harry would have to hope the threat to their lives was enough.

They reached the end of the walkway and Harry glanced back to Isaac. He didn't know what Amelia was capable of, or whether Isaac would be able to handle it.

Harry pushed Abu-Nazir towards the metal staircase, but he resisted. Harry hissed in his ear. 'Either walk or I'll throw you down and watch as you break every bone in your body.' He nudged him hard and held back a little, observing him move reluctantly.

Their pace was slower than Harry would have liked. He couldn't hurry them without drawing attention.

Halfway down, the same kid they'd met on the way up was now lying comatose, a needle and syringe by his side. He was the only person they encountered.

They hit the bottom and moved through the metal gate. Harry had allowed himself a small breath of relief but he regretted it when he saw what was up ahead. A parked car, internal lights on, suspension bouncing. Someone was having a good time. At least the two people in the car would be more interested in what they were doing than in four people walking by.

As they passed, Nazir dodged over to the car and, before Harry could stop him, he raised his leg and hammered his boot through the driver's-side window. Glass exploded, the sound deafening.

'You fucking prick,' said Harry, as Nazir dropped to the ground. Harry turned to see Amelia had followed suit and she was also now on the tarmac. Isaac looked shell-shocked. The back door of the car flew open and a young, wiry skinhead got out, pulling his jeans back on.

Nazir started to yell, nodding at the wound on his shoulder.

On the other side of the car, a young woman got out, in just a bra and short skirt. She started screaming at Harry – every curse he'd ever heard.

The tower started to wake up. Lights came on in windows. Shouts from the hallways.

Harry had badly misjudged this. He'd lost control.

Momentarily stunned, he didn't notice the young lad step over to him until he'd been punched in the stomach. He crumpled to the ground, winded.

Shadows formed silhouettes in Harry's peripheral vision.

'Oi, why's Singhy on the floor?'

'What the fuck have you done to Singh?'

The guy who had hit him searched Harry's pockets, removed the knife. 'It ain't Singhy.'

'Course it's him.'

A crowd had gathered around them.

Harry got his breath back, rolled over and scrambled to his knees. The turban fell to the floor.

Abu-Nazir shouted, sounding panicked, 'That Paki's a groomer – taking my girl for his mates. Got to stop him!'

Amelia joined in, backing up the claim.

Harry was thinking desperately of his next move.

Don't ever go into Saville Tower alone. Mandatory armed backup.

Harry didn't want to say he was a cop.

Amelia did it for him. 'That pig is fucking setting us up! Protects groomers! He's a bent copper! He raped me!' She spat towards Harry and the pantomime was complete.

The crowd started to murmur disbelief – no way a copper would come here alone, especially at night.

'Groomer!'

'Do him!'

The lad who had struck Harry, early twenties maybe, raised his hands and the crowd fell silent.

Ring leader.

He had tattoos of tears dripping from his left eye down his cheek. Stony-faced, pronounced jawline. He cocked his head to one side.

'Joe,' said the boy.

'Harry,' he replied.

'You a cop?'

Harry nodded.

'Groomer?'

'No. She's just kicking off cos she's under arrest.'

'What's the charges?'

'Soliciting.'

'And him?'

Harry didn't want to reveal Abu-Nazir's identity and they hadn't clocked it yet. 'Every bitch needs a hound.'

Joe sniggered and pursed his lips. 'Nobody comes into the Tower without a pass.'

'Singhy said I—'

'Singhy doesn't run this tower,' said Joe, pointing up at the building.

'And you do?' said Harry, unable to hide the smirk from his face. *You're just a boy.*

Isaac stood back, looking lost.

Harry's eyes darted between Joe and the crowd gathered around. Girls chewing gum, boys in hoodies with hands in pockets. Everyone was calm and nobody had their phone out. He'd heard that when shit kicked off in the tower, they'd learned not to film it.

'I got four tears,' said Joe, touching his face. 'One for each pig I put down.'

Harry sighed. Last thing he wanted was a fist fight.

'You wanna leave the Tower, you've got to earn it.'

'If I was white, would the rules be the same?'

'If you were white, Apu, you wouldn't have been stupid enough to try this in the first place.'

The girl who had been in the car came across to Joe. She ran her hands across Joe's chest, dragging her nails.

'Show him, baby,' she said to him.

Joe smiled and said to Harry, 'You put me down, you walk. Saville Tower rules.'

The crowd started to whoop and cheer.

Joe smiled. Touched the tears on his face.

Harry wasn't stupid. Joe had struck him hard. The kid knew what he was doing. Harry glanced at his bandaged left hand. He stood little chance.

Joe cocked his head to the side. 'You want to try, Harry, or lie down now and let the crowd have some fun?'

More jeers.

Another car pulled up beside them, its lights illuminating the area, music pumping loud. The crowd bounced to the music. They were ready for some entertainment.

A sense of despair crept over Harry.

The car's music system got cranked up, bass booming now.

Girls were dancing to the tracks, boys grinning, and all the while Joe kept smiling.

Harry pulled Isaac to one side and dropped his voice. 'This shit goes sour, take your chance and run.'

'Are you kidding? What about . . . everything else?'

'Find my colleague, DS Conway. Tell her everything.'

Harry moved towards Joe. 'Let's get this over with.'

Louder jeers from the crowd – a carnival atmosphere now. Didn't matter that across town thousands of lives were at risk. Here in Saville Tower it was all about this moment.

Joe danced to his left. The kid was light on his feet.

Harry stood firm, flexing his injured hand.

The kid flashed his fists in front of Harry, left–right jab hitting air. He smiled and touched the tattoos on his face. Four tears, one for each pig he'd put down.

Soon to be five.

SEVENTY-EIGHT

HARRY FELT A LIGHTNING-QUICK left jab followed by a thunderous right hook into his stomach. Air disappeared from his lungs. His vision blurred as he felt a third blow to his jaw. He was weightless until he hit the ground heavily.

Pain.

He struggled on to his side, air rushing back into his lungs.

Harry had expected feet to kick him when he was down but Joe had backed off. He and his girlfriend were celebrating his win.

Harry looked around. Nazir, Amelia and Isaac were still in the crowd, secured by some of Joe's entourage. He half wanted Isaac to make a run for it and get help, fearful that Joe was not a man he could beat. The only way he was getting out of this was to play dirty.

He wasn't going to die here, that was for damn sure.

Harry stood up. The crowd cheered. He massaged his side and touched his nose. His hand came away red with blood.

Joe's girl moved away and Joe smiled again.

Arrogant shit. Harry just needed to get close enough.

Joe danced around Harry, stayed out of range.

Slowly, Harry moved his right foot, pressing his toes into the ground and releasing his heel from his shoe.

Joe smiled, pearly white teeth flashing.

Harry inched closer. He threw out a left jab, slow and clumsy. Joe saw the punch coming a mile away. The crowd laughed.

Joe turned and laughed with them.

Harry flashed out another jab, his fist landing inches from Joe's face.

Before the kid could laugh at him again, he kicked out towards Joe. His shoe flew from his foot. Joe ducked.

With his opponent low and distracted, Harry lurched forward and threw as hard a punch as he could towards Joe's liver.

The kid was too quick and moved out of range.

A flash of fists.

Agony.

Blood in his mouth, tarmac under his cheek. And Joe was on top of him, angry, possessed.

Hands around Harry's neck, squeezing.

Joe's eyes were full of an anger Harry didn't understand. The world started to fade, his life being choked out of his body. Harry could do nothing.

The music suddenly stopped.

Joe pulled his hands away, allowing Harry an urgent breath, but kept a knee on his face. The crowd parted anxiously.

Harry heard dogs.

He saw Singh standing there, both of his Alsatians on a lead, straining to break free, barking aggressively.

Joe stood up, turned towards Singh and raised his arms as if to say, *What the fuck?*

Harry rolled over, trying to breathe, scanning the crowd for Abu-Nazir, Amelia and Isaac. They were at the back, surrounded by Joe's thuggish mates.

'Got to back off, Joe,' said Singh.

'The fuck has this got to do with you, Singhy? This is Tower business.'

'That prick owes me money.'

'So?'

'So, you do what you normally do and it makes collecting impossible.'

'You want me to back off so you can collect twenty quid from this pig?'

'If it was pocket change, I wouldn't have got off my couch to come out here. He owes me first. Your debt comes later. You know that's how it is around here.'

Joe looked around for support.

'Stand down, Joe.' Singh pointed at Harry. 'He doesn't pay then I'm ten large out. And that means prices are going to have to go up around here because I'll need my debt clearing.' Singh paused then added, 'Business is business.'

Joe's shoulders slouched. Whatever dealings he had with Singh, they were important enough that he had to back off.

'You help him get in here?' said Joe.

Singh pointed towards Abu-Nazir and Amelia. 'Those two fuckers need clearing off this estate. We don't need that kind of heat around here. That's bad business for everyone.'

'Who are they?'

'Ghosts. They were never here.'

'And if I say no?'

Singh didn't need to reply. He loosened the leads a little and both dogs bared their teeth.

Harry struggled to his feet. Each breath rattled and his nose wouldn't stop bleeding.

'OK, Singhy,' said Joe through gritted teeth. 'Pig's yours.'

SEVENTY-NINE

ABU-NAZIR AND AMELIA WERE in the back seat of Harry's car, tape Harry had got from Singh's store over their mouths. Nazir seemed to have realized the wound in his shoulder was not as critical as Harry had made out earlier.

Harry stood a little distance from his car now, trying to call Saima, news reports of a shooting at the Mehraj mosque filling him with dread. Her phone, as before, was dead.

'If anything's happened to you . . .' His words trailed off. He switched phones, reaching for the burner Tariq Islam had given him, and made the call.

Tariq answered on the first ring.

'The shooting at the mosque. What happened? Is Saima OK?'

The background noise was chaotic, clearly the Gold Command room. Tariq was evasive.

'I get it, you can't talk. Is she OK?' Harry asked again.

'Yes,' he said. 'Ops took a shot at an escapee. Can't say any more.'

Harry drew his hand across his face, suddenly exhausted. 'I've got what we need. All four. Tell the Patriots. I'll call again shortly.' He turned off the phone. He needed to think – choose what his next best move would be.

Isaac approached him looking concerned. 'Joe beat you up pretty bad. Your mouth is still bleeding.'

It wasn't Harry's mouth that was the problem but his chest. Felt like cracked ribs. Every time he took a breath it sent pain pulsing through his body.

'Just a scratch,' replied Harry, though even his rebuttal was delivered with a wince.

Singh struck a match and lit a cigarette, the end burning a furious orange.

'Appreciate the help back there,' said Harry.

'Fuck your thanks,' replied Singh, pinching the cigarette from his lips. 'Protecting my debt. Joe puts you in a coma, I kiss my ten grand goodbye.'

'Thanks anyway. Kid was untouchable.'

'No argument there. Only way a twenty-year-old can run that place. Ain't a man in that tower gets anywhere near him.'

'Seems you can.'

Singh sniggered. 'My dogs have their own reputation. Now you best piss off.'

Harry turned to Isaac and nodded at the car. 'Get in,' he said.

'One thing,' said Singh.

Harry turned to see him holding his phone up.

A flash as he took Harry's picture. Then two more of Abu-Nazir and Amelia in the back of Harry's car.

'Perfect,' he said, checking the images and smiling.

'The fuck's that for?' said Harry, irate.

Singh flicked his cigarette to the floor and stepped away. 'You've got the most hunted bastards on the planet. Reckon this shit you're doing is off the books.' He waved his phone at Harry then put it in his pocket. 'Insurance on your debt.'

'I gave you my word; my watch.'

Singh nodded. 'Still a pig, though. And you can take a pig out of its pen but, know what? It's still dirty.'

EIGHTY

THE PATRIOTS WERE ON the line.

'This is ACC Frost.'

Less than an hour since that sniper had pulled the trigger. News outlets were running wild, speculating that one of the terrorists had been shot dead.

Mustafa Khan, the escapee, had been taken straight to hospital. The sniper had missed the critical shot, hitting him in the shoulder, taking him down, not out. He was the only earner in his family, with a pregnant wife and elderly parents. The pressure had got to him.

This was going from bad to worse. The reality was, as the deadline diminished, there would be more incidents like this.

'You tried the tunnels, Frost.' The voice was disguised, just like before. 'How did you like our little surprise down there for your men?'

Frost said nothing. There were four other departments listening in, he couldn't put a foot wrong.

'And now this. Is the one who escaped dead?'

Frost had a decision to make. The Patriots wanted to hear

Mustafa was dead but he couldn't guarantee his organization was without leaks.

'Serious injury. The prognosis as yet unknown,' he said.

'You made the right call. Otherwise we may have had to act on it ourselves.' The voice paused. 'Do you have the four leaders of Almukhtaroon?'

'It is an ongoing operation.'

'You have three hours.'

The line went dead.

EIGHTY-ONE

INSIDE THE MOSQUE, EVERYONE who had been sleeping was now awake. An hour since the boy had been shot and everything appeared to be fracturing.

The gunshot had caused a ripple of hysteria.

The army were about to storm the mosque and everyone would die.

Because someone had escaped, the bomb would detonate.

Saima watched in horror as a surge of people, maybe two dozen strong, tried to storm the foyer from the grand hall. It sounded like they were being rebuffed and the doors were slammed shut.

Maria removed her phone and hurriedly typed a text.

Saima tried to get the phone from her. Had the enormous room not been so chaotic, someone might have seen the women engage in a struggle.

Maria swept Saima to one side and, before she knew it, Saima crumpled to the ground, unable to breathe. She hadn't even seen the blow.

Unable to move, she could do nothing except watch Maria's fingers dance across her phone before answering a call. As more people headed out of the room, Saima couldn't hear Maria's words. The phone was replaced, then Maria sat down on the floor beside Saima and said calmly, 'If they leave, this ends.'

As if the death of over a thousand people was routine.

Imam Hashim's voice boomed across the speaker system now, pleading for quiet and saying he had urgent news he needed to share with everyone.

Saima, her breath recovered, heard raised voices outside. The doors of the grand hall opened. The people who had tried to make a run for it returned, clearly irate. There were more people keeping leavers in than trying to leave themselves. For how much longer, Saima didn't know. She focused on the stage.

Hashim didn't mince his words. 'This is very simple,' he said, hands raised, tone aggressive – a different approach from before. 'If we break up in here and fall apart, we will lose. Do you not think these people want us to escape? So they can kill us all? So far we have stood together. Now, as we enter the final three hours of this standoff, we cannot – we must not – fail!'

Hashim had a remote in his hand and used it to turn on the large screen behind him, a live feed from an Arabic news channel covering the ten-thousand-strong crowd in Forster Square, candles held high – one enormous sea of light.

'Our friends did not return home when they were able. No. They are with us and the security services outside this building are doing everything they can to end this siege. We must play our part!'

A dissenting voice from the crowd interrupted. 'Doing everything they can – killing an innocent man!'

There were wide-reaching murmurs of agreement.

'Nobody has been killed. The boy who fled was not seriously injured. We are not the only ones under extreme pressure. We have a chance here – but if we give in and leave, then we each seal our own fate and that of everyone in this room. Quite simply, we all die. At least give yourselves the best chance you can.'

He pointed to the screen again. 'Have you ever seen such a coming together of our people? Are they trying to storm the mosque in outrage? Are they engaging in fights with those Far Right protesters behind them? No. They pray for us and with us.'

Saima didn't think his words were having the impact they needed. For the first time, he looked tired and uncertain. Moreover, the congregation was now clearly divided.

Saima felt that the closer they got to 6 a.m., the greater the chance of a mass exodus.

And for the first time she started to think of having her own shot at leaving.

EIGHTY-TWO

HARRY'S RIBS HURT. HE was forced to take slow, shallow breaths of air.

He'd checked his face in the car mirror. Cut eye, bust lip, blood-crusted nose. It was a long time since Harry had been in a fight like that. He flicked his eyes to the rear-view mirror and saw Abu-Nazir and Amelia staring at him.

What now?

Isaac had asked him twice. Truthfully, Harry didn't know. Every mile he put between himself and Saville Tower should have brought some peace but he knew he was heading towards the unknown. It could all be about to get a whole lot worse.

'Where are we going?' asked Isaac.

'Back to Azeez.'

'And then?'

Harry didn't reply. He swallowed, gagging at the taste of blood in his mouth.

'Are you OK?' Isaac's voice was uncertain.

'Marvellous.'

He didn't know how to talk to the kid just now. The Patriots wouldn't care that Isaac wasn't a true extremist. They wouldn't want to hear his story.

'You're worried about what happens to me now?' Isaac asked.

Harry's head was starting to pound.

As he entered Bradford, Harry pulled off the main road, once again using the side streets to reach the football stadium.

The Patriots' words were replaying in his mind.

Sacrifices must be made.

Difficult decisions undertaken.

Harry glanced at Isaac, conflicted.

Sacrifice.

EIGHTY-THREE

BACK INSIDE THE FOOTBALL stadium, Harry pushed Abu-Nazir and Amelia into the prison cell. They'd given up protesting through the tape over their mouths by now.

Azeez sat delirious in a pool of water, the ice bag just visible underneath him.

Harry took a photo of all four of them together, Isaac holding a copy of today's newspaper they'd found dumped by the food stands in the concourse. He could hardly believe he had them all. Isaac joined him outside the cell and Harry closed the door, locking it and handing the keys to Isaac. He trusted him fully now.

'Stay here and keep an eye on this lot for me.'

Harry made his way back to the concourse and found an exhausted-looking Ben standing by his car. Harry nodded towards the large metal gates.

'On the way in, saw a first-aid sign in the window next to that exit.'

Ben nodded. 'Player treatment room.'

Harry doubled over as a bolt of agony shook his insides.

'Christ, Harry, are you OK?'

He took a moment, the world going a little dizzy. He wondered just how many ribs Joe might have cracked.

'Any painkillers in that place?'

'I reckon so.'

Harry moved towards the room, keeping his breathing short and shallow. Ben unlocked the door. Harry scoured the room, seeing a small metal cabinet fixed to the wall. It had a sticker on it: *Controlled drugs.*

'You got the key to that?'

Ben shrugged, looking a little sheepish.

'Do you?' asked Harry, more insistently.

'Only supposed to open it when the team doctor's present. Laws and all that.'

'You can say I forced you.'

Ben seemed to understand the urgency. He flicked through his keys, found the right one and opened the cabinet, stepping aside. 'I'll have to say you made me do it, Harry.'

'You do that.'

Harry found several boxes of tablets and a bottle of liquid. He snatched at the bottle. Morphine solution 10mg/5ml. He had heard Saima speaking about the drug so many times, a common painkiller in A&E. There was also a small book in the cabinet: *Record of Administration.* He scanned it, seeing multiple entries – players' names and the same dose repeated time and time again: 10mg/5ml, with only one entry saying 20mg/10ml.

Hell with it. He unscrewed the top. Out of the corner of his eye he saw Ben looking grave. 'I know what I'm doing,' said Harry.

He swigged a mouthful, reckoning a tad over 10ml. He was a big lad and the pain in his chest was killing him.

'What have you heard about what's happening out there?' said Harry, closing the cabinet and sticking the bottle of morphine in his pocket.

Ben looked unimpressed.

Harry waited for an answer.

'Whoever got shot outside the mosque isn't serious. Media reported on it a few minutes back.'

That was smart, thought Harry. If it were true. Quicker they dispelled the notion of a dead worshipper, or a dead terrorist, quicker the heat got taken out of this.

'Them Muslims are in Forster Square. Holding candles.'

Harry heard the disapproval.

'Far Right reckon they are making a stand too. Fucking city is going to hell.'

Sitting alone in the dugout, Harry stared into the emptiness of the stadium. The morphine was starting to kick in, the edge taken off his pain.

He had 4 per cent battery left on his phone and dialled Saima. Straight to voicemail. Again.

Harry put his phone away and removed the burner unit, needing to call Tariq. Only thing was, Harry didn't want to hand over control of Almukhtaroon. With the shooting outside the mosque and the enormous crowd of Muslim worshippers in Forster Square, everything was primed for anarchy. Would it change Tariq's resolve? Would he be compromised by all of this? Harry didn't trust politicians at the best of times and the Home Secretary had proved to be a slippery son-of-a-bitch. Harry wanted to speak to the Patriots himself. Christ, he'd done all the work thus far, he'd be damned if he just handed it all over. For him, this was about Saima. He dialled Tariq, who answered immediately.

'Secure?' Harry said.

'Yes. Where are you?' replied Tariq, voice shaky.

'Close. I need to speak to the Patriots. Right now.'

'Why?'

'Because I said so.'

The line went silent.

'Bradford's unravelling. If it kicks off, we all lose. Time to end this, no compromises. You've got three minutes to get me the number or I walk into a police station with all four of these bastards and end this right now. Make it a much larger headache – four dead or a thousand?' Harry hung up.

There was nothing more to say.

It was a bluff. No way had he come this far just to hand Almukhtaroon over to the police.

The phone in his hand started to ring. Harry rejected the call and typed a hurried text.

Two minutes now. Send the number.

How could he know if he was doing the right thing? How could he know Saima would come home safely? He couldn't. And he hated it.

Harry's phone beeped a text message. A phone number. Harry didn't hesitate. He called the Patriots.

An international dial-tone.

'I have what you need,' he said, wincing as a sharp bolt of pain stung his ribs.

A pause.

'Civilian or security?' The voice was disguised.

'Civilian,' said Harry, afraid if he said he was on the force it might complicate things.

'We require photographic proof.'

'I have it.'

Harry was given another number to text the picture to and did so quickly.

The call disconnected.

He closed his eyes, focusing on the pain – his face, his ribs, his hands, anything not to think about Saima and what was happening inside the mosque.

He jumped at the noise of his phone ringing.

'Are you willing to kill them?'

Harry considered his response. 'I—'

'Either they die or everyone inside the mosque dies. If you won't decide, we'll put it to the people. You have ninety minutes.'

The line went dead.

EIGHTY-FOUR

IT ALL CAME DOWN to this. Four lives against a thousand. Just as Tariq Islam had said it would.

Harry had wanted control. Now he had it.

Isaac was the problem here. A choice between the other three and a thousand inside the mosque was no choice at all.

He couldn't sit here and think about it, a decision had to be made. He walked reluctantly back towards Isaac.

Harry heard noises coming from the cell, two voices.

But they were bound and gagged. Everyone but Isaac.

Was he . . .

Harry rounded the corner, saw the cell door open, keys in the lock, Isaac crouched beside Amelia. He squeezed inside the room.

'I had to take the tape off Amelia,' Isaac said. 'She was throwing up, would have choked if I hadn't done it.'

Amelia was drained of all her colour, eyes closed.

'Shame you didn't leave it five minutes,' replied Harry. It would have made at least one decision easier for him.

'There's a complication.' Isaac dropped his gaze to the floor. Fidgeting with his hands.

Harry looked at Amelia again. Pale. Vomiting. The realization hit him.

'Go on,' he said, energy draining from his body.

'She's pregnant,' said Isaac.

EIGHTY-FIVE

NINETY MINUTES BEFORE THE deadline and ACC Frost had a nightmare on his hands – either a nightmare or a lifeline, depending on how he could swing it.

A picture had emerged on Twitter of the four leaders of Almukhtaroon, secure, alive. None of them looked to be in a good way but somebody had them.

It seemed the photo had been posted by the Patriots themselves. It was followed by something else. Frost had stared down at his phone.

We, the people of this great country, will decide the fate of Bradford. Take back control!

4 leaders of Almukhtaroon dead?	96%
1000 innocent people dead?	4%

3,650,863 votes

It was increasing every minute, the early morning hour no deterrent. The world continued to watch Bradford.

The photo had inspired another raft of calls to the Gold Command hotline. Sightings of the Almukhtaroon leaders right across the city. No way Frost's men could act on them before deadline.

Most would turn out to be dead ends.

Right now, in a small room on the second floor, no windows, no glass panels, locked away from eager ears and prying eyes, Frost, Tariq Islam and Commander David Allen were deep in conversation.

'Can we get this vote pulled?' Tariq Islam paced the floor.

'We're looking into it but it isn't a quick thing to do,' Frost responded. He hated that Tariq was in the room.

'What else?' Tariq asked.

'We try to find them,' Frost said. 'We've got people analysing the photo now. We find them and we bring them into custody. We can't sit by and let the masses vote on an execution like this.'

The social media vote could not be ignored. With each passing second thousands were voting, baying for blood.

If Frost apprehended Almukhtaroon, that would be the end of the matter. They would be put into safe custody. They had not broken any laws.

The three most powerful people in this operation had one simple decision to make.

To uphold the rule of law.

Or to break it.

EIGHTY-SIX

HARRY HAD HAULED AMELIA out into the main concourse by the food stands, freed her hands and given her some water. Isaac had followed behind.

'Easiest way for you to get out of this is to play the pregnancy card.'

She'd been crying, eyes blood-red, blonde curls stuck to her face.

'My phone,' she said meekly.

Harry removed it from his pocket.

'Turn it on. The pin is 300979. Access my diary. Thirty-first of July. Midwife appointment. In my photos, go back a week or so – you'll find a picture of me holding a positive pregnancy test. That's how I told him, Abu-Nazir. If you need more, my latest orders on Amazon will tell you the rest.'

It was all there.

'You're not even three months and you're buying baby things?'

'It's my first. I'm excited.' Her voice was flat.

'Fuck,' said Harry, slamming her phone on the counter. 'Fuck me!'

Isaac slumped in a chair.

'Take us to a police station. Let us walk inside. Wash your hands of this,' said Amelia.

'My wife's inside that mosque.'

'Is she pregnant?'

Harry didn't reply.

'Call her. Ask her what she would do.'

All he wanted was to hear Saima's voice. He swayed a little on his feet, exhausted.

'Hands,' said Harry, gesturing for Amelia to raise them.

'Who cuffs a pregnant woman?'

'Says the bitch who put us all here.'

She suddenly exploded from her seat and slapped him, hard.

It shouldn't have hurt. The blows Harry had taken from Joe had done real damage. Her slap sent a thunderbolt through Harry's jaw into his brain. She went for it again but this time Isaac intervened before Harry could. They tussled and Harry grabbed for her, twisting one hand behind her back and slapping the cuffs on.

'This is your half brother or sister,' she screamed at Isaac. 'Can you live with yourself knowing you condemned them to die?'

She tried to lash out again. Harry wasn't sure if she wanted to get to him or to Isaac but he stopped her.

'Sit down or I'll lie you down,' said Harry.

She slumped into the chair, eyes raging.

Harry told Isaac to back away.

God only knew what this was doing to the kid's mind. He was alone, no one left in the world, and now he had the promise of a sibling. However much he hated his father, this would surely be too much for him.

Harry reached for his phone to try Saima again when a commotion from behind drew his attention.

'Armed police!'

He turned, horrified to see half a dozen officers with MP5 machine guns rushing towards him.

Military. Not police.

This was serious.

'On your knees! Hands in the air!'

One went to Isaac, a second to Amelia. Two came for Harry.

'Down! Now!'

Christ, how had they found him?

He kept his eyes up as he lay on the floor.

Ben stood in the doorway, arms folded. Harry had believed he could trust him. So much for old friends.

This was over.

EIGHTY-SEVEN

HARRY WAS LOCKED INSIDE the prison cell with the four leaders of Almukhtaroon. They were practically on top of one another, all handcuffed and gagged, watching the military guards outside their cell.

One hour to the deadline. And no cards left to play. Harry hoped the Patriots were bluffing.

His body was tired, aching, ready to switch off, but his brain was on high alert. Voices at the end of the corridor grabbed his attention. One he recognized. Tariq Islam.

Military personnel, faces still covered, grabbed Harry by the shoulders and led him outside, locking the cell behind. He was marched down the corridor into a small, dank room where his hands were freed and the tape over his mouth removed.

'You look like hell,' said Tariq, alarmed.

'What the fuck is happening?' Harry winced with the effort of speaking. He looked to Tariq's left, to a man in khaki he didn't rec- ognize, and raised his eyebrows.

'This is Colonel David Allen, elite military commander.'

'So?' said Harry, massaging his ribs. The morphine seemed to be wearing off, his insides feeling like they were once again being squeezed.

'I'll leave you two to talk this through,' said Allen and left the room.

'You want to sit down? Look like you need it.'

'Get on with it,' said Harry, staying where he was.

'I understand from your mate Ben that the kid may have been helpful.'

'He isn't like them.'

Tariq nodded. 'Amelia told our guys she's pregnant. That true?'

'Seems so.'

'Fuck,' whispered Tariq.

Harry shuffled to a chair and perched on the edge. 'It's over.' *Saima.* 'Can you get the military to storm the mosque?'

Tariq shook his head. 'High probability it will blow.'

'So, we do nothing?'

Tariq sighed. 'Up until twenty minutes ago, we had a play here,' he said, nodding back the way Harry had come. 'Until Ben dialled 999 and blew this wide open.'

Harry hung his head, foolish to have thought with everything going on that Ben wouldn't have recognized Almukhtaroon. If Harry had been in his shoes he would have done the same thing.

Harry turned towards Tariq, then back the other way, trying to find a position in which he felt slightly less pain.

'Before you came in, Allen and I shared a call with the Patriots.'

'Oh?'

Tariq closed the gap between them. 'We told them we have Almukhtaroon. That the woman is pregnant and we wouldn't bring her to the mosque.'

'The mosque?'

Tariq frowned. 'They said they'll release two hundred and fifty worshippers for each member of Almukhtaroon.'

'If you're not giving them Amelia, they'll only release seven hundred and fifty people?'

'They want the people responsible for making the UK less secure. I'm the Home Secretary, in charge of law and order, the one who tried and failed to prosecute Almukhtaroon.' He took a deep breath. 'The Patriots want four people. I'm going to take Abu-Nazir, Azeez and Isaac into the mosque and try to settle this myself.' Tariq waved his phone again at Harry. 'That's what has been agreed.'

'Who signed off on this?'

Tariq said nothing.

Harry understood. Tariq had made a deal with the military commander.

Frost didn't have a clue. He would think the Almukhtaroon had been lost to the night. Tariq, once again, was taking matters into his own hands.

'You've got a daughter,' said Harry.

'I'm betting my diplomacy works inside that mosque.'

'None of them will go willingly.'

'They won't know. Blindfolded, gagged, earplugged, handcuffed. They'll think we're doing our jobs and taking them into safe custody.'

Harry put his head in his hands. 'You can't do this.'

'If I fall with Almukhtaroon and it saves a thousand people, there's nothing better I can do with my life. Allowing a thousand Muslims to perish will ruin this country.'

Harry didn't push it any further. His thoughts, perhaps selfishly, were now on Saima.

'The mosque must have a cordon around it. How many officers on the ground? Few hundred? How the fuck are you going to get anywhere near it with your captives if Frost hasn't signed this off?'

'I don't know yet, Harry. I was hoping you might help me.'

EIGHTY-EIGHT

THIRTY MINUTES TO THE Patriots' deadline.

Harry was alone with Commander David Allen while his men, together with Tariq, got Almukhtaroon ready to leave.

What they were discussing was nothing short of mutiny.

'That's the plan,' said Harry, trying not to show Allen he was in agony.

Allen cracked his knuckles, his bulky frame seeming to fill the room. 'I've worked with my men for a decade. I know what they can deliver, and the degree of certainty. Now you want me to place all of my faith in you?'

Harry wanted to close the gap between them but didn't want to stand, afraid he'd collapse. His chest felt like it was fracturing. What he really needed was another morphine hit but the armed officers had taken the bottle from him when he'd been thrown in the cell.

'I secured Almukhtaroon. Hardly a walk in the fucking park.'

'That's what got you in this room.' Allen walked across to Harry. 'Stand up.'

Harry delayed it a second, gritting his teeth trying to disguise it from Allen, and stood up. He stared the commander in the face.

Allen put his hands out, one on each side of Harry's ribs, and pressed lightly.

Harry collapsed on to his chair and only partially suppressed a scream. He slid off it, ending up on the floor.

He rested his head on the tiles, eyes closed, unable to look at Allen.

'You're a mess.'

Harry took a few short, shallow breaths. 'Your men took some morphine from me. Another hit and I'll be fine.'

Allen crouched by Harry's side. 'I don't doubt you're a special kind of police officer. Hell, I know a soldier when I see one. I also know when a man's beaten.'

'Help me to my feet,' said Harry.

Carefully, Allen did so.

Harry put his hands on Allen's shoulder, not just for stability but because he wanted him to know he still had something left in the tank.

'Fine, I'm hurt. Almost down, but know what keeps me going? The thought of my wife in that mosque. My kid at home and my city on its fucking knees. I'll be damned if I let a little pain stop me now. You've heard my pitch – it's the best thing we have right now. Put me in the game. I won't let you down, sir.'

The men measured each other, Harry determined to show Allen he was able to see it through. *Bradford couldn't go down like this.*

Allen lowered Harry's hands from his shoulders. 'No commander wants to send his troops into a fifty–fifty. Know this, though, Harry. If you get to the doors and the hostages are not released, we will be forced to come in. Everything is set. I hope it doesn't come to that. I'll get you your morphine.'

Allen tried to step past Harry but he didn't move.

'The weapon I asked for? Do you have one? It's our only way in.'

A pause.

Allen nodded reluctantly and walked out of the room.

EIGHTY-NINE

HARRY SWIGGED AT THE liquid morphine.

'Easy with that stuff,' said Isaac.

Harry sealed the bottle and put it in his pocket, keeping his back towards Isaac so he couldn't see how badly he was struggling.

Broken ribs, for sure.

Outside Abu-Nazir and Azeez were being loaded into a Bradford City football van. Amelia had been left in the prison cell under armed guard.

'Did Tariq fill you in?' said Harry.

'Yes.'

'If we pull this shit off, you'll be able to sell your sketches for enough money to never work again.'

Isaac came to Harry's side. 'We need to go. Are you sure you can manage?'

Harry ignored the question. 'Did Allen show you . . . the weapon? Are you sure you got it? This is all on you now.'

'I can do this.' He put his hand on Harry's shoulder.

Tariq entered the room, phone in hand, and waved it at Harry. 'Are you all good?'

Harry nodded. 'Make the damn call.'

NINETY

SAIMA WAS INSIDE IMAM Hashim's office with Maria.

His face said it all – how had he not noticed her?

He handed the phone back to Maria. The call had been short, the Patriots claiming Almukhtaroon were soon to be brought to the mosque and that this was over.

Maria spoke dispassionately. 'As you heard, with each member of Almukhtaroon to enter the mosque, we will release a quarter of the followers. Your job is to tell everyone this is happening, organize them and ensure they do as we say.'

Hashim sat still, stunned into silence.

Saima felt he was thinking the same thing she was: could they really make it out of here alive so easily? Just walk out?

'What about me?' she said to Maria.

'You're of no interest to me any more. You and Hashim will be in the last group to leave. All we want is Almukhtaroon.'

'Why?' replied Saima.

Maria waved her phone at her. 'Six million votes have been cast. The people have decided.'

NINETY-ONE

THE BRADFORD CITY MINIBUS had blacked-out windows. Almukhta-roon were in the back, out of sight. Harry watched as Commander Allen raised his hand to the guard on the street. The military had control of the main route from Valley Parade stadium to the Mehraj mosque, a half-mile journey mostly straight down Midland Road. Each road block had stood down on Commander Allen's instruction.

They pulled up at the final blockade, the mosque directly ahead. To their left were hundreds of officers in full riot gear. It wasn't that that distracted Harry. It was the sight of thousands of people holding candles in Forster Square.

In the distance behind them, Harry could just see the Far Right protesters, placards raised.

The sound was deafening. Chants, shouts, a low hum of prayer.

Allen turned to Harry. 'Ready?'

Harry nodded.

'I need to hear it.'

'We're set,' replied Harry forcefully. The morphine hadn't

properly kicked in yet but he did have a warm, calm sensation in the pit of his stomach.

Allen turned to the row of seating behind him. 'Isaac – this is it.'

The boy looked tense. 'I'm ready.'

Allen handed Isaac a white-phosphorus grenade. Same size and shape as a regular one but instead of an explosive, it would release a noxious cloud of gas, the phosphorus burning people's eyes, temporarily blinding them. It was the perfect decoy.

'You pull the pin out, hold it safe while you get past the cordon. You only replace the pin when the mosque doors open and worshippers start to emerge. If they do not come out, I will authorize a full-out assault. At that point, you'll need to run.'

Isaac nodded, trying to appear resolute.

Allen confirmed the plan with Harry then turned to Tariq. 'Anything to add?'

'No,' he said, unlocking his phone and holding it to his ear. It was time to call the Patriots.

'We are here. Bradford City football van. At the perimeter. When we get to the front of the mosque, we'll stand aside to let the worshippers out.' Tariq hung up. 'We're on. As agreed, they are going to release seven hundred and fifty when we're at the door. The remaining two hundred and fifty worshippers will be held until we're inside the mosque. Harry, you'll wait outside and, once everyone is out, you retreat to the cordon with Allen. It's just the four of us going in.'

'Let's make this happen,' said Allen, as armed personnel approached the vehicle, weapons raised.

'God speed to you boys,' he added and opened his door. Isaac followed suit. The officers saw their commander and awaited instruction, weapons lowered.

That all changed the moment Isaac raised his hand, removed the pin from the grenade and shouted, 'Stand down! Or I'll drop the grenade and we all die!'

Harry was by his side, Azeez and Abu-Nazir between them,

unaware of what was happening, the blindfold, gags and earplugs in place. Harry braced himself for gunshots.

Allen and Tariq raised their hands, Allen shouting at his men, 'Stand down! He has a live grenade!'

Radios crackled, officers backed away hurriedly, putting maximum distance between themselves and Isaac.

Harry heard the noise of the crowds fall away, replaced by something else . . . the murmur of uncertainty. They'd seen something change at the perimeter but the van was obscuring their view.

Allen stepped towards his men, arms raised. 'We don't have control here. Back away, allow these men through the cordon!'

Harry was holding his breath, eyes on Isaac. He leaned closer and hissed, 'Don't look at them. Focus on the front door of the mosque. Walk forward slowly.'

Isaac yelled again for everyone to back away, voice shaky, hand trembling.

They had no choice, unaware it was only a phosphorus grenade. Having pulled the pin, his hand was now effectively a dead-man's switch. If he was taken out, he'd drop the grenade and they would all die.

'Move,' hissed Tariq as a gap in the cordon opened ahead of them.

Harry knew Gold Command would be getting these images live over CCTV. Frost would be shitting himself. *How the hell had this happened?*

They would claim that Allen and his men had stormed the football club and been caught by Isaac holding a grenade. They'd been forced to stand down and obey Isaac's demands for him and his crew to enter the mosque and end the siege.

They would tell them how Isaac Wolfe had turned on Almukhtaroon.

If they saw this shit through, he would emerge a hero.

Harry had simply gone after the Almukhtaroon as instructed

by his superiors. In the chaos of the night, they were banking on Frost forgetting that Harry had signed off.

And Tariq? He'd figure out his part.

Allen had joined his team now, relaying orders Harry couldn't hear but he saw the guards lower their weapons.

He wondered how many snipers in strategic positions around the mosque currently had their weapons focused on Isaac's head.

They couldn't shoot. It would be certain death for all of them.

Isaac shouted for Allen to walk them through the cordon. They wouldn't do anything stupid with their commander at risk.

They moved quickly but in an orderly way, Allen at the front, then Harry escorting Azeez, Isaac behind him, grenade raised, and finally Tariq with Abu-Nazir. It had been Allen's decision to put Isaac in the middle so a sniper's shot was more unlikely.

Halfway, Azeez stumbled then slumped to the ground.

'No sudden movements!' yelled Allen, turning to see what had happened.

Harry couldn't drag the bastard to his feet – he didn't have the strength left to do it. Allen stepped up, lifted Azeez from the floor and dragged him along.

Harry turned to Isaac. 'You good?'

'Ready to throw up,' he replied, pale and shaky.

They arrived near the entrance of the mosque about four minutes after they had broken through the cordon. The noise behind them was incredible, as if the whole city were whispering as one.

'Here we go,' said Harry, turning to Tariq. 'Do it.'

They removed the blindfolds from Abu-Nazir and Azeez's faces and took out their earplugs. Azeez barely knew what was going on, lost in a delirium. Nazir was a different animal. He started to struggle, realizing what was about to happen.

'Hey,' snapped Harry, stepping towards him. 'You mess this up and your wife and kid die. Back at the stadium, there's a gun at Amelia's head. Here, there's probably a dozen snipers itching to take you out, so stand the fuck down!'

Nazir's face screwed up in rage but he stopped fighting his restraints.

Tariq put his phone to his ear.

'What now?' said Harry.

'We wait,' replied Tariq.

Harry looked up. The sun had almost fully risen and he could see hundreds of armed guards, thousands of supporters and pro-testers in Forster Square, cameras trained on the entrance of the mosque, helicopters some distance away.

The entire world was looking at them, there on that step.

Harry checked the time on his phone: 06.00, the time the bomb should have gone off. For now, they had stopped that happening. He focused on the doors – they needed to open.

There were several clangs of metal and then the doors of the mosque were flung open and a steady stream of people started to walk hurriedly from the building, hands raised.

Harry held his breath, looking for Saima.

'It's working,' hissed Tariq, smiling.

Allen spoke hurriedly into a mic – Harry assumed it would be his team on the ground, ready to intercept the worshippers and take them into custody. They had to be certain nobody from the Patriots was among them.

It felt like an achingly long time for the seven hundred and fifty worshippers to exit.

Harry hadn't seen Saima. He'd seen many women emerge, and had assumed Imam Hashim would have prioritized getting the women out. Why hadn't Saima been among them?

Tariq's phone rang. He answered, listened to a short message then turned to Harry and Allen. 'They said that's seven fifty released. The rest when I take these three inside.'

Harry dropped his voice and leaned in to Isaac, who was shak-ing. 'Replace the pin in the grenade now.' Harry put a hand on his shoulder. 'I don't want you dropping that thing in there. Tariq reckons he can swing this.'

'He said he won't let them kill me.' Isaac was trying not to cry.

Harry nodded and lowered his voice to no more than a whisper so Tariq could not hear him. 'If you know it's going bad, pull the pin, throw it and run as fast as you can. You got that?'

Harry moved his body to block Isaac from the view of the crowds as he replaced the pin in the grenade. Last thing he needed was Isaac's head being taken off.

He raised his own hands above his head as he watched the four men disappear through the open door, Tariq hesitating, turning around to face the crowd and the hundreds of camera lenses no doubt displaying this on the world's media.

It would be all over the internet in moments.

Alone now with Allen, Harry dropped his gaze to the floor as the doors reopened and another stream of people started to walk out, heads down, hands raised, pace urgent.

Whether it was the adrenaline or the morphine, it didn't matter, but Harry couldn't feel any pain as he stepped closer, watching for Saima.

'Come on, come on,' he whispered.

He glanced down the path towards the bottom where worshippers were being searched by military personnel and ushered quickly away.

Something hit him.

The crowd.

The cameras.

The global media attention.

He glanced back to the front door, looking again for Saima.

Harry stepped a little closer to the entrance. The fact this thing might be drawing to a close gave him a sudden moment of clarity. He started to see things in a way he hadn't before. *Holy shit.*

The flow of people started to slow and, just as it ended, after a delay of no more than a few seconds, Saima Virdee stepped outside.

She saw Harry and started to run towards him.

'No!' he shouted, hands raised, alarming the few followers in front of her. 'Keep your hands up, Saima – walk slowly!'

She stopped, raised her hands and walked apprehensively towards him.

Harry patted her down quickly then threw his arms around her, kissing her.

'It's over,' he said.

She started to cry. 'God, I was so scared.'

'Harry, that's it, let's get out of here.' Allen's voice was calm and commanding.

In that moment, with his wife in his arms, and Commander Allen at his side, the noise of the past seventeen hours disappeared from his mind.

Harry Virdee understood. He had been played.

The bastard.

It was the way Tariq Islam had paused in front of the doors and turned back to the crowds, raising his hands like some sort of Messiah figure.

This had all started with Tariq Islam handing Isaac Wolfe to Harry. And now his sacrifice would be the enduring image of this siege.

Islam would be coming out of that mosque alive.

He pushed Saima towards Allen. 'Get her out of here.'

'Harry!' she said.

'Saima, I know what I'm doing. You have to trust me.'

'The hell you do,' said Allen, putting his hand on Harry.

He shrugged him away. 'Get my wife out of here.'

Harry walked to the entrance, hearing Allen dragging an outraged Saima away. Harry had been played and now, realizing his own life was not in any danger, Harry was going to put things right.

He opened the door and disappeared inside the Mehraj mosque.

NINETY-TWO

HARRY ENTERED THE MOSQUE calm and determined.

It was the twenty-minute warning the Patriots had given. Zero casualties in City Park. Tariq had placed himself centre stage for the whole operation, both on and off the books. Managing every angle. And just as the deadline had been reached, he had negotiated his way into the mosque after all the hostages had been released.

The question was – why?

Harry arrived in the main foyer, a spiral staircase to his left, two elevators to his right. The shutters were drawn across the floor-to-ceiling windows, blocking any snipers from seeing what was happening.

Which way?

Saima had told him the bomb was in the basement. Would Tariq have headed there? Harry needed to make a decision and fast.

He ran down the stairs. Inside the basement he found Isaac, Azeez and Abu-Nazir all out cold on the floor, hands and feet crudely secured with some sort of wire. He hurried towards them and checked for signs of life. They were all still breathing.

He found the white-phosphorus grenade in Isaac's pocket and shoved it in his own.

Suddenly he heard voices up ahead. Tariq Islam and one other.

He walked quickly towards them, rounding the corner to find an enormous wooden box, the bomb nestled inside.

'You should have stayed outside, Harry,' Tariq said.

Tariq stood with a young white woman.

She had to be one of the Patriots.

'You better start talking, and fast, Tariq,' said Harry.

Tariq shook his head, dismayed. 'Search him for a weapon and a phone.'

Harry removed the grenade from his pocket and pulled the pin, holding it high. 'Try it.'

Tariq frowned. 'Really?'

'You put me through hell, for what?'

'Put the pin back in and I'll tell you.'

Harry did no such thing. 'Tell me now.'

'It's a white-phosphorus grenade, Harry. It's not going to kill us.'

'Maybe. But it'll put you down while I cuff you both.'

Harry pointed at the bomb, the large screen displaying a timer that had stopped with only six seconds remaining.

'Start talking,' said Harry.

'This is Maria. She's a member of Group-13. One of my most trusted officers.'

'*Your* officers?'

'You never leave Group-13.'

Harry lowered his arm but kept his fist squeezed around the grenade, the pin still pulled.

'Power, Harry. That's what this is about. When I walk out of here, I'll be the hero of this saga, the most recognized face on the planet. It all but guarantees me the Prime Minister's job.'

Harry crept closer, eyes scanning the floor space for options and finding none.

'Power? Being Prime Minister doesn't buy you power. It isn't like being the President.'

'Not yet,' said Tariq, intercepting Maria, who had stepped towards Harry, Taser raised. 'You want to put the pin back in the grenade?'

'No.'

Tariq shrugged and spoke quickly and succinctly. He told Harry the world was changing. Powerful Far Right groups were emerging in the USA and all across Europe. And all the while, elitist career politicians with not an ounce of experience in the real world continued to dictate the country's policy in a twenty-first century unrecognizable from the one they'd imagined as children.

'We're headed for some major problems, Harry.'

The woman inched closer to Harry, Taser by her side. Once she was in striking distance, she was going to go for him, grenade or not.

'Better tell your pooch to stand down,' said Harry, nodding towards her.

'She has nothing to lose, Harry.'

'Radiation exposure in Korea,' she said. 'I've got maybe a year.' Her eyes shone.

The sacrificial lamb.

The perfect sleeper cell.

They were so close now that if Harry dropped the grenade, the phosphorus-burn would also injure him. They were calling his bluff and if it came down to it, he didn't know what the right call would be.

'What makes you so different from those politicians?' Harry pointed the grenade at Tariq. 'You seem more dangerous to me than anyone else.'

Tariq smiled. 'You just don't know when to quit, do you?'

There was a moment of silence as they all waited for one of them to make a move.

Tariq turned to Maria. 'Show him.'

'What?' she said.

'Show him why we did all this.'

She stared at him, incredulous.

'Either he's dead or one of us,' said Tariq.

'Are you sure?' she said.

Tariq nodded. 'I wouldn't have got him involved otherwise.'

Maria open a video on her phone.

'Drop the Taser and kick it away,' said Tariq. 'Give him the phone and let him watch it properly. Once he's seen it, he'll re-pin the grenade and we can get on with things. We can't be that far off a military raid.'

She did as he asked.

Harry retreated a little, hit Play and watched the clip. At first, he darted his attention between Tariq, Maria and the phone.

Two minutes in, he forgot they were there.

It showed the Prime Minister, Thomas Match, in conversation with two well-known billionaire businessmen and Tyler Sudworth. Their expressions said they were very pleased with themselves. The men congratulated each other on finding a scapegoat for the country's hardships, said how useful the immigrant population of the UK had been for them. They talked of targeting the Muslims, how satisfied they were with Abu-Nazir and his progress, and of growing hostility in the UK towards the immigrants. They spoke of social and ethnic cleansing, and returning the country to its indigenous roots.

The world had seen this before, in the 1930s and 40s.

All this hatred. It had come from these men.

These men in power, these men running the country.

The video didn't look or feel doctored. And Maria and Tariq had had no way of knowing in advance they might need this. They hadn't known Harry would be here.

He put the pin back in the grenade, placed it on the floor and said, 'How do we stop this?'

NINETY-THREE

'EXTREME SITUATIONS CALL FOR extreme measures. This is the only way we walk out of here.'

Harry didn't like Tariq's plan. Tariq wanted Maria to execute the three leaders of Almukhtaroon still unconscious on the floor.

'I get it but I can't sign off on the boy's murder,' Harry said.

Tariq suddenly pushed Harry, both hands landing flush on his chest, pain ricocheting through his ribs.

'You don't get sign-off. And I don't have time to run you through every minor detail. For now, Harry, you're either with us or against us. No civilians have died today – don't be the first.'

Harry wasn't sure he wanted to know the rest.

'The boy leaves with us. You'll say he was an embedded operative who helped bring Almukhtaroon down. You'll give him an award, a fucking medal if need be.' Harry glanced towards Abu-Nazir and Azeez. 'How'd you explain those two being killed, though?'

Maria pulled a gun from under her burka and put it to her own head. 'Do you know what radiation poisoning is like to die of?'

A true sacrificial lamb.

She handed the gun to Tariq. 'Better to die at the hands of my compatriots, civilized and honourable, than let my body burn from the inside. And it will cement Tariq's position as a true hero today.' She pointed towards the ceiling. 'He saved a thousand people.' She gestured to Isaac. 'Saved our insider.' Finally she put her finger to her temple. 'And took out the terrorist who killed Nazir and Azeez.'

Tariq stepped in front of her, looking at Harry. 'I need you to walk away.'

Harry rubbed his hand over his stubble, scratching it wildly. He opened his mouth to object but Tariq stopped him.

'Walk the fuck away and take the boy with you.'

There was nothing more to say or do.

Harry took one final glance at Maria, at the bomb behind her, the timer frozen on 00:06 seconds, and walked away.

He lifted Isaac from the ground, pain shrieking through his body. He had to put him back on the floor and drag him around the corner instead.

He waited. It felt like an age before Harry heard two gunshots: Abu-Nazir and Azeez.

Now for Maria.

Harry closed his eyes.

He wondered if Tariq would feel anything. He was far more complex than Harry had ever given him credit for.

Group-13, a brotherhood like no other.

A third gunshot.

There was a short delay before Tariq emerged, walking purposefully.

'You rescued the kid, didn't see what happened. The rest is on me. Got it?'

Tariq hit the button for the elevator.

Isaac was coming around now and Harry managed to unbind his hands and feet.

Tariq crouched beside Isaac, tone soft and compassionate. The change in his demeanour was astonishing to witness.

This guy was something else.

'You're safe. It's over. Harry got you to safety. Abu-Nazir and Azeez were killed by the Patriots before I could neutralize that threat. We'll debrief you fully when we are out of here. You OK to walk?'

Isaac simply nodded and Harry wondered if he'd registered that his father had just been killed. Perhaps the kid was in shock.

The three of them entered the lift heading for the ground floor.

They walked to the main doors of the mosque.

Tariq put his hand on Harry, halting him before they stepped through the doors to freedom.

'They'll take you to hospital and you'll be reunited with your wife. At some point tomorrow they'll want a debrief from you but I'll see you before then and we'll get this thing straight.'

Harry turned to leave but Tariq kept his hand firmly on his shoulder.

'OK?' he said.

Harry stared at Tariq's hand until he removed it. 'I got it.'

NINETY-FOUR

JOYTI VIRDEE HAD NOT really slept at all. She'd been watching the television on mute in her bedroom. Behind her, Ranjit was sleeping next to Aaron, arms cradling the boy.

Joyti had almost woken him up when the news had shown some kind of military operation under way at the Mehraj mosque. The footage had been cut short and, less than an hour later, it was all over.

Saima had called Joyti, crying. She'd cried even harder when Joyti had told her that her little boy was sleeping soundly.

Joyti looked over to her husband and her grandson, asleep on the bed. If she had known how to take a photograph on her phone, she would have. This was an image she never thought she would see.

What happened now was anybody's guess but right here, in this moment, Joyti felt a sense of peace she wanted to cling on to.

The clock by the bed started to beep loudly for its 07.45 alarm and disturbed both Ranjit and Aaron's sleep. She hurriedly turned it off and watched, heart in mouth, as Aaron sat up, rubbed his eyes and . . . smiled.

'Grandma, you still here!' he said, alert and happy.

Yesterday and all its worries were already gone from his mind.

Aaron turned to Ranjit and stared at him perplexed. 'You sleep in my bed?'

Ranjit smiled. 'I did. I was scared of the dark. I needed you to look after me.'

Aaron thought about this and nodded. 'It's OK. I get scared sometimes. I look after you.'

Ranjit glanced at Joyti and she knew in that instant that something had changed.

'You need a shave,' said Aaron.

Ranjit nodded. 'I like my beard. Do you want to touch it?'

'No. I don't like beards. Too scratchy. My daddy has a small beard. He rubs it on my face.'

Joyti lifted Aaron into her arms, allowing Ranjit to get out of bed. 'Does my little hero want breakfast?'

'I want my mummy.'

'She is coming. She will have breakfast with us too.'

Joyti glanced at Ranjit, who didn't respond.

What now? How did they move on from this?

Ranjit nodded to the window. A police car pulled up in the drive, the back door flying open.

Saima Virdee ran towards the house.

Harry laboured behind her, moving slowly.

They were safe.

Ranjit sat down on the edge of the bed, rubbing his hands along his knees. He looked anxious. 'I think this morning I will have my tea upstairs.'

Upstairs.

He didn't want to come down to see Harry and Saima.

Ranjit came across to Joyti and took Aaron from her. He kissed him and simply said, 'Goodbye, my little prince. You have lifted an old man's heart.'

NINETY-FIVE

THIS IS AMANDA MAWSON reporting live from Bradford where, in spite of the terrorist incident being brought to an end, a large police presence remains throughout the city. Transport links have reopened with Leeds Bradford airport announcing the resumption of flights.

Behind me you can see the Mehraj mosque, scene of one of the most audacious hostage situations we have experienced in modern times, and certainly the most high profile this country has ever seen. I can report that the bombing of City Park resulted in no casualties and while we understand that sixteen people remain in hospital, their injuries are not thought to be serious.

There are questions over what exactly happened inside the basement of the Mehraj mosque. No official statement has been given, but our sources have told us that both Abu-Nazir and Fahad-Bin-Azeez were killed in whatever took place when Home Secretary Tariq Islam and Detective Chief Inspector Harry Virdee entered the mosque. Indeed social media is full of unverified images of three bodies being stretchered from the building. As yet, the identities of those victims, especially the third one, remain unconfirmed.

With a conference scheduled for 2 p.m. at the Midland Hotel, the world's press is firmly camped inside Bradford. Just who are the Patriots? What will happen to the followers of Almukhtaroon? Do the security services expect a backlash and potential counter-measures from the Far Right?

This siege may have concluded, but for Bradford the past twenty-four hours will surely be only the beginning of a lengthy, complex investigation . . .

NINETY-SIX

HARRY HAD BEEN ADMITTED to Bradford Royal Infirmary.

Broken ribs. He had undergone several scans and numerous vials of blood had been taken from him. Eventually he'd even been given an injection of morphine.

He was getting used to that shit.

He was in a large comfortable side room. Outside he could see Saima ensuring everything to do with his treatment was in order. As yet, they hadn't spoken of what had happened in the basement of the mosque. Saima should have been at home but had refused to go. He could see Aaron sitting at the nurses' station, playing with a stethoscope, several nurses fussing over him.

Harry needed some sleep but his eyes were on the TV hanging above his bed. Sky News was broadcasting live from the conference hall of the Midland Hotel, journalists and television crews from all major channels reporting simultaneously.

ACC Frost and Tariq Islam took to the stage. Frost looked the more serious man. Harry knew why. He needed the streets of Bradford to calm, to end viral rumours on social media. It was . . . necessary. Last thing Bradford needed were reactionary forces, whether Far Right or otherwise, hitting the streets. This city knew all about that.

Harry had spoken to Frost but hadn't debriefed him. He hadn't known what to say.

Isaac had been taken into custody and Harry had made it damn clear he was not to be treated as hostile, and ensured Tariq had relayed the same message. Harry had not disclosed that Abu-Nazir was Isaac's father. That revelation could come later.

Frost opened up by running through key events of the past twenty-four hours, nothing the audience didn't already know. Camera shutters clicked ferociously, fingers tapped on laptops and pages of notebooks were ruffled. He spoke for under five minutes, ending his segment by stating that Harry had been an active member of his team, tasked with securing the leaders of Almukhtaroon, and had been compromised in the line of duty, which resulted in him being forced into the Mehraj mosque with Tariq. What happened thereafter, he said, was part of an ongoing investigation. He stepped aside for Tariq.

Harry couldn't bear looking at him and turned away from the TV. This was a game Tariq had played at such a high level that Harry could not allow it to go unanswered. He would not.

That, though, was for later.

Tariq covered some of what Frost had already said then, as Harry had expected, he made his move for political power.

'. . . what I will say is that the past twenty-four hours have reaffirmed the current political climate in the West. What I can tell you all is that what has come out of this is the revelation that Abu-Nazir and his partner, Amelia Rose, were in fact members of a covert Far Right organization and created the smokescreen of Almukhtaroon to conceal that reality. They used our fears to propel their own narrative and, indeed, their bank balance.'

There was a surge of incredulous chatter within the room. Tariq raised his arms, asked everyone to be calm and continued.

'We live in a time where identity appears to be up for grabs.

Where people are asked to pick a side depending on their ethnicity or religious values. This goes against the very ideology of a tolerant society. These divisions have been building for some time and we, not only as government but more widely, have allowed it to happen. Across Europe, Far Right gains have been building, no doubt aided by troubling messages coming from the United States.'

Tariq stared into the audience and paused. 'What happened inside the basement of the Mehraj mosque is currently under investigation and I cannot tell you any more than you have already heard. What I can say, however, is that it resulted in over a thousand innocent UK civilians being unharmed. I, for one, hold that above everything else.'

Another pause as he allowed the journalists to digest what he had said. Not quite condoning the death of Abu-Nazir but not far away.

'A thousand innocent UK civilians. Not a thousand Muslims or Asians or ethnics or any other word you want to use. But a thousand of us. We need to fix this country. Communities need to come together and embrace the common ground. Not by playing catch-up or continuing to do what has gone before, but by radically overhauling systems that encourage and tolerate division, whether financially or religiously. No more committee meetings and think-tanks and white papers. Simple, practical solutions. People first. People always. People together.'

Harry stared at Tariq, feeling like a grandstand finish was nearing.

'I have heard people saying that Bradford is broken. It is not. This country is broken. And I will finish by saying this. Starting tomorrow, I'm going to damn well fix it.'

He stepped aside as journalists fought for the right to ask the first question. Harry had heard enough and reached for the remote just as a journalist shouted out: 'Home Secretary, is your speech laying down the gauntlet for a prime-ministerial challenge?'

NINETY-SEVEN

TARIQ ISLAM WAS SITTING in Harry's room, his close-protection detail loitering outside on the ward.

Saima had taken Aaron home, closely followed by a security detail of her own. The media had swarmed around the house but she'd refused to stay in a hotel.

Tariq looked as tired as anyone Harry had ever seen.

'Two cracked ribs, I heard.'

'Three, actually.'

'I'm sorry, Harry. You need to know I mean that.'

'Park your bullshit elsewhere.'

Tariq leaned forward in his chair, hands clasped together, head bowed. 'You know what the real job of government is?'

'Its only job is to serve.'

'You're right. But not the people. Government serves itself.'

Harry raised his eyebrows.

'Westminster is the oldest old-boys' network in the world. Unlike other countries, we've never had foreign rulers – never been invaded or occupied. Westminster is still "Empire". You either embrace it or you're shown the door.'

'Get to the point, Tariq.'

'That video you saw was a snippet of a much bigger picture, Harry.'

Harry struggled to sit up.

'How did you get that video?'

'Group-13 has never officially existed. And yet, over the past eighteen months, my ex-colleagues have started to mysteriously disappear, presumed dead. I'm a threat to those men and they're trying to send me a message. That video was covertly filmed by Group-13. When you come after us, we don't take it lying down but this is a complex war we are fighting.'

Harry was confused. 'What do you mean, you're a threat?'

'I'm going to be the first Muslim man to become PM. And I don't fit with their rhetoric.'

'So you did do all this for power?'

Tariq got up from his chair and walked to the window, keeping his back towards Harry.

'No. I did it because behind closed doors the people who really run this country – the billionaires and finance companies who control the economy – are talking about overseas conflicts again. Yemen, Syria, another cold war with Russia. America continues to isolate itself in the most nationalistic of ways and here in Blighty we are, for the first time in generations, completely alone. I did what I did to make myself impossible to ignore and to force real, meaningful change. I'm going to go hell for leather after the hard-line right-wing societies and political entities to break them down but, at the same time, do the same with groups like Almukhtaroon. Abu-Nazir may have been playing a game to swell his bank account but there are others out there, true fundamentalists ready to take his place. I want a complete crackdown on all sections of hate speech and toxic nationalistic views. This country cannot afford to become like Italy, Spain, France, Holland, Germany, where the Far Right is growing in political power. We, Harry Virdee, are heading not only for another financial recession but this time also for a possible "cleansing" of UK passport holders. It's not for nothing that the current Prime Minister cut the policing and national security budgets by 20 per cent. How the fuck are you going to operate robust intelligence and security with cuts like those? It's not chance or an oversight. It's social cleansing.'

Tariq returned to Harry, stopping by his bedside. His face was flushed, eyes narrow, the tiredness replaced by something worse: a frightening resilience.

'You don't know this world of power like I do, Harry. There are plans in the most elite of circles, including government, to slowly move the centre ground to the right. Look back through history. Every hundred or so years, times change. Populations do. People turn on one another. I did what I did because I aim to topple the PM, and that will start tomorrow with a press conference like no other. I'll berate the toffs and the career politicians as pen-pushers with no real allegiance to the British way of life. I walked into the mosque with you so that that image would be the one that gets me the power I need to create real, progressive change. The whole world is talking about Tariq Islam and it's not my fucking ego I'm polishing, it's my credentials to become the first man of colour, the first Muslim PM in the UK. And my job will be to bring communities closer together and push the Far Right back to the fringes. Otherwise, we are all fucked.'

Harry's head was hurting. Some things made sense, others didn't. Why did they involve him? Why hadn't Group-13 just taken out Almukhtaroon themselves?

Tariq told him that had been the plan but, as he had already suggested, they were being systematically wiped out. Two days before, several key members of the organization had disappeared, ones critical to this operation.

'Everything was set. You were never part of this plan. No offence, but it's way above your pay grade,' said Tariq.

He told Harry that without their usual manpower, they had lost control of Almukhtaroon that morning. Only Isaac remained on their radar and he'd been the lowest rung. Tariq had targeted the only man he knew who stood a chance in Bradford.

Harry.

The remaining members of Group-13 were flat out ensuring the bigger plan with the mosques and security services went accordingly. Moreover, Harry was expendable; they were not.

'Thanks,' said Harry.

'You asked for the truth.'

'Why tell me all of this? Surely a bullet is what I should get. I could end you in a heartbeat.'

Tariq waved his phone at Harry. 'Globally I'm at ten million tweets. We live in a world of fake news. You wouldn't get far.'

Harry hated to admit it but Tariq was right.

'I'm telling you all this, Harry, so you don't stay up at night asking yourself questions you don't have answers to.'

Harry shook his head. 'No, it's more than that.'

Tariq smiled. 'It is more than that. Last year, in one monumental night for Bradford, with all the odds against you, Harry Virdee managed to pull off one of the greatest abductions and murders of our time. The best thing is, nobody knows it happened. You have a very specific set of skills, a very specific type of brother. There is one thing I am damn certain of . . .' Tariq helped himself to a glass of water, as if building up to what he had yet to say.

'In every major city in the UK I am making inroads. Putting "my people" in places they need to be, whether government officials or . . . otherwise. We need to cleanse this country in a far more radical way than politics currently allows. The world has changed. We either change with it or get left behind. Courts, jails and reform were before the digital age. Before the top one per cent of the world's elite fucked the rest of us. The one place I don't have eyes is Leeds Bradford, the fourth-largest catchment in the UK and a place I have no one I can trust to come with me on this journey.'

Harry shook his head. 'After what you did today—'

'—zero civilian casualties! Two people who deserved to die got their comeuppance and I put to rest a woman who asked me to end her life the way she wanted. Fine, I upset and frightened thousands of people and we had a few minor injuries but – perspective! Better twenty-four hours of turmoil then twenty-four years.'

'What was inside that bomb? Actual explosives?'

'Examination of the device will show it was fake. An extraordinary bluff.'

Tariq went back to his chair and removed his jacket from it, putting it on. His eyes looked so sore they almost made Harry's water.

'You're pretty golden, Harry. The brass doesn't have shit on you and you were just as much the hero as I was. You broke some rules? It was an unprecedented scenario.' Tariq pointed to the window and smiled. 'I've plans for Bradford, Harry. Plans for you. Don't judge me before you have heard them.'

NINETY-EIGHT

HARRY WAS HOME, SITTING in his living room, once again watching the news. Bradford remained the headline story.

This wouldn't be forgotten. A terrorist event of this scale would be subject to many 'commissions' and 'inquiries' over the coming years.

There were questions the public would want answering.

Who were the Patriots?

Would Tariq Islam stand trial for murder?

And many they would never know to ask.

Would Maria's identity lead back to Tariq Islam?

Would his role in this ever come to light?

Harry had none of the answers.

Saima had put Aaron to bed and entered the room, bringing with her a pen and piece of paper. She kicked the footstool over towards Harry and sat opposite him.

'Divorce?' said Harry, trying to crack a joke. He'd told her all about Tariq Islam but Saima hadn't said much.

She didn't smile.

Harry muted the television.

Saima placed the pen and paper on her lap, then said, 'How come we always end up here?'

'Here?'

She nodded towards his ribs.

'Bones mend.'

'Don't use that macho crap with me.'

Harry shrugged. 'But they do.'

'This city is going to ruin us, Harry. Don't you feel it?'

He didn't reply.

'We need a fresh start. No drama.' Saima put her hands on him. 'All I care about is my boy and my husband. The past forty-eight hours, in all this madness, I saw what really matters. I had so much time to think of you and Aaron alone, without me. Then about what might happen if I got out and something happened to you. I don't want to think that way any more.'

'I doubt I'll have a job anyway, Saima. I broke every rule there is.'

Saima rolled her eyes. She lifted the pen and began to write. Harry peered past her at the TV where a picture of him and Tariq Islam outside the mosque had a bold caption beneath it: *HEROES*.

He turned it off. You put everything on the line and got a few newspaper headlines, yet when all this died down, he was certain that the only thing in his future was a misconduct charge.

Saima handed him the paper she had scrawled on.

He stared at it and didn't react.

Just two lines.

'You don't need to be the saviour of this city any more. Gotham can find another Dark Knight. You've done enough. We just need to be "us", and everything else we'll figure out. Will you sign it please?'

Harry didn't move. He focused on the paper, on Saima, then back on the paper.

'Are you really asking this of me?'

Her expression said it all. In fact, it said more than Harry cared to see.

330

Saima was right.

He wasn't going to win here. Thoughts of Tariq Islam and his own brother Ronnie rolled across his mind.

Bradford's future was . . . uncertain.

Saima touched his hands and smiled. 'It's time. It is.'

Harry took the pen from her and scribbled his signature where she had left him space.

I, Hardeep Singh Virdee, formally tender my resignation with immediate effect from the West Yorkshire police force.

EPILOGUE

TARIQ ISLAM HAD BEEN true to his word and Isaac Wolfe was now something of a celebrity. The boy who pissed his pants and took anxiety medication was a distant memory.

Harry was standing by his side as Isaac laid a bunch of flowers on his mother's grave in Undercliffe Cemetery. The evening was warm and quiet, just the two of them by the headstone.

Harry had attended several meetings with Isaac and Tariq, where their story had been locked down before being shared with security services. Isaac had been given the chance to seal his file so that the fact Abu-Nazir was his father never came out.

He'd declined.

The other version was far stronger: the boy who had gone under-cover to become a spy, putting his country first, his toxic father a distant second.

The spin-machine had been hard at work.

Isaac had sold his comic sketches to a publisher for seven figures and was now one of the most eligible bachelors in England.

'Not half bad for eighteen hours' work,' said Harry.

Isaac smiled. 'Every time someone asks me whether I'm still a spy I say, "No comment" and it increases my social media reach by a few thousand.'

Harry put his arm around the kid. 'The world could do with a few more brown heroes.'

Isaac turned to Harry and hugged him. 'Like you, you mean?'

'Hey, don't squeeze me too tight. Ribs, remember?'

'Sorry,' said Isaac, breaking the embrace.

'I mean what I said. The shit you did out there – you're the real hero in all of this.'

Isaac put his hand in his bag and pulled out a handful of photocopied sketches. 'Here, I wanted you to see these first, before I submitted them to my publisher for next week's edition.'

Harry took them and tried not to laugh. It made his ribs scream. 'Are you kidding?' he said.

'Time Harry Virdee, or should I say Harri Verde, got his own edition.'

Harry flicked through the pages. 'I don't know what to say. Is this libellous?'

'It's all good stuff. Now *you're* famous.'

'Do I get any of that seven-figure action your publisher gave you?'

'Name your number.'

Harry waved the pages at him. 'I'm content with this. Nice touch.' He stuck out his hand and Isaac shook it. 'Farewell, Isaac Wolfe. London won't know what hit them.'

'You'll come visit, right?'

'Some time. For now, Bradford will do just fine.'

They shook hands, a few gentle slaps on the back, a bond they wouldn't easily forget.

'Someone told me you handed in your resignation – is that right? Or fake news?'

Harry went to answer, paused, then glanced around the cemetery. 'We're a long time dead, no?'

Isaac didn't reply.

Harry smiled. 'Don't worry, Isaac Wolfe. Whatever happens, I'm pretty certain Bradford hasn't seen the last of me yet.'

ACKNOWLEDGEMENTS

This one was tough! A seismic plot, which did indeed push me to my limits as a writer.

Huge thanks to my incredible editor, Darcy Nicholson. I'm not sure how we continue to do this! You push me to my limits and I appreciate it more than you realize. We are breaking boundaries and creating the sort of fiction that I always dreamt of writing. You work so hard on these books with me and continue to be my secret weapon. The entire team at Transworld is amazing, especially the copy-editing team. Thank you all, so much.

To former DCI Steve Snow, for allowing me to hound you, probably more than I should! I know I break the rules with my plots, but the fact that you are always there, guiding, advising and constantly trying to help me create the high-end drama I love to write is invaluable. Long may it continue! I've got to be honest, sitting there and watching your expressions as I twist and turn the plots is great fun! As you've told me before, 'If you were not a writer, Amit, I'd probably nick you . . .' Stay retired Steve! We have much more work to do!

To Rob Glover, for running me through a detailed plot strand which ultimately didn't make the final cut – but rest assured, it's coming!

Michael Shackleton, at Bradford City Football Club, for the generous access. Come on the Bantams!

Dr Jasjit Singh for assisting me with the finer points of Sikhism and Asian culture. I am so glad to have you on #teamVirdee!

My agent Simon Trewin for the continual support and for always being at the end of a phone.

To the 'Red Hot Chilli Writers' – Ayisha Malik, Vaseem Khan, Abir Mukherjee, Imran Mahmood and Alex Khan. Keep smashing the clichés guys! A wonderfully supportive space to be part of. Also, for the humorous hours of 'bakwas'. Keep it coming!

My family – I know it's hard when I'm writing and I 'disappear' into the fictional world I've created.

To the city of Bradford. Thank you for continuing to support Harry – he will always keep you safe!

Finally, my wife. This one was bruising! I couldn't have done it without you constantly telling me; 'one more page, one more chapter, one more hour . . .'

You are the only person I write for and I couldn't do it without you. Four books done and I've fooled you with the twists and turns each time! Seeing the look on your face when you finally read, 'the end' is the only reason I keep doing this.

I've said it before, I'll say it again:

Keep doing what you do – it makes me do what I do.

ABOUT THE AUTHOR

A. A. Dhand was raised in Bradford and spent his youth observing the city from behind the counter of a small convenience store. After qualifying as a pharmacist, he worked in London and travelled extensively before returning to Bradford to start his own business and begin writing. The history, diversity and darkness of the city have inspired his Harry Virdee novels.

Wakefield Libraries
& Information Services

This book should be returned by the last date stamped above. You may renew the loan personally, by post or telephone for a further period if the book is not required by another reader.